MINE AT MIDNIGHT

Ladies of the Order - Book 3

ADELE CLEE

More titles by Adele Clee

Lost Ladies of London

The Mysterious Miss Flint

The Deceptive Lady Darby

The Scandalous Lady Sandford

The Daring Miss Darcy

Avenging Lords

At Last the Rogue Returns

A Wicked Wager

Valentine's Vow

A Gentleman's Curse

Scandalous Sons

And the Widow Wore Scarlet

The Mark of a Rogue

When Scandal Came to Town

The Mystery of Mr Daventry

Gentlemen of the Order

Dauntless

Raven

Valiant

Dark Angel

Ladies of the Order

The Devereaux Affair

More than a Masquerade

Mine at Midnight

Mine at Midnight
Copyright © 2021 Adele Clee
All rights reserved.
ISBN-13: 978-1-8383839-6-1

Cover by Dar Albert at Wicked Smart Designs

CHAPTER 1

Hart Street, Covent Garden
Office of the Order

Nerves and excitement roused the same sensations, Eliza Dutton decided. Both left an empty feeling in one's stomach. Both left one's pulse racing and muscles twitching. She took a moment to catch her breath and gather her wits before knocking on the study door.

"Enter!" Mr Daventry called.

He was the master of the Order, the master of a group of enquiry agents who helped prove some people charged with crimes were innocent. While the men assisted those without the means or funds to help themselves, the ladies accepted paying clients.

Eliza opened the door and entered the room.

Mr Daventry's commanding presence left most men shaking in their boots. He stood to a height of over six feet, brushed his hand through his coal-black hair before pulling out his pocket watch and inspecting the time.

"Miss Dutton, as prompt as ever. I won't offer you a seat. We're leaving."

He had summoned Eliza to the office without explanation. It meant one thing. She was finally being given her first case, and they were off to meet a prospective new client.

A host of questions flooded her mind, but she couldn't act like a debutante at her first ball. As an enquiry agent, it was her job to maintain a professional air. She was to encourage confidence in her abilities, not jabber on like a witless fool.

"Is there anything I should know before we do so, sir?"

Mr Daventry narrowed his gaze. "Taking a case is not like picking a treat from a confectioner, Miss Dutton. It's not about what you find palatable. It's about recognising a client needs help regardless of personal opinion."

It was an odd thing to say.

So odd it aroused her suspicions.

"Is this where you tell me Lord Roxburgh is our client?" she jested. Mr Daventry knew she disliked the lord and often joked with the peer that he might hire Eliza to find his conscience.

Her stomach sank when Mr Daventry failed to smile.

"Lord Roxburgh is our client. We're heading to Hanover Square to see him now." He spoke as if she had no reason to dislike the lord, as if the thought shouldn't fill her with dread. "You have a choice, Miss Dutton. Accept the case and assist him with his dilemma, or I shall be forced to employ another agent."

Mr Daventry was known for his benevolence. Not any more. What had she done to deserve such a punishment? Had he given no thought to her harrowing experiences?

"Sir, with all due respect, Lord Roxburgh would stake his mother at the card table just to get a thrill. May I remind you, my father lost his fortune at the gaming tables?" He'd lost everything of value: his reputation, his home, his life. "Consequently, I cannot work with a man plagued by the same addiction."

Mr Daventry's gaze softened. "Lord Roxburgh's mother died years ago. One might suggest he stake his sister's reputation, but that is currently in tatters after an incident in the lord's garden. While Lord Roxburgh is our client, it's his sister, Miss Ware, whom we hope to save."

Lord Roxburgh had a sister? He didn't act like a responsible brother. Surely his reputation for being a scandalous rake had seriously affected his sister's prospects. And why would the Order become involved in a family matter?

"I know it's difficult for you," the master continued. "I know your father dragged you to the depths of hell. But Lord Roxburgh's case is different. And you must learn to let go of the past."

Let go of the past? How could she let go while still making fortnightly payments to a blackguard who owned a gaming hell?

"Lord Roxburgh provokes me. He is quite blatant in his use of innuendo."

Mr Daventry seemed amused. "You'll have to deal with more than innuendo if you work for me, Miss Dutton. I rarely make mistakes. I wouldn't assign you the case if I didn't think you could handle Roxburgh."

Mr Daventry gestured to the door. The discussion was over.

Eliza hesitated.

Every fibre of her being warned against accepting. Yet she loved being part of the Order, loved the security of living with other female agents in Howland Street. Mr Daventry was only thirty, but he was like the stable father figure she'd never had. It seemed she would have to learn to tolerate Lord Roxburgh and hope she had the skills to conclude the investigation quickly.

"Will you tell Lord Roxburgh he is to abide by my decisions? Will you explain he must take orders from a woman?"

Oh, she could almost hear the lord's salacious reply.

I only take orders from a woman in bed.

"You're in charge of this case, Miss Dutton. Lord Roxburgh will afford you the respect such a position deserves. This incident has shaken him. Consequently, he has more on his mind than seducing one of my agents."

Eliza suppressed a mocking snort. Lord Roxburgh might draw his last breath and still have time to appreciate a woman's figure. And he appeared to have developed a liking for women who worked for a living.

"Very well. I'm interested to learn more about the case."

The mile journey to Mayfair took thirty minutes, for the roads were busy with those taking advantage of a break in the chilly weather. Lord Roxburgh owned an elegant townhouse in Hanover Square, with a vast garden, Mr Daventry informed her.

"The garden is rather unique, redesigned by Roxburgh five years ago." Mr Daventry stepped up to Lord Roxburgh's door and hammered the lion head knocker. "As you know, he likes to entertain."

"Lord Roxburgh must have been quite young when he inherited."

"Roxburgh was fifteen when his father died. He came into his inheritance seven years ago, his maternal uncle being trustee and guardian until then."

So, by Eliza's calculation, the lord must be eight and twenty now.

"Having a huge responsibility at a young age must account for his love of reckless pursuits." The lord was unapologetic in his quest for pleasure.

"If we're to help him, we cannot make the obvious assumptions."

No, it was her job to remain impartial. But Lord

Roxburgh had a way of getting under her skin, and it was much easier to dislike him than to admit there was something attractive about his self-assured demeanour.

A footman dressed in dark green livery answered the door. Having already enquired after his master's availability, the servant welcomed them inside and escorted them to the drawing room.

Lord Roxburgh stood when they entered.

There wasn't a more sophisticated man in all of London. There wasn't a man with more charm and wit, a man with a more sensual grin. Every word breezed from his lips like a teasing caress, a subtle seduction of the senses.

Thank heavens Eliza was immune.

"Daventry, you came. You're certainly a man of your word." The lord's warm brown gaze settled on Eliza, and her stomach lurched the way it always did when in his company. "Miss Dutton." He swept a graceful bow. "While I felt sure we'd meet again, I hoped it would be under more pleasurable circumstances."

Spoken in his rich tone, the comment roused visions of moonlight strolls and stolen kisses.

"If I'm to take your case, honesty between us is vital, my lord." Eliza dipped a quick curtsey. "You should know I rather hoped our paths might never cross."

His smile lacked its usual sparkle. "One could never accuse you of being evasive, Miss Dutton. But I pray you will give this matter your serious consideration. Rarely do I leave myself open to scrutiny. If anyone must delve into my personal affairs, I'd rather it were you."

It was there again.

A sensual undercurrent.

A promise of something wicked.

Despite his impeccable dress and handsome bearing—he looked exceptional in his fitted blue coat—Lord Roxburgh seemed tired, weary. The man could drink, gamble and whore better than any of his peers. Which meant his solemn mood spoke of a serious problem.

"Please, sit down." Lord Roxburgh gestured to various chairs.

Eliza sat to his right. She would struggle to concentrate if forced to look at him directly. Mr Daventry chose the chair opposite.

"Should you not summon Miss Ware?" Mr Daventry glanced at the closed door. "It is her reputation at stake. Is she not our client?"

Lord Roxburgh appeared oddly nervous. "Lillian is left devastated by Saturday night's tragedy. Even with the power I wield, I've failed to silence the gossips. Half the *ton* has ambled past my door this morning. Mr Ashbury's parents came knocking, demanding answers, and Lillian has spent every waking hour in her bedchamber, sobbing uncontrollably."

Eliza was confused. Most parents would come crawling on hands and knees, begging the lord to spare their son a dawn appointment. "Mr Ashbury is the gentleman who ruined your sister in the garden?"

"Mr Ashbury is the scoundrel found murdered in my garden."

Murdered!

Eliza tried to suppress the rising panic. She'd been expecting to find a rogue and force a proposal, not investigate something as villainous as murder.

"Perhaps we should start at the beginning, my lord." Eliza ferreted around in her reticule and withdrew her pencil and notebook. It gave her a moment to settle her nerves. "You say your garden is the murder scene. Were you hosting an event?"

"I host a grand ball monthly during the season."

"And how many guests were in attendance?"

He shrugged. "More than a hundred. My secretary can

confirm the exact number. Bloom comes to the house every day at noon."

No doubt Lord Roxburgh had spent the night rolling dice over the green baize or propositioning someone's wife in an upstairs bedchamber.

Eliza made a note of Mr Bloom's name. "Might you explain what happened? When and where did you discover the body? Can you recall if there were any visible signs of an altercation?"

Lord Roxburgh stood. "We heard the screaming just after midnight." He took to pacing before the hearth, showing his muscular thighs to advantage. "Most people were taking supper, and a scream is nothing out of the ordinary at a rowdy event."

"One assumes you heard a woman scream."

He stopped pacing and fixed her with his arresting gaze. "My sister Lillian screamed. She was out in the garden taking air while the guests were occupied indoors. After finding Ashbury's lifeless body, she came bursting into the supper room, looking for me."

The young woman was outdoors alone?

"Your sister wasn't entertaining guests during supper?" Eliza thought that most odd, considering her brother was the host.

"Lillian complained of having no appetite and so retired to her room. There had been an incident with Ashbury earlier in the evening, and she wished to avoid him."

Mr Daventry frowned. "You let Ashbury stay despite his earlier encounter with your sister? I'm surprised you didn't beat him and throw him out."

Lord Roxburgh firmed his jaw. "I would have done more than throw him out, but Lillian failed to inform me of their … tussle. She only made her confession this morning."

"Does Miss Ware keep many secrets, my lord?"

"Not to my knowledge."

Young women always kept secrets. Perhaps Lord Roxburgh didn't know his sister as well as he ought. "But you say she was out in the garden when she should have been in her room?"

"Yes. She found Ashbury dead in the maze. The man had suffered a broken neck. There were no signs of a struggle."

Eliza considered the information. Why would a woman who had been accosted earlier in the evening venture outside alone? By pain of death, would she not have avoided a second confrontation?

"Doubtless your sister lacks the strength to snap a man's neck, hence why she's not the prime suspect in a murder investigation."

"Sir Oswald came and took our statements. They're delving into Ashbury's background, hoping to identify his enemies."

A man who accosted innocent women must have many.

"You're strong enough to break a man's neck, my lord." Eliza scanned his muscular arms. His coat clung to him like a second skin. While Lord Roxburgh oozed sophistication, his powerful physique said he could kill a man with his bare hands. "Perhaps you knew Mr Ashbury had propositioned your sister and so murdered him before taking supper."

The lord managed to smile as he dropped into a chair. "Think, Miss Dutton. Do you really believe that's how I would have dealt with the matter?"

No. Lord Roxburgh was by no means a savage. But the man was a confounding contradiction. How could such an esteemed figure live such a thoroughly sinful life?

Eliza reassessed her opinion. "You would have called Mr Ashbury out, my lord, shot him clean between the brows before he had a chance to fire."

Mischief flashed in his eyes. "Be careful, Miss Dutton. That almost sounds like a compliment."

"Do you not boast about being skilled at most things?"

"Only things you might find attractive in a man."

Oh, the devil was incorrigible. "I admire honesty and integrity, courage and strength of will. As a gambler, you lack the traits I find attractive." Gamblers were liars, thieves, mentally weak, yet Lord Roxburgh gave the impression he was anything but.

"Perhaps it's a topic open for debate, Miss Dutton."

Eliza might have offered a witty retort, but Mr Daventry put a stop to their banter. "Can you recall who else was absent from the supper room?"

Lord Roxburgh rubbed his sculpted jaw thoughtfully.

There was no denying the man was handsome. He had a magnetic appeal that drew women in droves. But why would a man who had everything risk it all on the turn of the dice? Perhaps if Eliza took the time to understand Lord Roxburgh's motives, it might give her an insight into her father's reasons for ruining their lives.

"Offhand, I can recall a handful of names." He gestured to Eliza's notebook. "Will you write them down, Miss Dutton?" He paused. "Mr Fraser and Mrs Stanley were missing, although I have it on good authority they were enjoying ... the decor in the library."

That was certainly a novel way of describing a liaison.

"The Harpers prefer to explore the garden when it's quiet and decided to forgo supper. And Lord Wright was smoking a cheroot on the terrace. Having lost a substantial sum at the card table, he couldn't stomach the guinea fowl."

"Did Mr Ashbury give a reason for remaining outside, my lord?"

"No doubt he was hunting for entertainment. He had much to celebrate. He won my vowel, too."

Eliza hid her surprise. Had he just admitted to having a motive for murder? He might be guilty of wasting his fortune, of corrupting his sister with his base morals, but every fibre of her being said he was innocent of the crime.

"When the constable searched the body, did he find the vowels in Ashbury's pocket?" Mr Daventry asked.

"Sadly, no. Wright was most desperate to have his vowel returned and tried to bribe the night watchman first on the scene. But the fellow refused to touch the body until the constable arrived."

Eliza had read about a watchman caught robbing a corpse and stealing a pocket watch. No wonder the fellow had been cautious.

"Your vowel was missing, too?"

"Indeed." The lord played with his signet ring, spinning it absently around his little finger. "Forgive me. I've not offered you refreshment. Will you take tea, Miss Dutton? I know Daventry will have brandy."

"Thank you, my lord. I shall refrain."

It was foolish, but drinking from his china seemed too intimate. When she brought the cup to her mouth, she'd lay odds he'd be watching with that wickedly intense stare.

"Is there a rule against drinking while working?" he teased.

"No, but rather than pass pleasantries, I'd prefer to focus on the case." If she hoped to catch a murderer within the week, she'd need to work quickly.

Lord Roxburgh cast a smile that would make most women sigh. "I admire your dedication to duty, Miss Dutton. But it's cold out, and you owe me a boon. I'll feel better knowing you've taken something warm inside."

Eliza's pulse quickened. She turned to Mr Daventry, who seemed to find nothing untoward in the lord's last comment. "Lord Roxburgh gave me the use of his carriage the night Miss Gambit went to Blackstone." Lord Roxburgh had appeared at an opportune moment, had been generous and flirtatious in equal measure. "He takes pleasure in reminding me I owe him a debt."

Lord Roxburgh arched a brow. "Did you not refuse to pay?"

"If a man cannot show benevolence, he deserves scorn, my lord." That said, gamblers were only generous when winning. The gifts were to compensate for the nightmares.

"As we'll be working so closely together, you should call me Roxburgh."

"As you're paying for my services, I would rather keep things formal, my lord."

He grinned. "So, you'll take the case?"

Did she have much choice in the matter?

Mr Daventry confirmed her appointment by saying, "Miss Dutton does not allow her personal feelings to affect her judgement. She knows how hard it is for a young woman facing a scandal."

Lord Roxburgh turned to her, looking most intrigued. "You do?"

Ordinarily, Eliza would curb her tongue, but this man needed to know why she disliked him. "My father gambled away his fortune and left me penniless. He was shot four times for failing to pay his creditors. I saved his life on three occasions but could do nothing about the lead ball lodged between his brows."

"My deepest condolences, Miss Dutton." Lord Roxburgh inclined his head. "Now I see why you dislike reckless men."

"How can I admire a man who's ignorant of his addiction?"

"How indeed," he said, his voice tight with regret. He turned to Mr Daventry. "You mentioned another agent. Perhaps it's wise to choose someone who won't find my habits offensive."

Eliza should have felt a rush of relief. Instead, she experienced the same crippling inadequacy she had when discovering the extent of her father's debts. And she felt something else ... a flicker of admiration for the man who would put her feelings first despite the gravity of his situation.

"No!" she suddenly blurted. "I would like to help your sister."

Being trapped by the weaknesses of one's sex proved stifling. And the lady would be the subject of distasteful gossip. Eliza was more than qualified to deal with society's scorn. Gossip did not leave a woman shivering from fear in the dead of night. Gossip did not march into a churchyard as Jeremiah Black had done, prise open a coffin and snatch a man's signet ring.

"As Mr Daventry mentioned, I shall not allow my personal feelings to hinder my work. You shall have my undivided attention, my lord. Should I prove a disappointment, you can request another agent."

"I doubt you could ever be a disappointment, Miss Dutton."

"And you must stop the silly talk."

"Silly talk?" Lord Roxburgh appeared amused, not offended. "I'm told my oral skills are second to none. It's to do with the way one rolls one's tongue."

Eliza sighed, but Mr Daventry intervened again. "You will treat my agent with the utmost respect while she's living here. You will do as she says. Answer her questions honestly."

Eliza jerked her head.

Had she heard correctly?

Had he said *living here*?

"Forgive me, but there's been a mistake." Eliza's heartbeat thumped hard in her throat. "You said living here, not working here." She almost laughed aloud at the ridiculous notion.

"That's correct." Lord Roxburgh's eyes brightened. "You're to move into my home with immediate effect. Did Daventry not tell you? You're to play the role of Lillian's live-in companion."

CHAPTER 2

Adam noted the panic in Miss Dutton's eyes. She could barely tolerate him for five minutes. How would she cope when forced to share an intimate meal with him each evening? Some paid companions were treated little better than servants. He intended to treat Miss Dutton as part of the family.

"Live-in companion?" Miss Dutton looked aghast. "I am capable of investigating the murder without moving into Lord Roxburgh's home." Giving a huff of frustration, she brushed imagined dust from her green pelisse. "Really, there's no need to inconvenience him."

It was by no means an inconvenience.

Lucius Daventry was the voice of reason. "If you've any hope of learning Miss Ware's secrets, you must befriend her, discover why she went into the garden alone at midnight. It might be crucial to the case."

"I believe it is crucial. The question is at the top of my list. Still, I don't see why I need to live in such close proximity."

She looked so beautiful when flustered. Adam liked

teasing her, liked seeing her blush, liked the fiery flash of indignation in her beguiling grey eyes.

"My secretary returned to the house on the night of the murder," he informed her. By all accounts, Bloom had appeared in the garden shortly after Adam heard Lillian screaming and remained until the magistrate agreed all guests could depart. "He said he had forgotten important papers and thought to slip into the house during the party, hopefully unnoticed."

"But you don't believe him," she stated.

"He's never given me cause to doubt his word, but I doubt him now."

Miss Dutton scribbled something in her little book.

"I need you to watch Bloom when he's here," Adam continued. "I need you to spend time with Lillian, yet your investigation will keep you out of the house for most of the day. If you live here, you can watch Bloom and befriend Lillian."

Miss Dutton pursed her lips.

"I wouldn't have suggested you stay were it not necessary," Daventry said with an air of authority. "Yes, paid companions are usually spinsters, but at five and twenty, some would consider you past your prime."

Miss Dutton's eyes widened in horror. "I may be unmarried, but it's not from a lack of offers. I received three proposals the day my father died. This is the life I chose. You may be assured of that."

Daventry raised his hands in mock surrender. "It was not a testament to your allure, Miss Dutton, merely a statement of fact."

Indeed, were it a question of allure, the lady would have a ballroom full of admirers. Miss Dutton brimmed with veracity and vitality, had an undeniable appeal that captured Adam's interest the moment they'd met. She called him out for his failures, didn't give a damn about his title. That made her unique, fascinating.

Miss Dutton cast her grey gaze upon him. "If I'm to stay here, I'll not lie to your sister. You will tell her I'm an enquiry agent playing the role of her companion."

Adam didn't jump from his seat in triumph but relaxed back in the chair and spoke in his usual languid tone. "I'll not lie to my sister, either. Together, we'll explain why you're here and what we hope to achieve."

"Oh." She seemed surprised he'd agreed. "This arrangement should last no longer than a week. I suggest we begin immediately. I can return to Howland Street later to collect a few items."

"You believe you can solve the case so quickly?" He'd rather hoped it might take a month. Although, for Lillian's sake, he wanted the matter dealt with swiftly.

"You shall have me for a week, no more."

Endless nights, he'd dreamt about having her once. Having her for an entire week was beyond his wildest expectations.

She consulted her notebook. "Do you have Mr Bloom's address?"

"He has a house in Brewer Street near Golden Square."

Miss Dutton nodded, then turned to Daventry. "Might you have a man watch the house for the next few days? I should like to know if Mr Bloom receives visitors. And might you make discreet enquiries into his financial affairs?"

Daventry stood. "I shall send Bower. And I'll have an agent visit Sir Oswald at the Great Marlborough Street office to inform him Lord Roxburgh is our client. He should be forthcoming with any new information."

Miss Dutton rose gracefully. "Should Lord Roxburgh make things difficult, I shall return to Howland Street and conduct my enquiries from there."

"Agreed."

Adam stood. "I assure you, Miss Dutton, I'm an exceptional host. You'll have no complaints. Indeed, I shall treat you so well you might never leave."

She arched a coy brow. "I swore an oath never to live with a gambler again. A week is my limit."

He was not ashamed of his need to take risks. It was part of coping with past traumas. Perhaps one day, he might tell her why he staked his life on the roll of the dice—why he needed to make sense of the confusion. For now, he'd give her the basic facts.

"Understand this, Miss Dutton. This house is entailed. Lillian's dowry is just that, hers, not mine. You'll not wake to find us destitute. I shall never marry. Never sire children. My cousin will inherit, and I don't give a damn if he's left with a pile of rubble."

"But you care about your sister," she countered.

"She's all I have."

His comment had a strange effect on her. She stared at him for the longest time, seemingly confused. "If we're to help Miss Ware, I suggest we refrain from discussing your visits to gaming hells."

Daventry responded. "If you're to catch a murderer, you'll want to understand every aspect of Lord Roxburgh's life."

Witnessing her grimace, Daventry offered words of reassurance. He told Miss Dutton to keep him updated on her progress, then bid them both good day and left the house.

Being alone with Miss Dutton was like being caught in a dangerous storm. The air thrummed with a powerful force, an intense rush that proved thrilling. He'd felt the same wild undercurrent upon their first meeting over a month ago, felt it more profoundly now.

She appeared oblivious and took shelter behind the barricade erected to keep him out. A barricade a man of athletic build would struggle to scale.

"Well, Miss Dutton? Do you wish to probe me further?"

She swallowed deeply. "I would like a tour of the garden. Can you show me all possible access points, show me where you found the body?"

"I thought you might like to meet Lillian first."

"I must understand how events transpired on Saturday if I'm to establish whether Lillian is lying." She must have noticed his mild irritation at the idea Lillian would be anything but truthful because she softened her tone. "Young women keep secrets. They fill their heads with romantic notions. She was outside for a reason. That reason seems obvious to me."

Adam couldn't imagine Lillian conducting secret liaison. She was too shy, too cautious, far too insecure.

"When you meet my sister, you'll know why I find the idea absurd." He saw an opening to learn more about Miss Dutton. "What did *you* dream about when you were nineteen? It might help me understand Lillian's motives."

Miss Dutton was no fool. "Our objective is to catch a villain, not delve into the workings of my mind. From what I hear, there's a queue of candidates offering themselves up for the experiment."

"Do I detect a hint of jealousy?"

"Jealousy implies I care. I do not."

"You care a little, else you'd ignore me."

"The clawing scent of your cologne makes that impossible, my lord."

Despite the stress of the last few days, he laughed. "Come, let me escort you outside lest we stand here exchanging quips all day."

She managed a smile. "Lead the way."

Adam escorted her through the house and out onto the terrace. The sun shone high in a bright blue sky, providing a welcome break from the spate of cold weather.

Miss Dutton stood on the stone steps and surveyed her surroundings. She opened her notebook and made a pencil sketch of the grand walkway—a central avenue flanked by high topiary hedges.

"Most gardens have pretty flower beds, neat borders and lush green lawns. Your design affords many hiding places, my lord. Why is that, I wonder?"

"While you're trained to understand a man's motives, Miss Dutton, you're wrong in whatever assumption you've made about me."

She descended the stairs. "And what assumption might that be?"

"That I designed the garden because I enjoy making love outdoors."

Her pale cheeks turned a pretty pink. "The term you use for an intimate act screams of hypocrisy. Do you expect me to believe you were in love with your last mistress?"

Adam grinned and tapped his finger to his nose. "We're not here to examine the workings of my mind, madam." He strode along the verdant walkway and stopped at the statue of Salus positioned on a plinth. "There's a reason you'll find hidden pockets in the garden. A reason I'll not share with anyone."

Miss Dutton considered the statue. "Greek or Roman?"

"To the Romans, Salus was the personification of health and welfare." He touched the stone and repeated the protection prayer silently to himself. "To me, she is the goddess of safety, which is rather ironic considering a man was murdered here."

Miss Dutton tilted her head, looking somewhat bemused. "It's rather ironic for a man who thrives on risk and danger."

"If only you knew me better, Miss Dutton, you might not find me so confounding." It was a problem he hoped to rectify during the investigation.

She came to the obvious conclusion. "It's to protect you from the hazards of gambling. You stroke the stone to bring you luck."

She was wrong.

Adam pressed his finger to his lips. "Gambling is a banned topic, remember. But regarding the case, Ashbury was found dead in the hedge maze to your left."

Miss Dutton muttered her frustrations, then strode to the end of the path. She turned left towards the lush green labyrinth. There was no chance of her getting lost or spending hours trying to find her way back to the entrance. The maze was merely a series of pathways with no end goal.

He found her pacing back and forth, deep in thought.

"What is it you find so troubling?"

She looked up at him, a frown marring her brow. "It must have been so dark, so cold. If your sister found the body here, she definitely came to meet someone. Someone she knows so well she wasn't afraid." Miss Dutton paused. "At her come out, did anyone show a keen interest? Did anyone make her an offer of marriage or behave inappropriately?"

Adam's stomach twisted into knots. "Lillian is unlike most women her age. She's quiet, unassuming, prefers her own company, dislikes attention." And had spent most of her coming-out ball hiding in the ladies' retiring room.

"Unlike her brother," Miss Dutton said in a light-hearted manner.

"Call it a weakness, but I'd rather suffer flattery than be ignored." He didn't wait for her to inform him flattery was another name for falsehoods. "As for my sister's dislike of parties, I bribed her to attend the ball last Saturday. It's why I was unsurprised when she retired to her room."

He'd promised not to send her to Somerset if she attended at least one social event this season. Lillian had let Moira style her hair, had worn their mother's diamond earrings, had even danced with his friend Lowbridge. All evening, she had been possessed by a restless excitement, and so he was wrong in his earlier testimony. He *was* surprised when she announced her need to escape to her bedchamber.

"When did you lose your mother?" came Miss Dutton's logical question, yet it was like she'd thrust her hand into his chest and ripped out his heart.

"Many years ago. Lillian was six years old and has next to no recollection of the event." Thank the Lord. Lillian knew of the tragedy, but it was never spoken about. "Our aunt lives in Somerset. Lillian spent time there as a child. She visits every spring but this year refuses to leave London."

"Did she say why?"

"She pointed out she's not a child anymore, and I should respect her wishes." His biggest fear was that she was slowly becoming a recluse. That, like their mother, she lacked the mental stability to survive in the world.

Miss Dutton sighed. "Is that why you have no desire to marry and sire an heir? Because you've spent your whole adult life caring for your sister?"

Adam folded his arms across his chest. "I love my sister. It's no hardship. I might offer a complex answer, but you're not here to discover why I've made certain decisions."

Her curious gaze lingered on his face. "Interesting."

He followed her out of the maze. "What's interesting?"

"You present your secrets like a box of chocolate delicacies. You open the lid and let me glimpse inside but slam it shut the moment I consider making a choice."

He laughed. Hell, there was a host of things he could say, but she was immune to his flirtatious banter. Not so immune when it came to piquing her interest. But then, enquiry agents had inquisitive minds.

"You dislike me, hoped our paths might never cross." An idea formed, one that would allow for a more personal exploration. "This case will no doubt take its toll, and I do not wish to make matters worse by burdening you with my sad tales."

"Sad tales? Like how you lost a year's income at the tables?"

"You'll never know." He gestured to the path leading to the opposite side of the garden and purposely changed the subject. "To the right, we have the rotunda." It was a Grecian style building with a dome roof, Ionic pillars, stone steps and balustrade. "I might tell you why I chose to have one occupy such a prominent position in my garden, but that would mean letting you eat a chocolate delicacy, and I'm rather voracious in my appetites."

With a confident tilt of the chin, she offered a challenge. "I'm sure I will discover the answer during the course of my investigation."

"Then you can read minds. I've never uttered the words to a living soul." He'd only uttered them to a ghost. He motioned for her to climb the steps, followed her and brushed dirt from the stone bench. "Let us sit for a while. I have questions of my own."

"What makes you think I would lay myself bare?"

Oh, the lady had such a delightful way with words. "Who proposed to you? And if you were left destitute, why did you not feel inclined to accept?"

She arched a coy brow. "How much did you lose to Mr Ashbury?"

Nowhere near as much as she imagined.

Adam waited for her to sit, then settled beside her. "Have you chosen this life because you're hiding, Miss Dutton? Hiding from your father's creditors, perhaps?"

Ah, her quivering lip said he'd hit a nerve.

"Are you hiding, my lord? Are you afraid to confront the truth? Do you whore and gamble as a means to patch a wound that has never fully healed?"

Damnation! The lady was far too astute.

"All these niggling questions. How will you sleep tonight?"

"I shall manage, my lord."

"Let's hope you can concentrate on the case. You wouldn't want to disappoint a man like Lucius Daventry." He paused purely for dramatic effect. "Of course, there's a way we might satisfy our curiosity."

Miss Dutton snorted. "Satisfying you will no doubt involve removing articles of clothing."

Adam slapped his hand to his chest as if her comment had hit like a barbed arrow. "On the contrary, you'll need to add a few more layers."

She looked at him through narrowed eyes.

"You'll need my help if you hope to solve this case." He raised a staying hand when she opened her mouth to protest. "I doubt my guests will answer your prying questions. You will need me in tow if you hope to make it past their trusty butlers. And you want matters over quickly."

"As quickly as possible."

"Then we must push aside the need to delve deep into each other's psyches."

"What do you suggest?"

Just as he knew there was a correlation between tragedy and human frailty, he knew Miss Dutton's experiences with a gambling man had her seeking a better understanding of the vice.

"Let's set aside a time, say, an hour each evening, where we might explore how the past has a bearing on our future. Let's meet here at midnight where I will answer any question you decide to pose, regardless how personal."

She shrank back. "In return, you expect me to answer your questions?"

"Yes, in your usual frank way." He gestured to the little notebook she carried. "We will spend the rest of the time attempting to discover who murdered Ashbury and why he did so in my garden."

She flipped open the book and scanned her scrawled notes. "Someone may have a vendetta against you. Do you agree to answer questions about your rakish habits? Do you agree to answer them during my investigation and not make me wait until midnight?"

"I concede someone may bear a grudge. I concede my debt to Ashbury is relevant, too." It was imperative she learnt to trust his word. Imperative for what reason, he was unsure. "My vowel was for the paltry sum of three hundred pounds. And no, I did not steal it back while inspecting his body."

Miss Dutton made another note in her book. "Someone did."

A gentle breeze caught a lock of black hair escaping her green bonnet. At midnight, he'd ask her to take her hair down. He'd spend the hour confirming his first thought. Miss Dutton was beautiful, inside and out. Of course, he would be forced to reveal his own torments. But it was the price he had to pay if he hoped to know her better, the price of making her his.

If only for an hour at midnight.

CHAPTER 3

"Good afternoon, my lord. How is Miss Ware?" A handsome man with blonde hair and neat side-whiskers appeared in the hall. He carried a leather portfolio practically bursting at the seams and was presumably the secretary.

"Shaken, as one might expect under the circumstances." Lord Roxburgh spoke in an even tone devoid of mistrust. "Allow me to present Miss Dutton." Lord Roxburgh looked at her with his striking brown eyes. "Mr Bloom is my secretary."

So, this was the man who lied about his reason for being in Hanover Square on the night of the murder.

After exchanging pleasantries and quickly deciding how she wanted to proceed, Eliza said, "I'm an enquiry agent hired by his lordship to discover who murdered Mr Ashbury."

Mr Bloom's eyes bulged.

Lord Roxburgh smiled. "Are we to tell the whole world why you're here, Miss Dutton? Perhaps I should put an announcement in *The Times,* have the crier march through the streets ringing his handbell."

"As your secretary, one assumes Mr Ashbury has knowledge of your private affairs, my lord." Eliza fixed Mr Bloom with a knowing stare. "As someone seen in the vicinity at the time of the murder, I'm sure he wants to confess."

Mr Bloom paled. "I assure you, Miss Dutton, I had nothing to do with the death of that poor man. I came merely to collect important papers."

"What papers?" Eliza noted the brief panic in Mr Bloom's angelic blue eyes.

"W-what papers?" Mr Bloom repeated.

"Yes. What exactly had you forgotten?"

"The erm ... the letter for his lordship's estate manager at Glendale."

Lord Roxburgh nodded. "Glendale is my seat in Worcester. I did ask Bloom to correspond with Mr Farthing."

That might well have been the case, but that was not Mr Bloom's motive for being in the house that night.

"So you did not come for papers, Mr Bloom, but for a letter?"

"Yes, a letter," the secretary said.

"Then his lordship must have dictated the letter on Friday."

"Yes, he did."

"Would you not have written it before leaving for the day and had it sent to post?" Something so important would have been dealt with before the weekend. "As his lordship frequently hosts balls, Mr Bloom, you would know the house was in chaos on Saturday, and Lord Roxburgh spent the day seeking a distraction. Would it not have been prudent to call then?"

Lord Roxburgh blinked in surprise. "I rode with a friend on Saturday, then played billiards at Boodle's." He folded his arms and fixed the secretary with an irritated stare. "You did write the letter because I franked it on Friday. Why the devil did you leave it here?"

Mr Bloom touched his hand to his throat—a classic sign he was drowning in his own guilt. Eliza eagerly awaited his reply, but then a gentle feminine voice cut through the silence.

"I thought I heard shouting." A young woman dressed in pale blue, her auburn hair styled in a simple chignon, came padding lightly down the stairs. "I feared it was Mr Ashbury's parents come to cause trouble again."

Presumably, this delicate creature was Miss Lillian Ware. And if she had spent days sobbing in her bedchamber, so dreadfully distraught, would she not be too afraid to face the Ashburys?

Eliza observed Mr Bloom's reaction. His countenance brightened considerably, and it was suddenly apparent why the lady ventured outside that night, knowing her brother was occupied in the supper room.

What surprised Eliza most was that a man of Lord Roxburgh's experience didn't know his sister was conducting a love affair under his roof.

"Thank heavens it's you, Mr Bloom." Miss Ware's nervous smile seemed genuine, though her eyes weren't bloodshot as one would expect from someone who had been crying for days. Her gaze skimmed past Eliza as if she were invisible and came to rest on her brother. "Have you heard from Sir Oswald? Has he made an arrest?"

Lord Roxburgh did not chastise his sister for her rudeness. "Allow me to present Miss Dutton. She's an enquiry agent, hired to discover who killed Mr Ashbury. And no, I've not heard from Sir Oswald."

The information acted as a restorative, reviving the lady's countenance. "An enquiry agent? You solve murders, Miss Dutton? How wonderful. Forgive me, I presumed you were my brother's ... erm."

"Paramour?" Eliza offered.

"Well, yes." Miss Ware seemed shocked and excited that Eliza had mentioned the forbidden word in front of two gentlemen. "I should have known better. Adam never brings ladies home."

Adam. Adam Ware. The strong, dependable name failed to reflect the complexity of Lord Roxburgh's character. And why would he bring a lady home? Lord Roxburgh was determined never to marry. Which was probably for the best, considering he usually kept a mistress and gambled to excess.

"Miss Dutton will live here temporarily," Lord Roxburgh informed his sister. "Should anyone ask, she's your paid companion. I pray you understand why such measures are necessary."

"I shall remain here for a week, no more," Eliza assured her.

Miss Ware's eyes widened in horror. "Paid companion? Am I expected to attend social functions? Oh please, Adam, no! After what happened last Saturday, I'm a social pariah." She gripped Eliza's arm. "Tell him, Miss Dutton. Tell him I hate the pretence, hate the pomp, hate the people."

Eliza had come to Hanover Square to solve the case, not become embroiled in family affairs. Yet she sensed this was a house of many secrets. It would serve all parties if they were brought to light, and there was no time like the present.

"Miss Ware, though I speak my mind, know my heart is full of good intention." Eliza had no option but to inform his lordship of the real reason his sister spent so much time at home. "I beg your forgiveness in advance. When you hear what I have to say, you might dislike me for a time. But a man has lost his life, and Lord Roxburgh has hired me to help limit the damage caused to your reputation."

Miss Ware stood statue-still, her eyes wide, her dainty chin trembling.

"Now, I suggest we retire to the drawing room and thrash the matter out there." Eliza gestured for Miss Ware to lead the way. "That includes you, Mr Bloom. Should you refuse, I shall advise Lord Roxburgh to terminate your employment."

As expected, Miss Ware gasped at the prospect of not seeing Mr Bloom every day at noon.

"Go on ahead, Mr Bloom. I wish to have a private word with Lord Roxburgh." Eliza hoped to give the couple a few minutes alone to decide whether they might confess. During which time, she would ensure Lord Roxburgh received his awakening.

As soon as Miss Ware and Mr Bloom strode into the drawing room, Lord Roxburgh gripped Eliza's elbow and guided her along the hall, out of earshot.

"Now I see why you command such an exorbitant fee." His voice was velvet smooth and full of admiration. "You handled my sister better than any governess ever could."

Eliza searched her mind for a polite way to call the man a fool. "My lord, please tell me you see what is going on here. Tell me all talk of Miss Ware's fragile nerves is a means of protecting her reputation."

Lord Roxburgh appeared confused.

Oh, dear! The man was clueless.

"Please tell me your experiences with the fairer sex amount to more than the rampant goings-on beneath the bedsheets."

"I understand women, Miss Dutton," he snapped, mildly annoyed.

"But you're blind to your sister's antics."

"Antics?" Lord Roxburgh straightened and folded his arms across his broad chest. "Being constantly in the doldrums is not a ploy for attention. Lillian is pale, has no appetite and rarely leaves the house."

Yes, Miss Ware was lovesick and probably fell into a state of melancholy whenever Mr Bloom departed.

Reluctantly, Eliza touched Lord Roxburgh's arm in the hope physical contact lessened the blow. "Your sister is in love with Mr Bloom. Why would she leave when he visits most days? That's why she insisted you treat her like an adult and not send her to Somerset. That's why she has no interest in attending balls and soirees."

Lord Roxburgh's gaze turned as dark as winter storm clouds. "In love with Bloom? God's teeth, you'd better be wrong."

"My lord," she began, pity—and the shock of discovering his heart wasn't made entirely of stone—forcing her to soften her tone. "Miss Ware arranged for Mr Bloom to meet her in the maze while you were taking supper. That's how she stumbled upon the body."

His cool reserve abandoned, the hard muscle in his forearm tensed beneath her fingers. Indeed, she could almost hear his blood roaring through his veins.

"If Bloom has laid a hand on her, he's a dead man."

"I see. You mean to help your sister by murdering the man she loves."

What had happened to the logical lord, the great intellectual who seduced women into bed with a devilish smile and witty conversation, the man so calm and self-assured?

He lowered his head and whispered, "As you appear to be a fountain of knowledge, Miss Dutton, what the devil would you do?"

Eliza snatched back her hand. Touching him while his mouth hovered mere inches from hers roused worrying sensations.

"Should you not seek confirmation? Should you not attempt to understand the full measure of the situation?"

Mr Daventry warned against reacting quickly. One's first assumption was often wrong. They were taught to focus on the facts, not race ahead, hurling accusations.

"I understand the situation." His sharp tone could slice through sinew.

Eliza scrambled to think of a way to reason with him. "Your sister is all you have. Will you ruin your only genuine relationship by over-reacting?"

Lord Roxburgh dragged his hand down his face and groaned.

"Don't be the tyrant she despises. Be the man she trusts and admires." Eliza spoke from personal experience. "Come. I must spend the afternoon listing the suspects and devising a plan. The sooner we deal with this problem, the better." And she still needed to ask him intimate questions about his private affairs.

The gentleman gave a resigned nod. "Daventry should charge double for your services. Your skills are highly underrated."

Eliza smiled. "Be careful, my lord. That sounds like a compliment."

"Don't imagine it will be the last."

"No, I'm told flattery is part of a rake's repartee."

They found Mr Bloom pacing the room, his hands clasped behind his back while Miss Ware marched beside him, almost frantic in her need to garner his attention.

They swung around when Lord Roxburgh entered. Poor Mr Bloom froze like a deer hearing the crunch of twigs in the woods. It was hardly surprising. Lord Roxburgh possessed a deadly stare and a formidable presence.

Miss Ware dashed tears from her eyes. "Adam, there's something Mr Bloom wants to tell—"

"You'll hear what I have to say first, Lillian."

"Perhaps Mr Bloom might like a brandy," Eliza suggested.

Lord Roxburgh's humourless laugh only added to the tension. "Perhaps I should give Bloom my racing curricle and seat in the House of Lords. He's keen to take everything else I treasure." He gestured to the nervous couple. "Sit down."

Mr Bloom and Miss Ware settled on the sofa. Hands clasped in their laps, they looked like children accused of stealing cakes from the kitchen, their lips pursed to hide the evidence of their gluttony.

Lord Roxburgh relayed Eliza's suspicions like they were

his own. Remarkably, he kept his temper, though occasionally balled his fists at his sides.

"You know me better than anyone, Lillian. You know I have every reason to despise secrets."

"But this isn't the same as *that* secret," Miss Ware implored.

Eliza was keen to learn of this mysterious secret and would add it to her list of questions for their first midnight meeting. Perhaps she shouldn't have agreed to the late-night liaisons, but learning about Lord Roxburgh's reckless pursuits might prove insightful.

"I've always wanted what's best for you," Lord Roxburgh continued. "I prayed one of us had made it thus far unscathed. Yet it appears your judgement is equally flawed."

Evidently, Mr Daventry had no need to joke about Lord Roxburgh's missing conscience. It hadn't jumped ship in a foreign port and scampered into the crowd but was hidden beneath the weight of his bravado.

"I wish Mother were here," Miss Ware blurted.

Lord Roxburgh stiffened at the comment. "Sadly, she's not."

A heavy silence ensued. Lord Roxburgh couldn't seem to find the words to continue despite speaking with such authority.

Eliza cleared her throat. "Mr Bloom. Can you confirm you arrived here on Saturday evening to meet secretly with Miss Ware? It's vital I understand what happened if I'm to prove Miss Ware is innocent of any crime." And there was the matter of repairing the damage done to the lady's reputation. Though that was probably a task beyond Eliza's capabilities.

"You don't have to answer," Miss Ware snapped.

"He does if he wishes to keep his position." Without Lord Roxburgh's recommendation, who else would hire him?

Mr Bloom turned to Miss Ware and captured her hand. "Lillian, this is a complicated situation made more problematic by my lack of fortune. But I should have spoken to Lord Roxburgh months ago when we—"

"Months ago!" Lord Roxburgh clenched his fists again. "Months! By God, if you've laid a hand on her, I'll wring your damn neck."

Full of indignation, Miss Ware jumped up and stamped her foot. "Mr Bloom is a gentleman. He treats me with the utmost respect." She turned to Eliza. "Be warned, Miss Dutton. My brother loves the thrill of the chase. Ladies fall in love with him, then he casts them aside. He is judging Mr Bloom by his own shallow standards."

"That's enough, Lillian." The lord's voice carried an ominous undertone.

"Is it? When will it be enough for you, Adam?" She directed her next statement at Eliza. "My brother took his last mistress to stay at the Marquess Devereaux's home. I ask you. Is that the mark of a gentleman or a scandalous rogue?"

"I said that's enough," the lord warned.

Eliza remembered the event because her colleague had been hired to discover who wanted to murder the marquess.

"I believe the marquess held an intimate party for close friends. In such circumstances, rules may be relaxed." The last thing Eliza wanted to do was defend Lord Roxburgh, but his reputation was not the one torn to shreds. "The question of what his lordship might do about your blossoming relationship is a private matter. For now, you must tell me—"

A loud knock on the front door caught everyone's attention.

Chin raised, Lord Roxburgh's footman walked past the drawing room.

"You must tell me exactly what happened when you stepped out into the garden on Saturday night." Eliza ignored the mutter of voices at the front door, though couldn't help but notice the speed at which the footman retreated. "Did anyone see you?"

Miss Ware seemed grateful for the distraction. "No. I left the house via the servants' door. It leads to the far side of the labyrinth." She cast a wary glance at her brother. "I'd agreed to meet Mr Bloom there at midnight. Afterwards, we were hoping to catch my brother in a good mood. Sadly, he lost at cards to Mr Ashbury and was a veritable grouch."

Lord Roxburgh muttered something beneath his breath. He threw daggers of disdain at his secretary and seemed to be a reasonably good aim because poor Mr Bloom inhaled so sharply he almost choked.

It was the butler's turn to march along the hall. Eliza heard him open the front door and speak to someone waiting outside.

"If you hate secrets, Adam," Miss Ware countered, "do not complain when I tell you the truth."

The butler appeared at the drawing door and cleared his throat. "Forgive me, my lord. Sir Oswald is here and requests an audience."

Relief raced through Eliza, bolstering her spirit. With luck, she'd be back in Howland Street before the clang of the dinner gong.

"Send him in, Greyson. We will all be relieved to hear his news."

Sir Oswald entered the room. Being a short man with an expanding waistline, every step left him gasping. Though his thin grey hair marked him past middle age, his florid face gave his countenance a youthful glow.

Eliza waited for Lord Roxburgh to introduce the magistrate and expected them to retreat to the study to discuss matters privately. But Sir Oswald took one look at Mr Bloom, and his cheeks ballooned.

"The chap is in here," Sir Oswald called to his man who was hovering in the hall, then he turned to Lord Roxburgh and apologised again for the intrusion. "Sorry to break the news, Roxburgh, but your secretary is wanted for questioning concerning the murder of Mr Ashbury."

"Murder! That's preposterous!" Miss Ware cried.

Mr Bloom's face turned ashen.

Lord Roxburgh suddenly switched allegiance. "Next time, you will state your business before barging into my home. As for my secretary, you'll not take him anywhere without a warrant."

A stocky man with a pocked face and squashed nose introduced himself as Sergeant Parks. He pulled a letter from his pocket and handed it to Lord Roxburgh. "The warrant, my lord."

"Roxburgh, I'm here at your behest. Did you not make me swear to catch the devil responsible?" Sir Oswald spoke with a touch of humility. "We've a witness placing your secretary in the garden at the time of the murder."

A fool could see Mr Bloom lacked the ruthlessness needed to break a man's neck. Still, Sir Oswald cared less about catching the real culprit and wished to deal with the matter quickly.

"Bloom was working late," Lord Roxburgh lied. "He heard my sister's screams and hurried outside to offer assistance."

Sir Oswald cleared his throat. "Lord Wright saw your secretary arguing with Mr Ashbury in the garden half an hour before Miss Ware discovered the body. By all accounts, your man grabbed Ashbury by his cravat and threatened to drown him in the Thames."

Mr Bloom made to reply, but Lord Roxburgh interrupted. "Lord Wright was three sheets to the wind and spent the evening muttering to himself on the terrace. Are you telling me you trust the word of a depressed drunk who lost a substantial sum at the tables?"

"If Lord Wright was in the garden half an hour before the murder, are you questioning him?" Eliza demanded to know. "He's the only person with any real motive." Not the only person, but Lord Roxburgh wouldn't kill a man over a few hundred pounds. "What possible motive might Mr Bloom have?"

Even if Sir Oswald had heard rumours about Miss Ware and Mr Bloom, he wasn't about to insult the sister of a peer. And when Lord Roxburgh introduced Eliza as one of Lucius Daventry's agents, the tubby fellow was forced to gasp another panicked breath.

"You can return tomorrow and question Bloom here." Lord Roxburgh maintained his stony expression. "If you fear he may abscond, then I give my word he'll remain in my custody until then."

Miss Ware looked at her brother as if he were the Messiah.

When deep in thought, Sir Oswald constantly twitched his nose. Perhaps he hoped the answer to his dilemma might be found in the notes of Lord Roxburgh's bergamot cologne. "I'll agree to your request but must insist on checking Mr Bloom's desk, his coat pockets and the leather portfolio he was carrying when he entered."

So, Sir Oswald had a constable watching Lord Roxburgh's house.

The magistrate was right to have his suspicions. Few employers would tolerate their secretary mingling with guests at a grand ball. And Mr Bloom could do nothing with an important letter at midnight and should have called at a more appropriate hour.

"Bloom has nothing to hide." Lord Roxburgh's comment sounded like a threat. "He works in my study. You're welcome to search the desk, but you have my word he carries nothing confidential in his portfolio."

"I'm afraid I must object to such harsh scrutiny," Mr Bloom said, having found a modicum of courage. "I don't see why it's necessary. What do Lord Roxburgh's personal papers have to do with a murder enquiry?"

He seemed most insistent yet had sat quietly with his hands in his lap until now. Indeed, he had not shot out of his seat to deny his involvement in the murder.

A sudden change in character is often a sign of guilt.

Mr Daventry's warning entered her mind.

The magistrate wasn't interested in important papers. He was looking for the missing vowels. Was Mr Bloom hiding incriminating evidence in his portfolio?

"I agree with Mr Bloom," Miss Ware suddenly chirped. "Why harass a man on the word of a sotted fool? It's outrageous."

If Miss Ware worked for Lucius Daventry, she would know that protesting the injustice of it all only deepened suspicions. And if Lord Wright was so inebriated, he'd have struggled to break Mr Ashbury's neck.

"Roxburgh, you must understand my predicament." Sir Oswald panted, for he clearly found the situation taxing. "I've procedures to follow. Confirm your man isn't in possession of the missing vowels, and I'll leave any questions until tomorrow."

Lord Roxburgh's mocking snort echoed through the room. "Even if, by some wild stretch of the imagination, Bloom had stolen the vowels, why the devil would he carry them on his person?" He paused, his expression darkening. "Unless you're suggesting I ordered my secretary to steal back my vowel. Indeed, it sounds like you're questioning my honour, not Bloom's."

"No! No!" Panicked, Sir Oswald waved his chubby hands in the air. "I assure you, it is just a matter of procedure."

"A matter of procedure? Have you emptied the drawers in Lord Wright's desk? Have you accused his staff of murdering a man to save their master paying a measly debt?" Lord Roxburgh answered for him. "No, you have not."

Sir Oswald shuffled uncomfortably, his cheeks turning crimson.

Lord Roxburgh displayed such strength of character, Eliza wondered why he needed to hire an enquiry agent.

"Leave now." Though Lord Roxburgh appeared calm, his voice carried the devil's own warning. "Return only when you've questioned Lord Wright and rummaged through his drawers. Return only if you have damning evidence against my secretary. In the meantime, I shall make my complaint to the highest authority."

Sir Oswald muttered an apology, ushered his sergeant out, and retreated.

Lord Roxburgh waited until Greyson closed the front door behind the men before exhaling a weary sigh.

When Miss Ware spoke, he raised a hand to silence her. "Don't. Don't say a word, Lillian. My temper hangs by the thinnest thread."

"It's imperative I take Mr Bloom's statement and have Mr Daventry sign the document," Eliza dared to say. She would demand a more detailed account from Miss Ware, too. "I cannot trust those at the Marlborough Street office to record the information accurately." They were desperate in their bid to find someone to blame.

"Agreed." Lord Roxburgh glanced at the leather portfolio wedged between Mr Bloom and the arm of his seat. "Is there anything you wish to say about Bloom's reluctance to comply with Sir Oswald's request?"

"Plenty," she began, assuming the lord had arrived at the same conclusion. "Mr Bloom will tell us how he came by the stolen vowels and why in heaven's name he is carrying them on his person."

CHAPTER 4

The last twelve hours had been nothing but chaos.

Bloom had not stolen the vowels from a dead man's pocket. Out of some misguided notion of punishing a corpse and saving Adam a few hundred pounds, Lillian had robbed Ashbury.

Lumbered with the evidence, Bloom had come to Hanover Square intending to confess. Consequently, the hope that Lord Wright had murdered Ashbury disintegrated along with the vowels burning in the grate.

After taking the necessary statements, Miss Dutton had left the house and had failed to return. Now, Adam sat alone on the stone bench in the rotunda, suspecting she'd told Daventry to send another agent, fearing she had no intention of meeting him for a midnight liaison.

He relaxed back just as the unsynchronised church bells across town chimed twelve. Disappointment flared. Then he chuckled aloud.

Why in the devil's name did he give a damn? Why did he want Miss Dutton to see him as someone more than a man whose past mistresses numbered a dozen? Someone more than a man who risked his funds because he was too damn scared to risk his life?

The patter of footsteps on the terrace caught his attention. Seconds later, Miss Dutton appeared, still wearing her forest-green pelisse. She'd dispensed with her bonnet, and a few teasing wisps of ebony hair brushed her cheeks.

Adam stood to the twelfth dong of the St George's bells.

"Thank heavens. I made it just in time." She smiled despite looking tired. "I told the jarvey I'd pay double if he got me to the square before the last stroke of midnight."

Adam covered his heart with his hand. "You'd give your hard-earned funds just to spend an hour in my company. I'm flattered, Miss Dutton."

"We had an agreement. As the daughter of a man who broke every promise, my word is my bond." When he invited her to sit on the bench, she frowned. "Is there room for two?"

Adam resisted the urge to say something salacious. "I'll stand if you feel uncomfortable. I presume you're staying and haven't come to inform me Miss Trimble is to take my case."

Miss Trimble was a busybody, employed by Lucius Daventry to keep house and care for his female agents.

"Don't mock Miss Trimble." Miss Dutton climbed the steps and perched on the bench. "She has an excellent mind and is well travelled. She can speak five languages."

"And yet Daventry hasn't hired her to solve crimes."

Adam flicked his coattails and sat beside her. He took a few seconds to appreciate their surroundings. The moon was visible behind silver streaks of cloud. The sprinkling of stars in the night sky, and the glow from the burning brazier, might easily put a man in an amorous mood.

"Miss Trimble is more than capable of solving crimes. She once worked for a gentleman who secretly kidnapped his own daughter and had his brother pay the ransom. She uncovered the plot."

That explained Miss Trimble's overly suspicious nature and why she was such a damn pessimist. "When I met her at Devereaux's wedding, I sensed her distrust of men." Miss Trimble had wrapped her protective wings around her ladies and glared at him as if he were the devil's spawn.

Miss Dutton nodded. "No doubt she has many stories to tell, but she rarely discusses her past."

"Well, we're not here to discuss Miss Trimble's secrets." Adam faced her fully, aware their knees were mere inches apart. "But I'm desperately curious to hear yours."

She looked him keenly in the eye, though he sensed her reluctance to discuss painful memories. "The hour is late, and I must relay all that has occurred this evening. Perhaps we can save all personal questions until tomorrow."

Ah, the classic distraction technique.

He'd not let her escape so easily.

"Unlike your father, I'm not one to break an oath. We can discuss the case while taking breakfast in the morning."

"But I'm told you rarely rise before noon."

"For you, I'll make an exception."

This time, her gaze fell to her lap. He liked the brief glimpse of vulnerability. Much like himself, she hid a lot behind her confident countenance.

"I'll begin," he said, wanting to wring this hour for all it was worth. "Is your mother alive? And if so, does she know you risk your life chasing criminals on London's dangerous streets?"

Miss Dutton's mouth thinned, but she answered. "My mother died in childbirth when I was nine. My newborn brother died that day, too. Things were never the same after that."

She had lost her mother and her brother on the same day?

Adam's stomach knitted into knots. "I feel your pain, Miss Dutton. Loss of any kind can have a profound effect."

He was desperate to change the subject lest she ask how his mother died.

"The depth of our sorrow is the measure of how deeply we loved."

"Indeed." Though he'd found it more complicated than that.

A brief silence ensued.

"What's the most you've ever lost at the card table?" she said.

Adam shrugged. He never kept a record of his wins and losses. Was reluctant to reveal anything but owed her the truth. "The worst loss was the night I staked my father's gold pocket watch. In terms of value, it's priceless. Thankfully, I repurchased the watch for a substantial fee."

Miss Dutton jerked her head. "Why would you risk something so precious?"

"Why indeed? But that's a question for another night." He decided on something more light-hearted. "Will you marry, do you think?"

She thought for a moment. "Perhaps. But I could never marry a man who gambles."

He wasn't the least bit offended. "Is life not a gamble? The odds are stacked against us, yet still, we chance our luck. Is gambling not an act of optimism? The hope of something better?"

"You're entitled to live how you please. Don't fool yourself into thinking it's a solitary pleasure. Everyone close to you suffers for your ignorance."

No one had ever spoken to him with such candour.

Adam inhaled deeply. "Like your perfume, the truth carries an irresistible bouquet. Both hold me equally enthralled."

Miss Dutton straightened. "If this is an attempt at seduction, you should know I'm resistant to your charm."

"Until you know me better, any attempt would be futile."

Adam closed his eyes and breathed the intoxicating aroma. "Your perfume says much about you. Notes of citrus assault the nostrils, much like your sharp criticism. Beyond lies the sweet scent of rose. A natural essence, free from artifice." He opened his eyes and fixed her with his gaze. "It's an alluring combination."

She gave a mocking snort. "You sound like the royal perfumer."

"The choices we make reflect something of our innate character."

"My mother wore this scent. My father bought it for her when life was good and suffering happened to other people. I used my advance from Mr Daventry to purchase a bottle, and though I apply it sparingly, it is rather potent."

Oh, there was a wealth of information in those few sentences.

She wore the scent because it brought hope of a brighter future. It was such a cherished memory she had made the extravagant purchase when she should have bought new boots. Yes, deep-rooted emotions often led to illogical actions.

"Your perfume is so unique I'd find you in a room full of women." He glanced at the lit brazier. They had a little time left before the fire died. "I believe it's your turn to ask a question. It may well be the last one of the evening, so choose wisely."

She might have consulted her notebook, but he knew the question dancing on the tip of her tongue had nothing to do with a murder case.

"Jealousy is a motive for murder," she began in a measured tone. "If I'm to understand why someone killed a man in your garden, I must know more about your romantic affairs."

"Ask because you wish to understand me, not a killer."

She gave a curt nod. "I'm told Mrs Thorne was your last mistress. That you parted ways recently. I know it's impolite to discuss a man's habits, but I must know if the rumours are true."

"Rumours?" He knew to what she referred.

"That you kept her as your mistress because she paid your gambling debts."

He found the gossip amusing and couldn't help but laugh. "You think I would take a woman to bed merely so she might settle my account at The Black Sapphire?"

Adam waited for her witty retort, but she froze, paled. "The B-Black Sapphire? That's the gaming hell you frequent?"

He shrugged. "Yes, amongst other haunts. Is it relevant?"

She blinked rapidly but gathered herself and shook her head. "Only that I heard the proprietor is ruthless when it comes to those who cannot pay. Not that you've had a problem settling your account."

"No." Based on her odd reaction, perhaps her father had visited the establishment and lost heavily at the tables. Jem Black was vicious when it came to recouping funds. But Adam would avoid the subject of her father's gambling debts for now. "In answer to your original question, Mrs Thorne did pay some of my debts."

"And you found that acceptable?" she asked in a haughty tone.

"As you've never been a man's mistress, it isn't right you should judge." Mrs Thorne's insecurities meant she was extravagant with her gifts. "The lady's husband shot himself, and I was a shoulder of support. Clearly, she felt the need to repay me for my kindness. Whenever I refused to accept her generosity, it only added to her distress."

"And you parted ways amicably?" she said, sounding less critical.

"Not amicably, no."

He'd parted ways the moment he'd laid eyes on Miss Dutton. It wasn't that he hoped to make an enquiry agent his mistress. But he'd felt that initial bolt of attraction, an exquisite type of madness that had him inventing tales of happy endings, left him contemplating the possibility that meaningful connections did exist.

Now fate had brought them together, Adam was torn between proving he was incapable of feeling any lasting emotion and wondering if it was simply that he'd not met the right woman.

"Mrs Thorne did not murder Ashbury because our arrangement had run its course." Besides, he'd been told she'd taken an extended trip abroad.

"And who replaced Mrs Thorne in your affections?"

Only you, he wanted to say.

"No one."

He'd seen Miss Dutton a handful of times this past month yet had thought about her daily. Indeed, he'd come to the conclusion he might be suffering from his mother's illness. It was out of character for him to dream, out of character for him to experience a frisson of excitement in anyone's company.

"So you see, the villain isn't a jealous woman on the rampage."

The church bells chimed the half hour.

Time was of the essence.

"Now, I believe it's my turn to ask a question," he said once the stillness of the night settled around them again. "What do you do for pleasure, Miss Dutton?"

"A working woman has little time for frivolous pursuits."

"Come now. I've seen the glint in your eyes when you whip me with your tongue. I speak metaphorically, of course, though should you feel inclined to act out your fantasy, know I'd happily strip off my shirt and let you have your wicked way."

Miss Dutton tutted. "One's tongue is hardly a formidable weapon."

"Trust me. The strike of mine in just the right spot would easily tear a groan from your lips."

She was quick to disagree with him. "You forget, I'm immune to your lascivious banter. Nothing you say could stir a reaction."

Oh, he would take great pleasure proving her wrong. "Perhaps we should return to this topic at a later date." And he didn't want to force her behind her barricade, not when he had every hope of breaking it down. "Perhaps you should tell me if you found anything pertinent when you questioned Lillian and that damn rogue Bloom."

Miss Dutton shuffled uncomfortably on the seat. "Your sister told the magistrate she went out into the garden because she'd lost her bracelet. I encouraged her to keep up the pretence. Indeed, if I'm to salvage anything of her reputation, I cannot have people believe she'd agreed to meet Mr Bloom in a dark corner of the maze."

Adam might have drawn attention to the fact she despised lies and untruths. He might have highlighted her hypocrisy, but he understood why she'd decided to support Lillian. And he admired her loyalty to her client. Still, he had no need to do either because the lady was suddenly overcome with guilt.

"I know it's wrong. I know it will probably come back to haunt me, but I spoke to Mr Daventry, and he supports my decision."

"As do I."

A hint of a smile formed on her lips. "I have faith in Miss Ware's account. There seems little point dragging her reputation through the mud when people already think badly of her."

"A lady seen alone in a garden will draw more than a frown."

Her sigh carried a wealth of regret. "Once, the same

might have applied to me. Yet here I sit in a garden with a scandalous rake, discussing all sorts of personal information."

"Is that why you're so keen to help Lillian?" Was it a means to heal old wounds, to cleanse the mind of horrible memories? "Did you suffer society's scorn when your father lost his fortune?"

Miss Dutton's eyes turned a stormy grey. He caught a glimpse of her inner turmoil, could almost feel a violent tempest brewing.

"My father was a gentleman, an academic who wrote many papers on scientific theory before my mother died." Her voice held disdain for a man who had proved a failure, a disappointment. "He was a respected member of the community until the gossips had their way and tore his reputation to shreds."

"I'm sorry you had to suffer that." For once, he sounded sincere.

"All the tales they told were true. But they condemned me for being nothing more than an innocent bystander." Her dainty hands balled into fists. "The world doesn't become a better place because of scientific advancements. It's changed by selfless acts of kindness. If someone had reached out to my father, I might not be in this predicament."

Adam had conversed with women on many subjects. Never had one left him contemplating how he might be a better version of himself.

"If it's any consolation, you're an excellent enquiry agent."

"You handled Sir Oswald so well I'm left wondering why you hired me."

"I can be persuasive, ruthless when required, but I'm not always objective when it comes to Lillian." And Ashbury's death had given him an opportunity to know Miss Dutton better. "The only way to help repair my sister's reputation is to force an influential peer to marry her."

Miss Dutton's light-hearted chuckle was like a cool breeze

on a stifling day. "Then you have a problem. Miss Ware said she will marry no one but Mr Bloom."

Damnation! What the devil had happened to sweet little Lillian? This infatuation had turned her mind to mush. The sister of a peer did not marry his secretary.

"She's not marrying Bloom."

"You'd rather see her miserable?" Miss Dutton sounded ready to fight for all women browbeaten by patriarchs. "You'd deny her the chance of true happiness?"

"Lillian might think she's in love, but she's had no experience of men. As for Bloom, the fellow saw an opportunity to advance the ranks and has convinced himself he feels the same."

I shall take care of matters while you're in Hampshire, my lord.

The bastard had taken care of more than Adam's upcoming engagements.

"Or you've convinced yourself it's all nonsense because you cannot face reality," came Miss Dutton's insightful reply. "But I have an idea how we might limit the damage to Miss Ware's reputation. Nothing will fix the fact that she was alone in the maze at midnight. Most people will presume you killed Mr Ashbury because your sister met him in the garden."

Had Adam known about Ashbury propositioning Lillian, he would have spilt the man's innards. "I fail to see how the *ton* might be convinced my sister isn't a harlot."

"When life leaves you floundering, you sink or swim."

Adam shrugged, still clueless.

"She must become the belle of the season. She must create such an air of mystery, weave such exciting tales that people hang on her every word. The *ton* must believe Miss Ware risked her reputation in an attempt to save Mr Ashbury's life."

Clearly, Miss Dutton had never entered enemy territory and been hit with the cut direct. "Lillian isn't strong enough. She'll crumble the moment she's snubbed."

"You underestimate her, my lord. She risked everything to meet Mr Bloom in the garden. She has your strength of will and is just as obstinate." Miss Dutton seemed keen to plead his sister's case. "And with you at her side, she'll have the confidence to tackle the world."

"Me!" Adam stood. "You expect me to attend the sorts of soirees one considers suitable for my sister? I'd die of boredom within the hour." But then a delicious idea entered his head. One that would make a dull party bearable. "Unless you came."

"Me?"

"Daventry can acquire an invitation to any *ton* event. Yes, you'll come as my sister's companion, and we'll spend the evening together. Perfect."

Miss Dutton jumped up as fast as a woman plagued with cramp. "I don't have the deportment or manners required to mingle in high society. I don't even own a gown."

The bells chimed the hour, leaving her no time to muster a better argument.

"Sadly, our midnight meeting is at an end." He gestured for her to descend the stone steps. "We can discuss the arrangements tomorrow." Tomorrow he'd send for the best modiste in town. Send for a dance tutor, too, for he would not forgo an opportunity to hold Miss Dutton in his arms.

"We're busy tomorrow," she snapped.

"Busy?" He couldn't resist teasing her. "You've thought of a wicked use for me, madam? I am but a slave to your wants and desires."

"What I want is for you to take the matter seriously. I'm to visit Mr Ashbury's apartment at the Albany tomorrow, and I need you to accompany me."

Visit the Albany?

Had the lady taken leave of her senses?

"You mean to visit an exclusive residence for bachelors

with a man most people consider a rakehell? Even if women were permitted entrance, it's sheer folly."

She tapped him playfully on the arm. "I'm not a fool, my lord. Mr Daventry has provided the necessary clothes and obtained the keys to Mr Ashbury's apartment. I'm to don a tailcoat and breeches and will use the name Mr Tiffin."

Tiffin! No doubt, that was Daventry's idea of a joke.

"I would not acquaint myself with a man named after a midday meal."

"Then choose a suitable name and inform me at breakfast."

Adam tried to muster another rational objection but instead envisioned the delightful Miss Dutton wearing breeches. Hellfire!

"I shall bid you good night, my lord, and remind you we must make an early start in the morning."

"How early?"

Adam doubted he'd sleep tonight. With his damn secretary staying in the house, he'd have his ears pricked, waiting for the slightest creak of the boards. He had warned Lillian to lock her door, but she'd developed a sudden affinity for reckless behaviour.

"You should be ready to leave at nine."

"Nine? So late?"

Her light laugh was music to his ears. "Mr Daventry agreed to send a man to watch Mr Bloom in your absence. He should arrive at eight-thirty."

"Do you always work to a tight schedule, Miss Dutton?"

"When one has a week to find a murderer, there's no time to slack." And with that, Miss Dutton flounced down the steps and disappeared behind the high hedge.

Yes, he'd definitely have trouble sleeping tonight. Miss Dutton would be thirty feet away, stripping off her clothes and seeing to her nightly ablutions. Having developed the habit of mumbling erotic fantasies while dozing, Adam would have to smother his face with a pillow.

On the bright side, he had much to look forward to tomorrow.

Sitting alone in a closed carriage with Miss Dutton would stir every nerve to life. And he suspected she'd never donned breeches before. Hell, he hoped they were beige. There was nothing like flesh coloured buckskins on a woman to show a man what he was missing.

CHAPTER 5

There was no such thing as a perfect plan.

The first problem occurred when Eliza descended the stairs of Lord Roxburgh's abode, dressed in her gentleman's finery. The lord narrowed his gaze and stroked his jaw while inspecting the cut of her breeches.

"Hmm. You must give me the name of your tailor, Miss Dutton. He knows how to show a shapely thigh to perfection." The devil studied her blue silk waistcoat with shocking intensity. "The idea is to create a sleek silhouette. I fear your peers may notice every delightful curve, though I'm certainly not one to complain."

Having spent thirty minutes strapping her breasts, she'd struggled to disguise them completely. "Some men carry a little more weight than others."

"Yes, you're certainly more endowed than most." His sinful grin brought heat flooding to her cheeks. "Again, it's by no means a criticism."

The second problem occurred during the short journey through Mayfair. Yes, the lord spent so much time observing her form he could probably sketch it from memory. But his comments about her voice resulted in a tense exchange.

"You move and speak too softly. If you're to pass for a man, you must be hard and rigid in all things." He rubbed his muscular thigh as if she should be impressed.

"One cannot hold a rigid stance permanently." She'd grown tired of his criticism. "The blood pumps too quickly. It's not good for the heart."

Lord Roxburgh found her response amusing. "A man must be stiff, firm in his ... manners and opinions."

"As you are, I suppose."

"Yes, and far more frequently of late."

Then she realised he was not talking about her movements at all. "Must everything be about your masculine prowess? Men who think themselves superior make the most dreadful lovers. My colleague worked for a modiste who testified to the statement's accuracy."

"As with all things, I'm an exception to the rule." He tilted his head to one side and nodded to the under-seat cupboard. "When I lent you the use of my conveyance, did you look to see if I kept ladies' undergarments stowed away? You seemed convinced you'd find evidence of my rakish habits."

Eliza recalled the night with clarity. He had been kind, helpful and provocative of manner. "Why waste time looking when I have no interest in the outcome?"

"Do enquiry agents not have curious minds?"

"Only when solving riddles. And your exploits are well documented."

"I thought we'd agreed the gossips exaggerate."

"I have yet to see evidence to support your claim."

He glanced out of the window, suddenly noticed they were about to leave Bond Street for Piccadilly, tapped the roof and informed his coachman to park close to the Burlington Arcade.

The third problem was not that she felt naked walking along Piccadilly in buckskin breeches or that her ill-fitting beaver hat practically obscured her vision. It wasn't that Lord

Roxburgh gave his calling card to the porter at the Albany and lied about being invited to Mr Ashbury's apartment (or set as it was called by those fashionable gents who had taken residence).

It was something far more disturbing.

The front door to Mr Ashbury's apartment was wide open.

And someone was rummaging around inside.

Eliza's pulse raced. Despite spending many nights terrified out of her wits, she'd never had to confront her fears. But for an enquiry agent, catching criminals was part of the remit. What else could she do but attempt to apprehend the fellow?

Like a true gentleman, Lord Roxburgh acted as a human shield and gestured for her to follow behind. Had there been no need for silence, Eliza would have reminded him who was in charge.

Upon entering the drawing room, she caught sight of the intruder snatching strewn paper from the floor. He was tall and slender with ginger side-whiskers and a bald pate. The blackguard had ransacked the apartment, turned over chairs, slashed cushions and canvas paintings. Every drawer in the walnut desk was open.

Lord Roxburgh cleared his throat. "Who the devil are you? And what the hell are you doing in Ashbury's drawing room? Explain now, or I shall throttle the truth from you while Copeland fetches the constable."

For a moment, Eliza forgot she was Mr Copeland but quickly nodded. It was better to play the mute friend than get thrown out for being a woman.

The fellow swung around and firmed his jaw. "Never mind asking who I am. Who the blazes are you?"

"It's the height of bad manners to answer a question with a question." Lord Roxburgh crossed the room, stepping over discarded books and a broken decanter though glass crunched beneath his booted feet. "Etiquette permits I might shoot you for your insolence."

Despite his previous objection, the intruder raised his hands in surrender. "I live upstairs. I heard banging last night and came to warn Ashbury I'll not tolerate his antics. The door was open, and I feared the man had fallen and cracked his head on the grate."

Did the gentleman not know of Mr Ashbury's death? Or was it an excuse to explain why he was rummaging around in the man's apartment?

As the agent in charge of the case, it was her job to ask questions.

"What is your name, sir?" Eliza deepened her voice but probably sounded much like a dandy. "Have you not heard of the tragedy?"

Through narrowed eyes, the man appraised her attire. "Tragedy?"

"Mr Ashbury is dead." There was no point mincing words. "He was found murdered on Saturday." She refrained from saying exactly when or where.

"Murdered? Good Lord!" The middle-aged man paled. He might have stumbled back and dropped onto the sofa were it not covered in down feathers. "Who would do such a thing? Other than having to warn him about whistling on the stairs, he seemed like such a pleasant chap."

Not so pleasant. He'd accosted Miss Ware and ripped her dress.

"You couldn't have heard Mr Ashbury banging about last night," Eliza said. "You heard the intruder and, quite possibly, the murderer. The culprit is still at large. Judging by the state of things here, he is likely to return."

The fellow pulled his coat tighter across his chest and shivered. "Have the trustees been informed? They'll need to post a guard on the door. They'll want to warn all the residents."

"Not yet. Let me escort you back to your rooms." Lord Roxburgh gestured to the hallway. "I suggest you remain indoors until I've summoned the magistrate and alerted the trustees."

Rather than appear grateful, the gentleman grew instantly suspicious. "How do I know Copeland isn't the murderer? Maybe this is a ploy to get rid of me so he can rip this place apart again."

"If he is the murderer, isn't it better to run upstairs before he breaks your damn neck?"

Keen to bring an element of calm to the situation and get rid of this man so she might begin her investigation, Eliza decided honesty was the best policy. "I am an enquiry agent, not a murderer. This is Lord Roxburgh, my assistant."

Lord Roxburgh glanced at her and arched a brow. He drew a silver case from his pocket and handed the gentleman his pristine calling card. "State your name, then I demand you return to your apartment. You're hindering our progress."

It seemed Lord Roxburgh was correct in his earlier assertion. When a man hardened his tone, appeared rigid in his stance, a formidable force in the room, the weak cowered at his feet.

"The name is F-Finch, my lord." The man inclined his head. "Forgive my impertinence. This is all rather worrying. The Albany caters to respectable gentlemen. We've never had an incident like this before."

"Which is why I insist on escorting you upstairs so Copeland can continue his investigation."

Mr Finch offered his assistance, but Lord Roxburgh ushered him out of the property. Eliza waited until she heard the echo of footsteps on the stone staircase before rifling through the scattered paper.

Amongst various receipts, she found unpaid bills amounting to a thousand pounds, love letters though none bore evidence of a lady's name. Perhaps, Mr Ashbury enjoyed entertaining married women. She folded the letters and slipped them into her coat pocket.

Lord Roxburgh returned. "I suggest we hurry. Finch seems rather agitated and is likely to summon the board." He motioned to the pile of papers she'd gathered. "Did you find anything of interest?"

"No, just bills and love letters." Eliza gestured to the slashed cushions. "The murderer was looking for something. Something small enough to hide in an obscure place."

"Ashbury was on a winning streak. The villain emptied the desk drawers so may have been looking for his vowels."

"Then we should search for Mr Ashbury's diary." If they could piece together Mr Ashbury's movements this last week, it might bring them closer to finding the killer. "In all likelihood, he met with the person who broke his neck and ransacked his home."

Lord Roxburgh rubbed his firm jaw. "Shall we move to the bedroom?" Spoken in his rich tone, every syllable sounded suggestive. No doubt he'd used that phrase countless times before.

"The bedroom?" Eliza's pulse fluttered in her throat.

"So we might search Ashbury's personal effects." Amusement glinted in his eyes. "I'm not about to ravish you in a murdered man's home, Miss Dutton. Besides, most of what you've heard about me is entirely untrue."

"Then why not work to correct the misconceptions?"

The rogue winked at her. "If only you knew me better, you wouldn't need to ask. Come, we should check Ashbury's clothes. And it might be an idea to interview his valet."

Last night, before her midnight liaison with Lord Roxburgh, she had discovered that Mr Ashbury's valet and maid had been redeployed to his parents' abode in Curzon Street.

"Monsieur Sapiere is on my list of people to question." She presumed Mr Ashbury's manservant would know everything about his late-night habits. "Now, let us continue our search before Mr Finch returns."

Mr Ashbury's bedchamber looked like a chaotic winter scene. Goose down feathers, ripped from the pillows and scattered about in a panic, covered the floor in a white fluffy blanket. The intruder had emptied Mr Ashbury's armoire and flung the garments about the room, dragged bedsheets and blankets off the mahogany tester bed.

Lord Roxburgh retrieved a tailcoat from the pile and rifled through the pockets. "One gets the sense the intruder left empty-handed. He left no stone unturned."

"Yes, I can almost hear his groans of desperation." Eliza searched the open drawer in the nightstand, finding nothing but a book, a tinderbox and candles. "We can rule out burglary. Mr Ashbury's silver cuff links are here on the nightstand."

"I've found a card for a gaming hell."

"A gaming hell?"

"The Black Sapphire."

The Black Sapphire!

Any other three words might have piqued her curiosity. Those three words chilled her to the bone. Jeremiah Black owned the gaming hell she was forced to visit fortnightly. Jeremiah Black had shot and killed her father. She had no proof but had borne witness to his vile threats.

"Was Mr Ashbury a frequent visitor?" Eliza was a frequent visitor, though only entered via the back door and never ventured farther than Mr Black's office.

"Yes, Ashbury was a regular patron." Lord Roxburgh turned the card over in his hand. "That's odd. There's a Latin phrase printed on the back. I have the club's card, but the reverse is blank. *Victor Ludorum*."

Victor Ludorum!

Her father had owned the same card, stuffed in his desk drawer, though his was tatty around the edges. Now she knew two men who'd possessed that card. Both were dead. Instinct said she should keep the information to herself. Only a fool gathered evidence against Jeremiah Black.

"It means victor of the games, does it not?"

Lord Roxburgh frowned. "Indeed. You read Latin?"

No, she'd consulted her father's book of Latin quotations.

"I've heard the phrase before."

"Where?" Now he sounded like an enquiry agent.

"I—I don't recall," she said, being deliberately evasive.

He slipped the card into his pocket, threw Mr Ashbury's coat to the floor, and crossed the room. "Understand this, Miss Dutton. Speak your mind. I despise being misled." He spoke with a fervency that belied his cool demeanour. "I can tolerate anything but that."

She remained silent, though her mind was at war with itself.

"As a logical man, I shall make the obvious assumption."

"And what assumption is that, my lord?"

When he captured her elbow with surprising gentleness, it was evident he'd read her mind. "Men come from miles around to gamble at the Sapphire. As you never attended public school and had no means of hearing the phrase, I'll wager your father had a similar card. I'll wager your father gambled at the popular club owned by Jeremiah Black."

Jeremiah Black!

She might have held her mettle had they been discussing anyone else, but it was as if the rising swell of emotion was controlled by an otherworldly force.

Tears welled. "If you're so insightful, perhaps you should solve this case on your own." The urge to flee, to leave London as she should have done after Jeremiah Black's first wicked threat, came over her again. "If you disapprove of my need for privacy, perhaps you should hire another agent."

Eliza tried to shrug out of his grasp, but his hold became as firm as his intention. "I need you, Miss Dutton. I need your help with this case and with Lillian. Where she is concerned, I find myself torn between forcing her to abide by society's strict example or letting her follow her heart's desire."

Eliza couldn't fault his honesty. "I don't envy your position."

"What does one deem more important? Reputation or love?"

"Your friend, the Marquess Devereaux, chose love. He married a courtesan's daughter and is blissfully happy." It was hard to believe Eliza's colleague was now a marchioness. "For me, the question is whether Miss Ware really loves Mr Bloom."

"Perhaps it's my cynical nature, but I suspect not."

Only when witnessing how Miss Ware behaved in a ballroom full of eligible gentlemen, would the truth become apparent. "Miss Ware possesses an understated beauty. If we select the right party, many men will seek to gain her attention."

"We?" A smile played on the lord's lips. "Then you agree to help salvage something of my sister's reputation?"

Eliza realised he still had a hold of her elbow. Never had she thought to be comforted by this rogue's touch. "Let us continue our search of Mr Ashbury's abode and leave all personal questions until tonight." Or tomorrow night. Or they might get round to it at some point during the week. Or never at all.

He released her. "Then I look forward to our midnight liaison."

In a bid to change the subject, she scanned the room. "If the intruder didn't find what he wanted, perhaps the item is still here."

"Then let's begin in the hall and work methodically."

"Agreed."

While Eliza crouched beneath the console table in the

hall and searched for secret letters, Lord Roxburgh examined the walnut parquet. She peered behind pictures, examined a bust of Julius Caesar.

With few furnishings in the dining room, they finished their search there quickly. It was the drawing room with its cluttered mahogany cabinets and array of gilt pictures that proved tiresome.

"It would help if we knew what we were looking for." Eliza noted the smashed decanter, the smell of liquor and the stain on the Aubusson rug. "The intruder emptied the brandy decanter. Perhaps we're looking for a small item made of metal—a ring or rare coin."

"Perhaps. Ashbury may have accepted a ring as payment for a debt but then refused to sell it back." Lord Roxburgh opened the back of a gilt mantle clock and checked inside. "There's nothing here. Perhaps we should return to the bedchamber." He cast her a wicked grin. "To continue our search of Ashbury's belongings."

The bedchamber was in such a state of disarray it was impossible to conduct a thorough inspection. And if the intruder had turned everything upside down and left empty-handed, in all likelihood, they were wasting their time.

"Imagine you had a secret, my lord, and wished to hide something at home. Where would be the ideal place?"

Asking the question sparked fragments of a memory: shouting from the study, her father pleading with a stranger. He had told the visitor there was nothing of value in the house. Less than an hour later, Eliza had witnessed her father hurrying upstairs, clutching his metal money tin to his chest.

She shook herself from her reverie and looked at Lord Roxburgh, though he appeared equally lost in a troubling thought. It would be rude to disturb him, and so she watched the lines deepen on his brow, watched his sensual brown eyes darken with a pain that spoke of hidden secrets.

He dragged his hand down his face, pinched the bridge of

his nose. "Forgive me." His voice lacked the playful tone that often marked him as shallow. He cleared his throat to suppress a crackle of emotion. "My mother hid her diary beneath a loose board in her chamber. We should attempt to clear the floor and look for indents."

Why would his mother hide her diary?

And why would the memory have such a profound effect?

Suddenly, midnight couldn't come soon enough.

"I recall my father hid a metal money tin somewhere in his study." He had cradled the thing as if it were a newborn babe. "He brushed dirt or soot or cobwebs off it as he climbed the stairs. The gentleman who called that night had scoured the house looking for coin and left with nothing but a rosewood tea caddy."

"Keepers of secrets are masters of disguise."

"We need to stop searching and start looking."

Lord Roxburgh nodded.

They stood in silence, observing every minute detail, though she was slightly distracted by the musky notes of his bergamot cologne.

"The maid would have prepared the fire for Ashbury's return," he mused. "She laid the fire in the drawing room but not in this room."

Eliza noted the clean grate. Mr Ashbury would have washed and undressed in his bedchamber before settling down for the night. Though the weather had improved, there was still an icy nip in the air.

"The coal bucket is full. There are no clumps on the floor. If the intruder was looking for a small item of jewellery, why didn't he empty the copper bucket?"

Lord Roxburgh gestured to the fireplace. "Who can say? Shall we empty the bucket, Miss Dutton?" He crossed the room, took hold of the copper tub and turned the contents out on the hearth. His smile died as he scanned the black lumps. "There's nothing inside but coal."

Feeling equally deflated, Eliza took hold of the bucket. It was surprisingly shallow. The internal dimensions seemed at odds with the outer dimensions. One knock on the bottom revealed the reason for the discrepancy.

"The bucket has a false bottom." Eliza prodded one corner, and the metal bottom flipped out. Beneath was a silver box, twelve inches square. "I believe we've found a motive for murder, my lord." She removed the box and handed it to Lord Roxburgh, then brushed coal dust from her hands.

Lord Roxburgh placed the box on the bed and gently opened the lid. Nestled amid red velvet was an odd assortment of objects, all small, all different.

Eliza reached for the silk rose attached to a piece of white fabric. It was clipped to an invitation. "It might have been torn from a woman's gown. The invitation is for a ball held by Lord MacTavish."

Lord Roxburgh thought for a moment.

"I recall MacTavish's daughter had a come out in London as well as in Edinburgh. Such a soiree would fail to hold my interest, but I may have been forced to attend with Lillian had she been inclined to venture from her room."

Interesting. Particularly since Mr Ashbury had torn a decorative flower from Miss Ware's gown.

"And you've heard no gossip relating to Lord MacTavish?"

"None." He gripped the corner of the invitation and pointed to the date. "As the ball was three weeks ago, we should speak to MacTavish."

"Indeed." Eliza picked up a silver snuffbox. The lid was engraved with a battle scene. The underside bore the initials D. F. "You said Mr Fraser was absent from the supper room. I don't suppose his name is David."

"No, Daniel. But I've never seen him take snuff." Lord Roxburgh was more interested in the letter tucked beneath a ruby brooch. He peeled back the folds and read the missive.

"The letter is from a Mr Minchin. The name sounds familiar. It's a declaration of love and mentions a rendezvous at a property off York Street near the Regent's Canal."

Eliza jerked her head, unsure if she'd heard correctly. "Mr Minchin professed his love for Mr Ashbury?" It called into question the other letters she had found in the drawing room, though Mr Ashbury had been in no hurry to hide those. "Were you aware Mr Ashbury had a fondness for men?"

Lord Roxburgh snorted. "Ashbury was a known lothario, an unscrupulous seducer. He tended to favour the wives of—"

A knock on the front door captured their attention.

No doubt Mr Finch had come to check their progress.

"Quickly. Stuff the items into your pocket." Eliza slipped the brooch and the likeness of a young woman into hers. "Hide the box under the bedsheets."

Lord Roxburgh obeyed, then they made for the front door.

It was Mr Finch.

"Any luck hunting through the debris?" Mr Finch peered over Eliza's shoulder as if she were harbouring a fugitive. "I left a note with Hamilton's maid—he's on the board— informing him of poor Ashbury's death, and thought to see if you required an extra pair of hands here."

A prickle of suspicion reminded Eliza not to trust this man's word. "We've inspected every room and have been instructed by Mr Ashbury's parents to lock the door on our way out." Though whoever killed the gentleman had surely stolen his door key.

"I can do that once I've tidied a little." Mr Finch's expression turned solemn. "One imagines his mother might visit, and the mess will surely cause further distress."

"The magistrate insisted we secure the property upon our departure." Lord Roxburgh offered a friendly smile. "But thank you, Finch. Do you have a card? We might take advantage of your generosity should we have need to call again."

Mr Finch shook his head. "I'm afraid not. I lost my card case at the races and have yet to purchase a replacement."

The hairs on Eliza's nape prickled. It sounded like one of her father's excuses. Losing things was a habit, and she had worried about his memory. Then she noticed her father's unique cigar case in a pawnbroker's window in Kingston, and it all made perfect sense.

"Do you live with your brother, Mr Finch," she said in her most firm voice. She turned to Lord Roxburgh. "Isn't Finch the name of the gentleman you play billiards with at Boodle's? Did he not say he lived here?"

Being an intelligent man, the lord understood her intention. "Ah, Frederick Finch. Yes, he said to call on him at the Albany." He turned to Mr Finch. "Forgive me, did you not introduce yourself as David?"

"Donald," the man replied. "But no other Finch lives at the Albany."

Donald Finch.

The snuffbox might belong to the annoying neighbour upstairs who admitted to having a gripe with Mr Ashbury, regardless of how petty.

"Donald. Yes, I should have remembered as it was my father's name." Lord Roxburgh stepped over the threshold and patted the man on the upper arm. "You have my card. Send word should anyone attempt to enter Mr Ashbury's set."

And with that, Eliza locked the door and slipped the key into her already full pocket.

Twice she had to remind Lord Roxburgh not to cup her elbow while escorting her along the Rope Walk and back through the main building.

"Don't give the gossips an excuse to invent stories about your bed habits," Eliza teased. "Roxburgh seen fondling a man at the Albany? What will people think?"

"In those breeches, it's obvious you're a woman."

"Mr Finch didn't think so."

"Finch needs spectacles."

They continued exchanging amusing quips during the carriage ride to Hanover Square.

As if Eliza hadn't enough to deal with, she encountered her fourth problem the moment she crossed Lord Roxburgh's threshold.

"Quickly! Hurry!" Miss Ware raced to greet them, her face wet with tears. "You must hurry. Mr Bower left five minutes ago. He headed east towards Regent Street. Hurry." She clutched a piece of paper as if it were a lifeline.

Lord Roxburgh gripped his sister by the upper arms. "Lillian, calm yourself. Breathe. What prompted Mr Bower to leave the house? Did Ashbury's parents call again?"

Miss Ware struggled to catch her breath. "No, it's Mr Bloom." She thrust the crumpled paper at her brother and burst into a sob. "He's left, run away, and says he's never coming back."

CHAPTER 6

The first clang of the St George's bells echoed in Hanover Square. Adam had eleven seconds to race through the house and arrive at the rotunda before the last stroke of midnight.

He'd not seen Miss Dutton since they'd left to hunt for the absconder, since they'd both headed off in different directions hoping to catch Bloom. Doubtless, they'd not have time to talk about anything but the case tonight. A heaviness settled over him as he lamented the missed opportunity to know her better.

Adam's heart leapt to his throat when he exited the grand walkway and saw Miss Dutton sitting on the stone bench. Despite building his life on uncertainties, it was reassuring to know she had kept her promise.

"Forgive me," he panted as the last chime vibrated in the night air. He mounted the steps and exhaled a deep breath. "I would have been here before time, but I had to explain Bloom's sudden departure to Sir Oswald. The magistrate insisted I sup with him and blamed me for downing half a decanter of brandy when his footman came to refill the glasses."

"Men and their vices." She shuffled to the edge of the seat.

Moonlight cast its silver sheen over her silky black hair, over the delicate line of her jaw and throat. "Women rarely live life to excess. Why is that, do you suppose?"

The question caught him off guard. "Men are considered weak if they show any sign of vulnerability. They must find other ways to tackle their demons."

"Women often commit their thoughts to paper which can be cathartic."

In Adam's experience, writing was the catalyst that precipitated a tragedy. "Do you keep a diary?"

He'd sworn never to read a person's private thoughts, even if they had departed this world and it gave a better understanding of their torment. Hurtful words carried a negative vibration that burrowed into the heart, causing irreparable damage.

Her sigh held a wealth of regret. "I wrote a letter to my father to say how he'd hurt me, but decided to burn it rather than add to his burden. It went some way to easing the ache." Her gaze swept over him before lingering on his face. "You said your mother kept a diary and hid it under the boards. You seemed troubled by the memory."

So much for focusing on the case.

He'd not realised he would be the subject of much scrutiny.

Should he speak the truth or lie?

"My brother drowned in the lake at Glendale many years ago." Sebastian would have been five and twenty next month. "My mother used her diary as a means of understanding her grief." That was as much as he could cope with tonight.

Miss Dutton swallowed deeply and pushed to her feet. "My condolences, my lord. Such things never leave us. Our hearts remain a little less whole for our experiences."

He hadn't the strength to explain the devastating event that followed, so inclined his head by way of thanks and gestured for her to sit.

"I know we've spoken about this before, but I'd rather you called me Roxburgh. I cannot abide formality between friends."

After hearing his harrowing revelation, he doubted she'd object.

"Of course." She patted the bench with her gloved hand, encouraging him to sit beside her. It was by far another welcome development. "Perhaps we should focus on the case. Tell me what happened when you left this afternoon."

He was glad of the distraction. "I know you didn't find Bloom at his home address because Daventry arrived to speak to Sir Oswald. He explained Bloom was still at large. I searched the coaching inns with stages departing today—The Spread Eagle, The Bell and Crown—searched every ticket office and can be sure Bloom isn't booked on the first passage to Boston."

"I spoke to his neighbours. Mr Bloom lives alone but is visited by a young couple on occasion and by two men of a similar age. Mrs Rampling, who lives next door, believes the men attended Oxford together."

There were a few reasons to explain why Bloom had darted through Hanover Square and disappeared into the midday crowd. Perhaps he thought Adam would call him out for disrespecting Lillian. Perhaps he feared Sir Oswald would arrest him and fabricate evidence. Perhaps he had seen the murderer and was in fear of his life.

Adam relayed his thoughts to Miss Dutton.

"The note Mr Bloom left suggests his only motive was to protect Miss Ware and save her from further embarrassment." She looked up at Lillian's window. "She's been beside herself with worry and needs your reassurance all will be well."

How could he make such a promise when the opposite was often true? Experience had taught him to fear the worst.

"Did you speak to her about trying to salvage something of her reputation?"

"Her only focus is finding Mr Bloom. She refused to entertain the idea of repairing some of the damage done. I explained, identifying the murderer and solving the case is the best way to help your secretary."

Adam listened, a little in awe of this woman's mental strength. Maybe it was easier to remain objective when one's emotions weren't engaged. "How is it at five and twenty you can look at problems so rationally?"

The question caught her by surprise. It must have made her remember all the harrowing scenarios that had shaped her character because her brows knitted together, and her lovely bow-shaped lips took a downward turn.

"When a child is forced to behave like an adult, there is no time for idle daydreaming," she said.

"You had to grow up quickly?"

"A child should not have to lie awake at night to ensure her father doesn't choke on his own vomit." Water filled her eyes, but she kept the tears at bay. "A child should not have to give her most prized possession to a man desperate to stake it in a game of chance."

For the first time in his adult life, Adam felt a slither of shame.

He was in danger of revealing too much, yet avoidance was a skill he'd mastered. "Yet those experiences helped hone your skills. You're a woman of logic and great intellect. You have a capacity to solve complex riddles, to use reason and good sense."

"Roxburgh, everything comes at a price." She spoke his name with a warming hint of familiarity. "I'm a woman who's forgotten how to dream. My heart is empty, depleted. I would rather be the silly girl skipping down the street than the sensible one who has seen the worst of humanity."

When a person spoke of deep sadness, the normal instinct was to convince them they were wrong, wrong to feel pain and sorrow, wrong not to focus on the good things in their life. Sometimes, a person just wanted to be heard. He knew that.

"You have every right to feel cheated. I know we joked about revealing our secrets during the midnight hour, but know I am here to listen should the memories keep you awake at night."

When she met his gaze, she seemed confused. "Why do you not let others see your generous nature? Why do you hide behind the libertine's mask?"

Adam laughed. "I am a libertine."

"You said the gossips exaggerate."

To a certain extent. But his desperate desire to make love to this woman marked him as morally weak. "Miss Dutton, you need only say the word, and I'd ravish your mouth in a heartbeat."

Despite the slight blush rising to her cheeks, she narrowed her gaze. "You really are a man of many contradictions."

"Hence why you're taking steps to know me better." Every hour spent together fed his need to know more. "As for my generous nature, did I not loan you my carriage during your desperate race across town last month?"

"Only because you want me in your debt."

"You still owe me a boon."

She raised her chin. "I have no intention of paying."

"But you always keep your promises, always pay your debts." He'd not meant to compare her to her father. "Perhaps if a man were rewarded for his generosity, it might encourage him to be charitable again."

It was Miss Dutton's turn to laugh. "I agreed to take your case. Consider that payment enough. Besides, kindness is its own reward."

"Is that why you're being nice to me when you'd rather our paths hadn't crossed?"

She shrugged. "Perhaps you're not as shallow as I thought."

Adam smiled. "Is that another compliment, Miss Dutton?"

"It's a statement of fact." She clasped her gloved hands in her lap and shivered. "It's bitterly cold tonight. Perhaps we won't stay outside for the full hour."

"Shall I go inside and fetch a blanket?" Being late home, he'd not instructed Greyson to light a brazier. He would make sure the butler knew to light one nightly.

"No. It's been a long day, and we should retire soon. I shall remember to bring one next time."

Adam's pulse quickened with anticipation. He wasn't thinking how he might sleep tonight, but planning what he might ask her tomorrow. He lived for today, never thought of the future. Was it not foolish to become emotionally invested in an event that might never occur?

"I spoke to Mr Daventry about what we found at the Albany." Keen to be out of the cold, Miss Dutton spoke quickly. "He arranged a meeting with Lord MacTavish. We're to visit him tomorrow at his house in Pall Mall."

Daventry certainly worked quickly. One might think the bastard son of a duke had more influence than the King.

"We might call on the Harpers and Daniel Fraser while we're out. See if Fraser misplaced his snuffbox."

"You said he was in the library with Mrs Stanley at the time of the murder. We will need to take her statement, confirming that was indeed the case."

"That might prove a problem." They could not call at the lady's home address and would have to catch her during her frequent shopping trips to town. "Mr Stanley will not take kindly to the news he's a cuckold. He can be irrational when the mood strikes."

"Irrational?" Miss Dutton pursed her lips and stared at the night sky. Those shrewd grey eyes said she was busy contemplating how it was relevant. "What if Mr Ashbury was a man for hire? What if Mr Stanley knew of his wife's infidelity and sought to punish her lover?"

"Assuming the snuffbox in Ashbury's possession belongs to Fraser, it's hardly an item one might use to torment a man."

Miss Dutton sighed. "You're right, of course. Yet something tells me there's more to this than Mr Ashbury stealing a few worthless trinkets." She reached into her pelisse pocket, withdrew an oval miniature and handed it to him. "I took this from the silver box in Mr Ashbury's bedchamber. Have you seen this woman before? Do you recall her likeness?"

Adam studied the portrait. The lady looked no older than eighteen. Indeed, her bright blue eyes cried of youthful innocence. Her golden blond hair framed her face like a halo.

"No, never. It's probably one of the best paintings I've seen. The poor ones rarely look lifelike. The artist captured her delicate features perfectly."

Miss Dutton leant closer, so close he felt her breath against his cheek. "There's an elegance about her demeanour. She's definitely a gentleman's daughter. Mr Daventry knows everyone in the *ton*, but he's never seen her."

"I believe Daventry is well acquainted with Lady Perthshore. She keeps abreast of the latest gossip and may shed light on our mystery woman."

Their fingers brushed as Adam returned the miniature. The gentle touch tightened the muscles in his abdomen. How was it a man experienced in every intimacy could be aroused by something so innocent?

Miss Dutton brushed her gloved finger over the image. "Every instinct warns of another tragic tale."

"Perhaps it's time we were both a little more optimistic."

Her eyes brightened. She might have replied, but Lillian

appeared in the garden, clutching her wrapper tightly across her chest.

"Forgive the interruption, Miss Dutton." Lillian gave a watery smile and had clearly been crying.

Miss Dutton pushed to her feet. "No need to apologise. We were discussing the case, but it's late, and we have a busy day tomorrow."

Lillian looked at Adam. "May I speak to you before you retire? I've given up trying to sleep."

"Of course. Let's go inside where it's warm." Disappointment flared when he turned to Miss Dutton. Though he'd have her to himself again in twenty-four hours, the next stroke of midnight felt like a lifetime away. "Good night, Miss Dutton. Am I expected to rise before the cock crows?"

"Nine should suffice." She descended the stairs, clutched Lillian's forearm in a gesture of reassurance. "I shall leave you to tell your brother I have no need of a modiste or a dancing tutor. Good night."

Adam watched her depart, the confounding need for her leaving him as restless as a caged animal. And although Miss Dutton soon disappeared behind the high topiary hedge, out of sight but not out of mind, he was certain she'd command his dreams tonight.

"WHAT IS THIS ABOUT?" Lord MacTavish spoke with a Scottish brogue. The fellow towered over most men, and his wiry red beard was so long it almost touched his tartan waistcoat. "Daventry said I'd be interested to hear what ye have to say, though I cannae think why."

Adam waited for Miss Dutton to sit and then sat next to her on the green damask settee. Though the drawing room was in keeping with English styles, paintings of sprawling

Highland mountains and vases of dried blue thistle gave one a glimpse of the Lord's Scottish heritage.

Adam gestured to Miss Dutton. "As I explained, my colleague is an enquiry agent working for Lucius Daventry. I am merely her assistant, and so I shall leave her to explain the nature of our visit."

Miss Dutton cleared her throat. "As you may already know, a gentleman by the name of Mr Ashbury was found murdered in Lord Roxburgh's garden during a ball last Saturday." She paused. "Did you know Mr Ashbury?"

MacTavish relaxed back in the wing chair and stroked his red beard. "I cannae say the name's familiar."

"Mr Ashbury was in his late twenties, with wavy brown hair and a handsome countenance. He gambled at The Black Sapphire and was known as somewhat of a libertine."

MacTavish gave a mirthless chuckle. "That description applies to half the men in London. And a man who values his neck does nae gamble at the Sapphire."

No, only men who liked living on the edge wagered at Jem Black's establishment. Men who needed to know how it felt to dice with death.

Miss Dutton remained silent, though she fixed MacTavish with a curious gaze. "Then we're sorry to have troubled you." The lady stood, forcing them to stand, too. "During our search of Mr Ashbury's apartment at the Albany, we came across evidence to suggest you did know him. Best we hand it to the magistrate at the Marlborough Street office, though the constables are unreliable and often open to bribery."

Adam bid MacTavish good day and was about to follow Miss Dutton to the door when the lord said, "Wait! Happen I did know him. I didnae mean to lie, but I'll not have the world know of my arrangement with that black-hearted devil."

Miss Dutton turned and offered MacTavish a warm smile. "You can trust us to keep your secret. Tell us of your dealings with Mr Ashbury, and we shall return what he stole from your daughter."

Miss Dutton had taken a leap of faith, but after learning Ashbury had ripped a silk flower from Lillian's gown, it was logical to assume MacTavish's daughter had suffered the same slight.

MacTavish gestured for them to sit. "I'll tell ye the whole story, though I cannae swear I'll nae curse that blackguard to the fiery pits of hell."

They returned to the settee.

"Miss Dutton is a skilled enquiry agent and understands your frustration," Adam said. "I'll not lie to you. My sister's reputation is in tatters because she found Ashbury's body in my garden." Lillian had spent an hour last night apologising for the tragic mistake. "People will assume they were involved in a dalliance, particularly since the rogue propositioned her and tore a silk flower from her gown earlier in the evening."

Miss Dutton cleared her throat. "What Lord Roxburgh means to say is that you can trust us implicitly. Any information you provide will be used to shed light on Mr Ashbury's nefarious deeds, in the hope of catching a murderer and lessening the blow to Miss Ware's reputation."

MacTavish gave a weary sigh. "Ye'll nae repeat it to anyone else?"

"Only to Mr Daventry as part of our ongoing investigation. But he is already aware of the evidence recovered from the Albany."

After giving the matter lengthy consideration, MacTavish said, "The devil accosted my daughter, Ailsa, at her come out ball. He tore her gown and threatened to use it as evidence to suggest she'd been free with her affections." He muttered something murderous in Gaelic. "A few people noticed her torn gown, and so I couldnae take a chance."

Doubtless, Ashbury planned to blackmail Adam. That would have been a serious mistake. People mistook his air of sophistication for weakness. They assumed, like all dissolute rogues, he lacked the capacity to feel genuine emotion.

They'd be wrong.

He would have shot Ashbury dead for hurting Lillian.

"Did Mr Ashbury want money?" Miss Dutton removed her notebook and pencil from her reticule. "Were you supposed to pay for his silence?"

"Aye, at first." MacTavish's gaze dropped briefly to his lap. "I'm ashamed to say I paid him a thousand pounds. I was told to leave it with the innkeeper at The Swan in Cheapside. She handed me a room key in exchange, said I'd find what I needed there. But that wicked devil left me a note demanding further payment."

"He wanted more money?" Miss Dutton spoke with the compassion of a woman who'd once felt equally helpless.

Anger flashed in the lord's eyes. "He wanted me to steal the Duke of Dounreay's cufflinks. The gold pair bearing his crest."

"Steal cufflinks?" Miss Dutton said incredulously.

Adam was equally puzzled.

"Somehow, the devil knew I was to dine at Dounreay's mansion house last week. I was told to steal the cufflinks, and Ashbury would meet me personally to make the exchange."

"Was this before Ashbury was murdered?" Adam asked.

"Aye."

"But you didn't steal the cufflinks?"

"I'll nae steal from my brethren," MacTavish cried. "I feigned illness and had Dounreay reschedule, then contacted a goldsmith in Ludgate Street and commissioned him to make a copy. Ashbury said he'd give me one week else the *ton* would learn of Ailsa's loose morals."

A tense silence ensued.

MacTavish had a motive for murder. But how did one accuse a lord of committing a vile crime? Thankfully, Miss

Dutton decided to broach the subject. Coming from an enquiry agent, it didn't sound like such an insult.

"You had every right to break the blackguard's neck, yet I suspect you did not."

MacTavish firmed his jaw and made an impassioned speech. "I swear on the blood of my forefathers, I didnae kill the blighter."

"And you didn't hire anyone to kill him?" Miss Dutton said, her tone by no means accusatory. "You didn't visit the Albany, steal into his apartment and ransack his rooms?"

The lord's cheeks coloured. "Aye, I visited the Albany many times, but the blackguard must have been staying elsewhere. I couldnae kill him without taking back what he stole from Ailsa."

"But you've never been inside his rooms?" she attempted to confirm, relentless in her need to discover the truth. "As you said, you had every reason to search for the torn piece of gown."

As if the walls had ears, the lord leant forward and lowered his voice. "I went there, aye. The door was open, the place a shambles. I searched for the torn piece of gown but to nae avail."

"And you saw no one else?" Adam said, wondering if Mr Finch had seen the lord. Finch was one of those neighbours who knew the comings and goings of everyone in the vicinity.

MacTavish shook his head.

The lord spent the next few minutes telling them about Ashbury's arrogance, giving a description of the woman who took payment at the inn in Cheapside, and speaking of his shame, for a man with warriors' blood did not cow down to a liar and a crook.

Miss Dutton stood. "I suspect Mr Daventry will want to keep the evidence until the case is concluded. But I wish to put an end to your daughter's torment." She reached into her reticule, removed the invitation and the shorn silk and studied it for a few seconds.

Already on his feet, MacTavish gasped as he realised he was staring at the simple piece of material that might have brought about his daughter's ruination.

"Take it. I shall suffer the consequences." Miss Dutton handed the evidence to MacTavish, then turned to Adam. "Rest assured, my lord. This will in no way hinder my investigation. I shall do my utmost to ensure Miss Ware can walk the streets without fear of insult."

Adam studied her. Sometimes, those who'd significantly suffered proved the most benevolent. It was Adam's turn to feel embarrassed. He'd spent more than a decade focused on nothing but his own pain.

"There is no one I have more faith in than you," he said.

"Thank you for understanding, and for the undeserved compliment."

MacTavish cleared his throat. "Is there a way I might help yer sister, Roxburgh?" His green eyes glistened with gratitude.

Adam was touched. "I'm sure Miss Dutton will help ease my sister's burden, but I thank you all the same."

"Perhaps you might do me the honour of attending the ball I'm hosting for the Duke of Dounreay on Saturday. I couldnae cancel though I feared Ashbury might have an accomplice, that he'd make an appearance and continue the devil's work." He clutched the torn silk in his fist. "There's nae need to worry anymore."

Adam considered the offer.

Bring Lillian to a ball full of Scots?

Equally, as the event was for the esteemed duke, there would be many English aristocrats in attendance.

"I fear our presence would cause a stir, MacTavish. I fear the duke will take issue with us using his lavish party for our own end."

"Och, Dounreay does nae take kindly to tittle-tattle. I'll

confide in him, explain my purpose. He'll be accommodating. I promise ye that."

Miss Dutton seemed keen on the idea. "If Miss Ware does as instructed, it would help limit any damage done. And one dance with the duke will smooth the rippling waters."

Adam turned to MacTavish. "Miss Dutton will require an invitation. She is also acting as my sister's companion until we've found the man who murdered Ashbury."

MacTavish nodded. "I'd be honoured to have yer company, Miss Dutton."

"Then it's settled," Adam said before Miss Dutton could protest.

Before bidding them good day, the lord reiterated what it meant to have the offending article returned and reassured he would do his utmost to quell the gossip come Saturday.

Adam escorted Miss Dutton to his carriage, parked further along Pall Mall. "Lillian said you've no need of a dance tutor. By all accounts, you dance very well." He'd hoped for an opportunity to test her skills at their next midnight meeting.

"During one of my father's winning streaks, he happened to own the debt of a dancing tutor. I received weekly lessons for a year, though have never danced in front of an audience."

The prospect of holding her in his arms brought a rush of excitement. "You'll need practice then, and I shall be your tutor." He'd be anything she wanted him to be given a chance.

She cast him a sidelong glance. "I have no intention of taking to the floor and will be there in a professional capacity."

Adam smiled to himself. He would use bribery if necessary, use every skill he had mastered in the pursuit of pleasure. While their main objective was to help Lillian, he had a wicked purpose of his own.

CHAPTER 7

Determined to be the first to reach the rotunda, and with a wool blanket tucked under her arm for good measure, Eliza descended the stairs fifteen minutes before midnight.

After leaving Lord MacTavish's abode and discovering Mr Fraser was away from home, she'd spent the afternoon alone, interviewing Mr Ashbury's parents, trying to determine if they knew why someone had murdered their son. It had been a taxing few hours full of howls and heartbreak because poor Mrs Ashbury had struggled to contain the raging swell of grief.

Oddly, Eliza had missed having Lord Roxburgh there to quell the rising tide with his calm comments and relaxed reserve. Indeed, she had spent the time battling her own tangle of emotions. Emotions that had nothing to do with Mrs Ashbury's unwavering praise for her devious son and everything to do with her slanderous comments about Lord Roxburgh.

The need to defend the lord had left Eliza biting her tongue and fidgeting in the seat. Still, she couldn't quite understand why she liked Roxburgh when every ounce of logic said she should despise him. She was mildly flattered by his interest, found him amusing, even though she gave every indication he was a thorn in her side.

"Miss Dutton." Roxburgh appeared from his study, carrying two goblets of brandy. He was dressed entirely in black as if wickedness was the theme tonight. "I see you've brought a blanket. I thought a nip of amber nectar might stave off the chill."

Warmth filled her chest at the mere thought of sipping the spirit. Or was it Roxburgh's sinful smile that had such a profound effect?

"After the stresses of the day, I may need more than one glass."

"Some things are best taken slowly, best savoured."

Eliza arched a brow. "Why do I suspect you're referring to something other than brandy?"

"A man cannot help but have amorous thoughts when in the company of a lady he admires."

"Then perhaps you'll need more than one glass, too. It must be frustrating knowing I'm resistant to your charm."

When he laughed, it occurred to her that she rather liked the sound. It reminded her of the blissfully happy hours spent with her friends in Howland Street. The house was quieter now that Julianna and Rachel had moved out and married.

Perhaps that was the story of her life.

Somehow she always ended up alone.

Roxburgh stepped closer and handed her a glass. "Lift the brandy to your lips and take a sip. It will fortify you against the frigid breeze."

Needing to suppress a wave of sadness, Eliza did as he asked.

"Allow the silky spirit to roll over your tongue." He studied her expression, watched the movement of her mouth. "Is it not a melange of intoxicating flavours? Does it not cause a rush that slows the mind yet quickens the pulse?"

She welcomed the burn as the fiery liquid trickled down

her throat. Yes, her mind relaxed while her pulse raced. Sipping brandy suddenly seemed like an erotic experience.

"So, you have an excellent appreciation for perfume and liquor."

"I have an appreciation for anything that stirs my senses."

"Like women," she teased.

"Indeed." Mischief danced in his bewitching brown eyes. "Perhaps I should assess you in the same way I assess brandy."

"You mean to taste me, Lord Roxburgh?" The comment left her lips before she realised it sounded shockingly inappropriate.

Lord Roxburgh's eyes glazed. "Make no mistake. I'd devour every inch of you given a chance." His voice was so soft and rich and intimate she imagined tilting her head back, imagined feeling his hot mouth on her neck. "But as you're repelled by my advances, I've no choice but to sample you with my eyes."

"Your eyes?" she repeated, battling a flutter of excitement. "How novel."

"Hmm. Like identifying the best cognac, I shall discern that one alluring quality that separates you from all others." He gestured to the hallway. "Come. I shall make my assessment in the moonlight."

Eliza walked with him through the house and garden. Fire blazed in the two braziers positioned next to the rotunda. Cushions of gold brocade covered the stone seat. Lit candle lamps created an ambience ripe for seduction.

"My motive is to keep us warm," he said as if reading her thoughts, "not lure you into sin. Sit and sip your brandy while I make my detailed appraisal."

Intrigued to know what he found appealing, she settled on the bench and had him hold her glass while she draped the blanket over her lap. Their fingers brushed when he returned the vessel, the sudden jolt of awareness stealing her breath.

Roxburgh sat beside her. He tossed back his brandy and then studied her with unnerving intensity.

"Your hair is as dark as the night, soft like silk, but that's not what sets you apart. Your grey eyes are compelling. They possess a magical ability to change according to your mood, from silver to green to a delicate pale blue. But it's not that."

Roxburgh was certainly a man of great rhetoric. He had her hanging on his every word, longing to hear what else he found attractive.

"It's not your luscious lips, though they're shaped in a perfect bow, are a mouthwatering rose hue."

"Then what sets me apart from other women of your acquaintance?"

Roxburgh smiled. "Perhaps it would be wrong of me to say."

"It's something inappropriate, then." She should have known he meant to tease her. "Something a gentleman would never repeat."

His piercing gaze pinned her to the seat. "It is something indescribable, intangible. It is everything and nothing."

Stunned, Eliza jerked her head. "You have such an eloquent way with words you must be able to offer an explanation."

He narrowed his gaze. "You'll think me foolish."

"I am not one to judge." That was a lie. She had judged him from the moment they'd met. She thought the worst of him merely because she saw similarities to her father.

After a lengthy silence, he said, "It's the way the air shifts when you enter the room. The way it steals my attention like a silent call to the soul. It's the sense I've known you before, long before you took this divine form. When I'm with you, I find myself wishing I were a different man, a better man, your man."

"Oh," she said, shocked and touched in equal measure.

Lord Roxburgh was a skilled lothario. He could spark a

fire in a cold heart. He could alter a rigid opinion in seconds. He could make a woman want things she'd never dared dream of before.

"They're not the words of a seducer," he assured her, "though the thought of having you keeps me awake at night."

Merciful Lord! Never had anyone spoken so frankly. Even a devil like Jeremiah Black only intimated he was interested in more than the fortnightly payments.

"My lord, you certainly know how to stir a reaction." Indeed, she was breathless—a little dizzy—from the shock. Yes, the shock, that explained why she was dazed.

"I would prefer anything to your disdain, Miss Dutton. I hope to earn your respect, hope you come to understand why gambling has been such a purgative experience."

His odd choice of words only added to the confusion. But she saw an opportunity to ask the questions foremost in her mind.

"Then help me understand."

"Ask me anything, and I shall answer honestly."

Eliza took a sip of brandy to steal her courage. "Why did you risk losing your father's watch when you could afford to place a substantial bet?" People only risked precious items when desperate.

Roxburgh gave a half shrug. "I wanted to feel my heart pounding in my chest, experience the wild panic, see if at any point it would subside and I'd come to terms with my decision. I wanted to see if there would be a moment when my emotions disengaged."

Puzzled, Eliza stared. "And was there?"

Those dark, unfathomable eyes searched her face. "No. Losing the watch only reminded me of the pain of losing my father."

"And that was a good thing?" she tried to clarify.

"No."

"Why?" She pondered what it all meant. What made this

man such an enigma, and how was it similar to her own father's plight?

"I believe the next question is mine, Miss Dutton."

Eliza huffed in frustration. "Ask what you will, but we're returning to this subject as soon as I have answered."

Roxburgh inclined his head. "Who proposed marriage, and what prompted you to refuse?"

Thankfully, he'd not asked about Jeremiah Black or if her father had gambled at the Sapphire. Nor why she had accepted Lucius Daventry's offer of a comfortable home and a good income.

"Mr Flanders was the first to call. He owns the neighbouring estate in Kingston-upon-Thames. Though he's a kind and considerate gentleman, he's a widower with three unruly children."

"You weren't keen to play the doting mother?"

"Had we been in love, I would have taken on a dozen mischievous urchins. Nothing would have kept us apart."

"Ah, so you'd choose love over security and your reputation."

Eliza laughed. "There is nothing left of my reputation. But yes, I would never marry for convenience, hence why I declined Mr Sharrow and Mr Boreland."

"So, you're looking for a love match."

"I am not looking for anything."

"I think you are." His rakish gaze took to wandering again, over her hair and mouth. "And what of your physical needs? What happens when you feel that inner stirring, that need for release?"

Good Lord! It was one thing to discuss personal matters with one's friends after stealing a dusty bottle of liquor from Miss Trimble's pantry. Downing the contents had certainly loosened their tongues. But to discuss such matters with a gentleman. Never!

"If you knew me better, you wouldn't need to ask."

Roxburgh's laugh was like a teasing melody, a siren's song to lure unsuspecting maidens. The deepening crinkles at the corners of his eyes only added to his appeal.

She took a moment to appreciate the sight and to let him feel that rush of euphoria. "Why would you want to remember the pain of losing someone? Surely you would avoid having your heart ripped from your chest again."

His amusement died. Before he donned a mask of arrogance, she caught a glimpse of the vulnerable man hiding behind the facade.

"That's a question for another time," came his smooth reply.

"No." She reached across and gripped his forearm. "You cannot invite me to play this game and then shut me out. It's the height of bad manners."

Roxburgh looked at her dainty hand and sighed. "That's what sets you apart from all others, Miss Dutton. Your courage in the face of adversity." He laid his strong hand on top of hers. "If I tell you, I fear you will see me as something less than what I am."

Eliza tried to concentrate but was acutely aware of the heat spreading from his palm. It excited the senses while rousing every fear.

"I think you want me to see you. People assume they have the measure of you, and yet you show them nothing but the false version."

"I'm a man of many secrets."

"But I think you're tired of hiding."

"I have no choice but to hide."

"Then share the burden. Tell me why you looked like a lost boy at the mention of your mother's diary. Tell me why this garden is designed so you can steal away from prying eyes. Trust me with your story."

Roxburgh swallowed deeply. He lowered his gaze while he

battled with the dilemma. After a prolonged silence, he muttered a curse.

"I shall tell you the facts," he said, despair already etched on his brow. "But I cannot discuss what happened, not tonight. Once we've spoken, I shall bid you good night and retire to my chamber. Please do not think ill of me."

Eliza nodded. Her heart thumped wildly in her chest. What was this secret that could crush a man as powerful as Lord Roxburgh?

She firmed her grip on his arm, a gesture of support.

His lips thinned, though it seemed an age before he spoke.

"My mother blamed herself for my brother's death." The weight of his torment rang in every strained syllable. "Sebastian couldn't swim. With my mother being a woman who lived in fear of life, she insisted on giving him lessons. He drowned. She couldn't save him and couldn't live with the guilt."

The implication of what that meant was not lost on her. "Your mother died not long after the accident?"

Roxburgh went to speak but was forced to cough away the emotion choking his throat. "She drowned, too, though her death was not the accident the coroner claimed."

He snatched his hand away abruptly and stood.

Eliza knew he meant to leave but hadn't expected it would be so soon after his sad revelation. Guilt stabbed at her conscience. This wasn't a game of questions invented by a seducer. This was a man desperate to reach out and not knowing how.

"Wait. Sit a while." Instinct said she should comfort him, draw him into an embrace. "We can talk about something else, anything else. Stay."

Roxburgh bowed gracefully. "Good night, Miss Dutton. Forgive me. You're the last person I'd want to leave sitting alone." And with that, he turned on his heel, descended the stairs and disappeared into the night.

"YOU'RE CERTAIN THIS WILL WORK?" Eliza stood with Lord Roxburgh at the entrance to the mews, a mere hundred yards from Mr and Mrs Ashbury's home in Curzon Street. "What makes you think Monsieur Sapiere will get an opportunity to escape the house?"

Roxburgh smiled though it was evident from his tired eyes he'd had little sleep last night. She had spent hours awake, too, wishing she'd not asked the question, feeling his immense pain.

"Valets are notoriously nosy creatures. My note will do more than pique his interest." He spoke in a jovial tone that in no way reflected his inner torment. "And as Mrs Ashbury refused your request to question the Frenchman, I don't see we have an option."

According to Mrs Ashbury, servants could not be trusted to give an accurate account of a man's affairs. They lacked the breeding needed to understand the complexities involved in being a gentleman.

"What did you write?"

He'd torn paper from her notebook and scribbled a few lines on the page. Since breakfast, Eliza had studied every facial expression, looking for signs of suppressed emotions. Lord Roxburgh wore his self-assured mask well.

"*Victor Ludorum*. I said he'd understand the consequences if he failed to meet me."

"What makes you think he knows what it means?"

"A valet would search his master's coat pockets before airing the garment and returning it to the armoire. There's a reason he didn't remove the card and place it on the nightstand."

"Of course."

It was then Eliza spotted Mrs Ashbury leaving the house in her mourning clothes, stopping briefly to lower her black lace veil. She turned right towards the mews.

"Don't turn around." Eliza shot behind Lord Roxburgh's broad frame. "Mrs Ashbury is approaching. She's bound to recognise me. Monsieur Sapiere must have shown her the note. Hide me. Hurry."

"What the devil," Roxburgh said but quickly came up with a solution. "Wrap your arms around my waist. Rest your head on my chest. Let her think you're weeping."

There was no time to consider an alternative.

Eliza stepped closer. She slipped her arms around Roxburgh's lean waist and buried her face in his chest.

Heavens! He smelt divine.

Touching him roused the oddest sensations.

Their bodies melded together, a perfect fit.

"Make a sobbing noise." The devil took to rubbing her back in soothing strokes. "You deserve someone better," he said smoothly, playing the role of confidant. "You deserve someone who loves you, someone who can show you the joy true happiness brings."

He sounded so convincing his words proved comforting. She found herself sagging against him, lost in his warmth, overwhelmed by his unadulterated maleness.

"Stay with me. I'll keep you safe, then you need never be afraid again." He wrapped both arms around her, protecting her in a masculine cocoon, drew her tight against every hard muscle. "Say the word, and I shall grant your every wish, your every desire."

Tears welled in her eyes. Oh, it had been so long since she'd felt a tender touch. Even though the embrace was a means to hide from Mrs Ashbury, Eliza slid her hands up his back, hugged him tightly, silently prayed the moment might never end.

Roxburgh inhaled sharply. "We tread dangerous waters, you and I. But then our need is as fathomless as the depths of the deepest ocean."

Eliza daren't look up at him.

Daren't ask him to explain this profound need.

They stood there for a minute, maybe more. Mrs Ashbury had surely passed, but it was a hoarse, feminine voice that forced them apart.

"Are you the gent what sent the note to Monsieur Sapiere?"

Eliza jumped back and took to straightening her pelisse.

Roxburgh met Eliza's gaze and smiled before facing the young maid, who appeared no older than twenty.

"You work for the Ashburys?" Roxburgh asked.

"That depends who's asking."

Eliza stepped forward. "Do you remember me? I called yesterday and spoke to your employers. We wish to ask Monsieur Sapiere a few questions regarding his time working at the Albany."

The woman considered them through narrowed eyes. "He's tending to the master and sent me to tell you he'll meet you in half an hour at the church." She gestured to the building further along the street.

Roxburgh straightened to his full, intimidating height. "Tell him I'll hunt him down, have him on the first ship to Calais if he fails to attend." He paused. "Did you work at the Albany?"

The maid seemed reluctant to answer. "Only these past two months, to replace the maid what left in a hurry."

"And how did you find your employer?"

She glanced back over her shoulder as if expecting to see the devil standing there. "There's men what brag about being wicked, and there's men like Mr Ashbury."

"You mean men who are inherently evil?" Eliza said.

"Gluttons what feed on another's suffering." Again, she looked behind. "I must go. If Sapiere don't come, it's 'cause he's scared."

"Scared?"

"Scared to find out what that beast was really doing." And with that, she hurried away.

"Interesting." Roxburgh watched the maid retreat, then turned to Eliza and offered a wicked grin. "Perhaps we should embrace again while we wait for Monsieur Sapiere. We wouldn't want Mrs Ashbury to amble past and see you. You could stroke my back in the same sensual way, breathe the same satisfied sigh."

The man was incorrigible. Truly incorrigible. "We should wait in the church, away from prying eyes." Away from all temptation.

"Excellent idea. We might confess our sins while there."

Eliza laughed. "Unlike you, I am without transgression."

He leant closer. "Come now. Had you looked up as I held you, we would have kissed. You would have drunk deeply from my mouth. That first rush of euphoria can be a potent aphrodisiac."

"You think too highly of yourself, my lord." Eliza fought to stop a blush rising to her cheeks. What alarmed her most was the glaring accuracy of his statement. "You forget I'm being paid to play a role."

He was not deterred. "I know a genuine sigh of pleasure, Miss Dutton. I suspect we'd be rampant with passion once we started."

Her mind conjured all sorts of lewd imagery.

A shiver ran from neck to navel as her traitorous body responded. So much for being immune to his charm. Then she remembered Lord Roxburgh was a man of illusion. He created a fantasy far removed from stark reality.

Eliza cleared her throat, keen to play this devil at his own game. "Yes, rampant to the point of madness, I suspect. But I'm paid to think logically. Having met your match, logic says you'll be besotted." She tapped him on the chest. "Then I'd have no choice but to cast you aside. Best we keep things on a friendly basis as I would hate to break your heart."

She strode past him before he could offer another witticism.

He caught up her with near the entrance to Mayfair Church. "So this is a test of my resilience."

Eliza ignored the comment. She crossed the threshold, the cold air instantly penetrating her bones, the musty smell irritating her nostrils, and gestured to the nearest pew. "Let's sit close to the door. We don't want to give the valet an excuse not to speak to us."

"Choose the second pew from the back. Then the man might sit behind without anyone suspecting he has an ulterior motive for being here."

They shuffled into the pew.

Fearing Roxburgh wished to continue their earlier conversation, she insisted on spending a moment in silent prayer. That only made matters worse because he bowed his head and sighed as if he carried a great burden.

Then an unusual looking man slipped into the church. His black coat was trimmed in gold velvet, his long hair fastened back with ribbon. He scanned the rows of pews, noticed them and sat behind as Roxburgh predicted.

"I have but five minutes to spare, monsieur," Sapiere said in a thick French accent. "This, it is about a dead man, *non?*"

Roxburgh did not turn around. "Your previous employer ruined my sister's reputation. I am keen to shed light on his nefarious dealings."

In a moment of madness, Miss Ware had ruined her own reputation. Still, had she not stumbled upon Mr Ashbury's body, no one would be any the wiser.

"The man, he played a dangerous game."

"What sort of game?"

Monsieur Sapiere paused. "Blackmail."

They had gathered that much from Lord MacTavish.

"Why resort to blackmail when his skill at cards was renowned?" Eliza asked. "And why force his victims to steal from others?" What was so important about the Duke of Dounreay's cufflinks?

Monsieur Sapiere muttered something in French. "That, I do not know. But Monsieur Ashbury, he was a collector of trinkets, trinkets he traded."

"You left The Black Sapphire's card in his coat," Roxburgh stated. "Is it not your job to empty his pockets?"

"Monsieur Ashbury, he did not want anyone to see the card."

"Because it has something to do with *Victor Ludorum*?"

"As I said, monsieur, he was playing a dangerous game." Sapiere shuffled closer. "I heard Madame Ashbury talking. She said her son took the deeds to his *appartement* from the bank. That he had staked them in a game of chance, yet no man has come forward to claim his winnings."

Roxburgh hummed. "Ashbury didn't look like a man who'd lost his home at the gaming tables." The devil had been far too smug.

The Frenchman stood. "I must go. I can say no more. But you will take this as proof." He dropped a letter into Eliza's lap and then hurried from the church.

Eliza glanced at the letter, her heart missing a beat.

The seal was broken, the wax as black as Mr Ashbury's soul.

She stared for so long, Lord Roxburgh nudged her gently. "Are you going to read the missive?"

"Yes, of course."

Her hands shook as she gripped the paper. Every instinct said she knew what she would find inside. While her pulse thumped in her throat, she peeled back the folds.

"Well?" Roxburgh said, giving her nary a second to consider the message written on the page. "Who sent it?"

Eliza forced her gaze past the black scrawl to the identifying mark at the bottom. "There is no name, nothing but this ugly black stain."

"But you recognise it?"

"Yes, it's the signature of Jeremiah Black."

CHAPTER 8

To say Miss Dutton was terrified of Jeremiah Black was an understatement. While Adam suspected her father had gambled at The Black Sapphire, her reaction to seeing the ebony stain on the paper confirmed it was the case.

She said nothing while ushering him out of the pew, while rushing from the musty building as if her life depended upon breathing clean air. She offered no explanation while hurrying to his conveyance, made no apology for taking command of his vehicle and instructing his coachman to ferry her to Hart Street.

During the thirty-minute journey, navigating Pall Mall and other busy thoroughfares, she spoke only to repeat the same phrase.

"I shall explain everything once I have spoken to Mr Daventry."

"Can I not read the letter and draw my own conclusions?"

She handed him the missive, but he saw nothing to cause her distress. It was merely a few lines informing the Ashburys their son had staked the deeds to his Albany apartment in a card game.

"Ashbury owned the property. Most men lease an apartment."

Perched on the edge of the seat, Miss Dutton kept her nose pressed to the window as if willing the carriage to gain momentum. "Be warned. There's a chance Mr Daventry will assign another agent to your case."

Assign another agent?

Like hell he would!

Adam tried to quell the rising panic that had nothing to do with his worries about Lillian and everything to do with the fact he needed to spend more time with Miss Dutton.

"I don't want another agent. I want you."

"The letter complicates matters."

"Why? Because you were able to identify the signature?"

"Because it involves Jeremiah Black." Fear clung to every strained word. It sliced through her confident facade to leave her visibly shaking.

Adam was busy considering his response when the carriage clattered to a halt outside Lucius Daventry's house in Hart Street, one used as a business premises for his agents.

Miss Dutton snatched the letter from Adam's hand. "Forgive me. You couldn't possibly know what this means, but I shall ask Mr Daventry to visit you later today to discuss your options."

"No need. I'm not leaving."

"But I could be hours."

"I'll wait."

He'd managed for a month, surviving on chance meetings and brief conversations. He could wait a few hours in a plush carriage.

Her half-hearted smile spoke of an inner turmoil. "While I suspect Mr Daventry will remove me from the case, if he agrees, I would like to accompany Miss Ware to Lord MacTavish's ball. It wouldn't feel right deserting her completely."

The news lifted his spirits. He might have shown his gratitude had she not flung open the door and jumped to the
pavement as if the vehicle were ablaze.

Adam watched her race into the house, clutching the
letter in her gloved hand. Had her father owed Black a debt?
Was there something in the letter that had sparked a frightening memory?

He leant back against the leather squab and considered
what he'd learnt this morning. Yes, Sapiere had confirmed his
master was in league with the devil. But that was not the
thought uppermost in Adam's mind.

Holding Miss Dutton in his arms had been a novel experience. For a man who had dabbled in every vice, he'd not
expected to find it so arousing. Yet while he'd been hard in
the place that mattered most, painfully so, the solid wall
around his heart had softened.

If he'd suffered that from a mere embrace, what would
happen when they eventually kissed? And they would kiss.
He'd sell his soul for one taste of her lips.

Indeed, he fantasised about the slow melding of their
mouths while observing the comings and goings in the Hart
Street office. He knew all Daventry's gentlemen agents, but
he did not know the dark-haired man leaving through the
front door, wearing a stern expression.

The fellow stalked towards Adam's carriage with a confidence that said he'd been in many fisticuffs during his service
to the Order. He rapped hard on the window.

Adam leant forward and opened the door. "You come
bearing bad news, I suppose."

"I come with a flask of brandy and a word of warning."

"Unless you mean to move me along, which would be a
serious mistake because I refuse to leave without speaking to
Miss Dutton, climb inside."

The man hauled his athletic frame into the conveyance,
dropped into the seat opposite and slammed the door shut.

"I presume you work for Lucius Daventry."

"In a fashion. I'm here with my wife, who used to be one of Daventry's agents."

As only two of Daventry's female agents had recently wed, one to Adam's friend Devereaux, he knew this gentleman's name.

"You're Eli Hunter. Miss Dutton mentioned she attended your wedding recently." It was while reassuring Lillian that true love did exist, and she would one day marry the man destined to be her match, whether that be Bloom or some other lucky fellow. "Have we time for brandy, or shall we cut straight to threats and intimidation?"

Hunter grinned as he reached into his pocket and removed a silver flask. He handed it to Adam. "We'll drink first, drink a toast to Daventry and his machinations."

Adam noted the engraving on the flask as he unscrewed the top. "*Facta, non verba.* Acts, not words. That's an interesting motto."

"I judge a man on what I see, not what he tells me."

"What if that man is a master of disguise?" Adam pulled the stopper and swigged the brandy. "Would it not make your judgement flawed?" He took another sip, wiped the mouthpiece and handed the flask back to the man who stared with unnerving intensity.

"Are you asking me to believe you're not a wastrel?"

"I don't give a damn what you believe."

Hunter swallowed a mouthful of brandy. "Daventry has a reputation for pairing like-minded people. I fail to see how you have anything in common with Miss Dutton. Daventry is known for his accurate appraisals. Perhaps he's made his first mistake."

"Or you've made the wrong assumption," Adam challenged. "Maybe Daventry can read minds and see through the constructs we use to keep people out. Maybe the question you should ask yourself is whether you should choose a new motto."

The tension in the air proved palpable.

But then Hunter laughed, and Adam realised he didn't need to punch the man sitting opposite, didn't need to ruin his new coat.

"You do realise his agents always marry their clients."

"Then perhaps Daventry *has* made a mistake. I have no intention of putting a noose around my neck." And so what was it he wanted from Miss Dutton? A friend? A companion willing to partake in intimate relations? Did he want more than a bed partner?

Hunter shook his head. "Marriage was never a consideration for me. Yet here I sit, wed and blissfully happy."

Doubtless, Hunter had never seen the destructive power of love.

A man was stronger for refusing to succumb to the experience.

"It matters not. In all likelihood, Daventry will assign another agent to my case. I am merely waiting to discover my fate."

At any moment, Miss Dutton would leave the house and break the news he was dreading. Which brought him back to the nagging notion that he wanted more from her than an opportunity to test his seduction skills.

"Daventry has one other agent, though is considering her for a case in Kent. Despite Miss Dutton's pleas for him to reconsider, it's my understanding he wishes her to confront her nightmares."

Confront her nightmares?

What the devil did that mean?

Hunter sat forward and opened the carriage door. "You'll need more than fine clothes and a sharp wit if you're to help her."

Adam tugged his cuffs, accepting the challenge. "How foolish of me. I thought I was the one in need of assistance."

"Daventry believes your lives are inexplicably entwined, your goals one and the same." Hunter arched a mocking brow. "You'll need more than a devilish charm if you mean to solve this case. I doubt the murderer will agree to don fencing clothes and flex his foil."

"I'll reiterate my earlier point," Adam said, his tone laced with warning. "I'm a master of disguise. Don't doubt my capabilities. Beneath this expertly tailored garment is a savage who would rip out a man's throat the moment he overstepped the mark."

Hunter vaulted to the pavement. "Miss Dutton will need a savage if she's to emerge from this mess unscathed. Inform her now if you're not up to the task." Then he closed the carriage door and marched back to the house without a backward glance.

Adam muttered a curse. He had spent his life avoiding complications, avoiding the crippling emotions that made men weak. He had embraced the role of profligate—men had to have a purpose—and he'd been so bloody convincing he'd lost himself beneath the sleek swagger.

Then he'd seen Miss Dutton, and something in his world shifted. He recalled the moment with perfect clarity, a rarity for him. She'd walked into the room, the instant connection hitting him like a lightning bolt, almost knocking him off his feet. Everything before that moment seemed like a rehearsal, a means to idly pass the time before his real life began.

If she'd been open to his advances in the beginning and not given him every reason to think she despised him, perhaps his attachment to her might have waned.

Adam leant back and closed his eyes, choosing sleep over attempting to make sense of his emotions. One thing was certain. Miss Dutton was in command of this show. All he could do was play his part and hope she was pleased with his performance.

ELIZA STOOD ALONE in the hall of the Hart Street office, gripping the doorknob while she contemplated her fate.

Should she return to the study and inform Mr Daventry that he'd made a mistake hiring her? Should she leave the comfort of the house in Howland Street and find work elsewhere? In a quiet town, far away from the perilous streets of London.

But that would not solve her problem.

She would still owe Jeremiah Black two hundred pounds, still have to venture into his disreputable club and deal with the degenerate. But then she wouldn't have the security of knowing Mr Daventry was at hand, ready to charge into the fray with reinforcements.

The alternative sent the fear of God racing through her.

Should she tell Roxburgh the truth?

Should she investigate Jeremiah Black as a murder suspect?

Mr Daventry's position had been clear. Jeremiah Black played a dangerous game. After making the final payment, Eliza could find she owed another debt. One she had no hope of paying. One that bound her to the villain for good.

She considered her options again.

Both came with certain risks.

"Few people have the true measure of Lord Roxburgh." Mr Daventry's voice echoed through the hall. "Few have seen him as I have. Strong. Dependable. A man willing to fight for what he believes."

Eliza turned to find him watching her from the study

doorway, his dark eyes conveying some sympathy for her plight.

"I have every faith in you, Miss Dutton. I have faith you'll make the right decision," he said before disappearing into the study and closing the door.

The right decision was trusting Lord Roxburgh.

There was certainly more to the lord than she'd first assumed. The problem wasn't that she couldn't depend upon him. He was a man of his word. Every instinct said he'd be by her side while she tackled this case. It was what he did to her, his arousing comments, his tender touch.

He'd been seducing her from the moment they met.

She'd been too naive to notice.

Had you looked up as I held you, we would have kissed.

Undoubtedly.

To make matters worse, she was beginning to believe he needed her, too, needed the pleasurable rush to obliterate the nightmares.

Eliza made her decision. She exhaled deeply and opened the front door. Each step towards his carriage brought renewed faith. This was her course now. Somehow she would muddle through.

Raising her hand to stay Roxburgh's coachman, she gave her direction as Howland Street and then climbed into the lord's conveyance.

In repose, Roxburgh lounged back in the seat, his eyes closed, his muscular arms folded across his chest. He made no move when the carriage lurched forward and gathered speed. He breathed slowly, deeply, at peace from his troubles.

Deciding not to wake him until they reached Howland Street, she took the opportunity to study him closely. The man was a magnificent specimen of masculinity. He filled every inch of his expensive coat, every inch of his tight-fitting breeches. She'd felt the firmness of every muscle while held in his arousing embrace.

Her gaze drifted from the golden highlights in his dark brown hair to his full lips. No doubt they were soft and warm and carried a subtle hint of brandy. No doubt they moved expertly over a woman's mouth to create havoc with her insides.

"Such an enigma," she uttered to herself, feeling immense regret that their partnership would soon be over.

He spoke then. "You're so deliciously warm and wet, Miss Dutton," he whispered in a wickedly velvet voice. "Open your legs, love ... wider ... let me taste you as I've longed to do since the moment we met."

Taste her? Taste her!

This devil was determined to rouse a reaction.

"I suppose you find teasing me amusing. While I suspect you wish to punish me for keeping you waiting, I suggest you keep your lewd thoughts to yourself."

He mumbled incoherently before saying with absolute clarity, "I can make your body shudder with pleasure."

Eliza swallowed deeply.

Was it her imagination, or had it become rather hot in his carriage?

"Lord Roxburgh!" Only a sybarite muttered erotic musings in his sleep. "Roxburgh! Wake up!"

"Do you need me inside you, love, pushing hard?"

Good Lord! Her body responded instantly to his lustful comment. Heat pooled between her thighs, and she became acutely aware that she felt so ... so darned empty.

"Roxburgh!" She kicked his foot, dared to grip his knee and shake the devil. "Wake up, else I shall crack you with your coachman's whip."

He blinked and opened his eyes, took a moment to gather his wits before straightening and dragging his hand down his face.

"Miss Dutton?" He glanced out of the window with some

surprise, realising they had left Hart Street. "Why did you not wake me?"

"Trust me, I tried. Numerous times."

He narrowed his gaze, then recognition dawned. "Ah. I can be quite free with my thoughts when sleeping. I don't suppose I gave a boring account of what I ate for breakfast this morning?"

Eliza cleared her throat. "You seemed keen to eat something."

Roxburgh laughed so hard his eyes sparkled. "I pray you were my dinner companion, Miss Dutton. That talk of our meal whet your appetite. That you'd consider dining with me every night of the week. Perhaps break your fast with me, too."

She inwardly smiled. "I prefer to dine alone, my lord. When one is in control of the menu, one is guaranteed satisfaction."

His grin turned sinful. "You're rather good at this game. But I can whip up a delicacy that will make your mouth water."

"After what I just heard, I don't doubt it. But I suspect you'd be dribbling uncontrollably were I to lay my dishes on the table."

"I'd be like a boy in a confectioner's shop."

The air between them shifted.

They stared at each other, their need palpable.

"Should you ever need me to sample your culinary skills, Miss Dutton, you need only say the word." Roxburgh tugged the hem of his waistcoat and shifted in the seat. "Am I to assume that having your company on this journey means you're still my agent?"

Eliza paused to gather her courage. "Mr Daventry thinks I should trust you with the truth. That while I'm being paid to solve your problem, you might help me solve mine."

He considered her for a moment. "Where you're concerned, my benevolence knows no bounds."

Why was that? What did he find so appealing? Was it merely that a rake liked a challenge? Was it all part of his game?

"I'm told I may need my pugilistic skills if I'm to be of service. That you may need me to strip out of this fine coat and reveal the beast beneath."

"Mr Hunter came to speak to you?" He had threatened as much, and Mr Daventry had offered no objection.

Roxburgh nodded. "To share his brandy and remind me what it means to be a man. Apparently eloquence can be a hindrance, can make a gentleman appear weak."

"While I wish he had remained indoors, Mr Hunter is simply caring for the welfare of his wife's friend. And his fears are groundless. I personally find your manner full of vigour."

The devil winked. "Should you need proof I'm in my prime, I guarantee you won't be disappointed." He sat forward. "Now, tell me what your problem has to do with Jeremiah Black."

Needing to get this part over with quickly, she inhaled a deep breath. "My father gambled at the Sapphire. He had a card bearing the same Latin phrase. Mr Black attended my father's funeral where he proceeded to prise open his coffin and steal his sovereign ring."

It was the height of disrespect. The heirloom had been the last thing left of any value, a means to bribe Saint Peter.

Roxburgh frowned. "And no one thought to stop him?"

"I was the only person in attendance." Eliza swallowed past a hard lump in her throat. "Word got about that he was shot by the notorious owner of a gaming hell."

"And that's why you're afraid of Jeremiah Black?"

She shook her head. "Mr Black possessed the deeds to my home. When he came to claim his winnings, he informed me that my father owed three hundred pounds and that debt was now mine."

"But you're not legally responsible."

"I am aware of that, but Mr Black made threats giving me no option but to pay." He'd not hurt her, had spoken so softly when reminding her he'd take her in payment instead. "I visit the Sapphire every fortnight to pay him twenty pounds."

"Twenty pounds? I don't know what Daventry pays you, but it seems a huge ask for a working woman." Roxburgh sounded deeply concerned. "I shall give you the money, and you can clear the debt today." Anticipating her answer, he added, "If you won't take it from me, then take it from Daventry."

To Roxburgh, it was a pittance. Still, she was touched by his concern.

"Unbeknown to my father, I had been saving money for years. When he died, I sold what little furniture we had. I have enough to settle the debt, but Mr Black insists I visit fortnightly and pay in instalments."

Roxburgh sat back and considered her through narrowed eyes. "Then Black wants something else from you." His insight was remarkable, though he was no stranger to the wicked schemes of men.

"I fear he will produce another debt, fear he plots one of two things." Both possibilities sent an icy shiver up her spine. Both made her want to cast up her accounts. "He wants me for his mistress and has intimated as such. Or he intends to blackmail me into doing something criminal."

Roxburgh gave a troubled sigh. "Now I understand Hunter's warning. Did Daventry know this when he hired you?"

"No. At least, I don't think so."

Mr Daventry had heard of her plight because her father had been firm friends with Atticus Atwood, Daventry's deceased father-in-law.

"After seeing the letter bearing Black's threatening mark and knowing I'd have no choice but to investigate his involvement, I had to explain my situation to Mr Daventry."

Roxburgh fell silent.

When the carriage turned into Howland Street, it jerked him from his reverie. "Is there a reason we've come to the Order's house and not Hanover Square?"

Knowing he would be displeased with this new development, Eliza struggled to form the words. "Staying with you is no longer prudent." Odd she felt another pang of regret. Was it not what she'd been hoping for? "I need time to consider how I might approach the problem with Jeremiah Black, and Mr Daventry feels my remaining in Hanover Square might place your sister in danger."

Roxburgh sat bolt upright, mild panic flashing in his handsome eyes. "But I need you. As your client, surely the decision should be mine."

"It's not just that. Miss Trimble must alter a gown for me to wear to the ball tomorrow night and so needs me here for more than a few hours."

A sadness seemed to wash over him. "And what of our midnight liaisons? We made a pact, agreed to meet for the duration of the case."

She'd come to understand his need to confide in someone. Beneath the disguise lay a man struggling with his painful past. Whether he'd meant to or not, Roxburgh had seduced her with his honest answers, his heartbreaking stories.

"I shall do my best to visit Hanover Square tonight." Perhaps it was wrong to continue meeting. At some point, they would go their separate ways, and yet the midnight hour would forever hold a special place in her heart.

His shoulders sagged in noticeable relief. "I shall bring blankets and wait for you in the rotunda."

She should tell him about the other developments in the case. Mr Daventry had sent men to look for Mr Bloom, visit the Regent's Canal address, and question the innkeeper in Cheapside. But that could wait until tonight.

"Please tell Miss Ware that we shall speak at length tomorrow. Tell her to send word should she need to see me before then."

Roxburgh appeared grateful as he opened the door and alighted. He held her hand and assisted her to the pavement. It took every effort to calm her racing heart, to smile and bid him good day.

"With luck I shall manage to sneak away," she said as he climbed into his coach and dropped into the seat. "It shouldn't be too difficult."

"Then I shall look forward to our illicit encounter with much anticipation." Roxburgh held her gaze. "Until tonight."

"Until tonight."

Eliza watched his carriage charge away along Howland Street while considering the momentous tasks ahead.

Getting Miss Ware to play the enchantress and have the *ton* eating from her hand would require a miracle. The odds of tackling Jeremiah Black and bringing him to his knees was a feat too impossible to comprehend.

And yet, both seemed achievable when compared to her most pressing dilemma. Being held in Roxburgh's arms this morning had opened the flood gates and caused a deluge of new emotions. The real difficulty now was remaining objective in his company, keeping her distance while crippled with this intense need.

CHAPTER 9

Despite the later hour, Greyson answered the door promptly. Roxburgh's butler welcomed Eliza into the house and asked if she would like an escort to the garden.

"Thank you, Greyson, but I shall find my own way. I must collect a few things from my room, hence why I'm half an hour early."

"As you will, ma'am. Ring if you need assistance." He left her to her errands and trudged back through the hall.

Eliza hurried upstairs to the pretty pink bedchamber Roxburgh had selected for the duration of her stay. She found her valise and thought to pack but a wave of sadness engulfed her.

It wasn't that she'd miss the comfortable bed or Cook's superb scrambled eggs. It wasn't that she'd miss the rides in a plush carriage or the taste of fine cognac.

She would miss Roxburgh's company, the intelligent conversation, the heated looks that made her giddy. She would miss his witty quips, miss the surprising revelations as he discussed his troubled past.

A knock on the chamber door drew Eliza from her romantic musings. She turned to find Miss Ware standing in the doorway, dressed in nightclothes, her auburn hair tied in a single braid.

"You came," the lady said with immense relief. "Adam wasn't so sure, but I knew you would."

Eliza smiled. "I'm a little early for my meeting with your brother but had things to attend to here."

"Adam is in the garden. He's had a footman light the braziers and candle lamps. He'll be thrilled you made the time and enjoys your midnight discussions tremendously. Indeed, I rarely see him so enthusiastic."

Recalling the lady's harsh criticism of her brother, Eliza thought to correct any misconception. "Ours is a working relationship. Lord Roxburgh has been a perfect gentleman and has in no way beguiled me with his charm and wit."

That wasn't entirely true.

Roxburgh didn't have to try to make himself appealing. Although Eliza liked him, she wasn't so foolish as to fall in love with a rogue.

"Despite his faults, my brother is naturally charming. It's never his intention to push people away. He rarely gets close to anyone." Miss Ware offered a coy smile. "But he's different with you."

"Different?" The word was more a croak of surprise.

"More himself."

Yes, he was nothing like the man she'd first met at her colleague's wedding. "Probably because our situation requires complete honesty." Eliza saw an opportunity to ask a pressing question. "Can I be assured you have been equally frank?"

Miss Ware glanced at the hem of her nightgown.

"Miss Ware?"

She looked up. "Please, call me Lillian."

The lady was stalling. "What haven't you mentioned?"

"Don't be cross. It's nothing to do with what happened to Mr Ashbury. It's ... it's that I'm not sure I can attend the ball tomorrow. I've gone over the script as we agreed, but I fear I lack the confidence to be convincing."

Eliza's heart softened. She knew how it felt to face a room full of vipers. "I shall be beside you every second of the way."

Lillian wrung her hands, the worry lines on her brow deepening. "It's the looks and the whispers I cannot abide. They hit like a rainbow of barbed arrows, each one sharper than the last."

Moving her valise aside, Eliza patted the bed. "Come and sit down. It's too cold to stand in the corridor."

Lillian Ware padded across the room and sat next to Eliza on the plush bed. "It's why I hate going about in society. People make snide comments about my mother, suggest I have the same weak constitution. Heaven knows what they'll say about me now that I've been seen alone in the garden with a dead man."

They would tear her apart like vultures attacking a rotting corpse.

"The spiteful comments people make merely reflect their own state of mind. Have you ever heard a happy person saying terrible things? No, only miserable people slander others."

Lillian nodded. "Judge less ye are judged. I've often thought it the motto of the *ton*."

"I told you how cruel they were when my father was shot. Like me, you have a choice. You can cower before them or hide in the shadows. Neither will prevent them from saying hurtful things. Or—"

"I can do what my brother does so well, wear impenetrable armour capable of withstanding a horde of marauding Vikings."

It was Eliza's cue to laugh, but sadness enveloped her heart. A man shouldn't have to bury family secrets. He shouldn't have to assume a different identity and hide a wealth of good qualities just to stop the vultures pecking. Sadly, that was the nature of high society.

"Wear your armour for a few hours. But when you're home, with the people you love, let them see the kind, compassionate woman beneath."

Lillian's eyes glistened with unshed tears. Silence filled the room before she said, "Do you think Mr Bloom will return?"

Eliza reached for Lillian's hand and gave a reassuring squeeze. "I don't know what prompted Mr Bloom to run. I cannot promise things will be as they were before, but I know you're strong enough to deal with whatever happens."

A rush of confidence suddenly possessed Miss Ware. "I shall make you proud, Miss Dutton. I shall don my mask and give an excellent performance."

"If we're to be firm friends, you must call me Eliza. Rest assured, I shall be waiting in the wings to offer my support."

Lillian suddenly lurched forward and hugged Eliza. When she straightened, she seemed happier than she'd been in days.

"You should go now and find my brother."

Eliza would wait for the first stroke of midnight before hurrying to the garden. "I've time to pack before the bells of St George's chime the hour."

"If you go now, you won't find him seated in the rotunda."

Curious, Eliza frowned. "Where will I find him?"

Lillian swallowed deeply. "When they hauled my mother's body from the lake, Adam ran away. He hid inside Glendale's vast maze, slept there for two nights. I was six, but I remember being scared I'd lose him too."

Emotion tightened Eliza's throat. "Is that why he built a maze here?"

Lillian shrugged. "By day, Adam is the focus of much attention. By night, he wanders the garden alone, disappears into the shadows where no one can see him."

The vision of a frightened boy weeping in the darkness tore at her heart. There'd been no one there to hold him, comfort him, reassure him he was loved. He'd have felt trapped, suffocated, consumed by the emptiness.

"Then you're right. I should go now." Eliza jumped to her feet and kissed Lillian on the forehead. She thanked her before hurrying downstairs and out into the garden.

Roxburgh was not relaxing on the stone bench in the rotunda, surrounded by the fiery glow of lit braziers. She found him sitting on the ground in a corner of the hedge maze, head bowed, hiding in the darkness, at one with the shadows.

"Roxburgh," she called softly.

He sat statue-like, silent, enveloped in a coldness that clung to her like a winter's frost. Seeing him sitting alone near broke her heart in two.

"Roxburgh."

He glanced up as if hearing the distant mutterings of a ghost.

She was intruding but refused to leave him suffering. "It's cold. Come and sit in the rotunda where it's warm. I'll summon a footman to fetch refreshments. We're both in need of a stiff brandy."

Though he looked at her directly, he was still buried in the dark depths of his misery, entrenched in the nightmares, unable to scramble back to the light.

Where was the scoundrel who teased her incessantly?

Where was the libertine who stirred lust even when in slumber?

While she found both men entertaining, she was bewitched by this lost man's spell. A host of feelings overtook her all at once. A need to comfort a friend. A desire to kiss the man awake. A yearning to satisfy the crippling ache within.

She closed the gap between them and dropped down beside him. With tentative fingers, she reached out and pushed the errant lock of hair from his brow.

"Don't sit here alone."

She touched him, smoothed her hand down his muscular arm, stroked his jaw, sought to stir his senses back to life. Then she lost her mind completely. Cupping his cheeks, she leaned forward and pressed a warming kiss to his lips.

Roxburgh inhaled sharply, jerking awake, meeting her gaze.

Seconds passed before he moved. Then he cupped her nape, closed his mouth over hers and drank like a lonely boy thirsting for affection.

She let him take what he needed, a virgin's elixir that somehow worked to restore his vigour and heat his blood, the life force of a novice who desired to see him whole again.

The air about them turned tense, restless.

He broke contact, the wicked glint in his eyes confirming the libertine had joined the party. Oh, how she welcomed the sight of the scandalous rogue.

"Miss Dutton. I'd convinced myself you wouldn't come."

"I'd have moved heaven and earth to keep my vow." The hunger in her veins did not abate. It didn't help that his mouth was so close.

"You're probably wondering what I'm doing in here." Suddenly captivated by a stray lock of her hair, he brushed it back behind her ear as if it were a prelude to seduction.

"It had crossed my mind, but Lillian is quite forthcoming with information. I'm told Glendale's maze is vast in comparison."

He took a moment to reply. "I come here to remember, to prepare myself for disappointment." He made no reference to his mother, and Eliza was not about to resurrect a ghost. "Although I did not anticipate the night taking such a satisfying turn."

Embarrassment warmed her cheeks. "You looked so hopelessly lost. It's why I kissed you. It's why you kissed me back."

A sinful grin played on his lips. "That wasn't a kiss, love. It was a mere taste. The dipping of a toe in lust's waters." He captured her chin between his elegant fingers. "Perhaps we should paddle, for I still have a desperate need to find my way home."

She had tasted his despair, swallowed his pain. Had felt the fortifying wholeness that came with any benevolent act. Nonetheless, she'd distinguished something else on his tongue. The promise of pleasure. The tantalising taste of temptation.

"What makes you think I'd help you a second time?"

"You're as curious as I to know if it will be as good as you imagine." He brushed his mouth gently over hers. "Can you feel the rush of anticipation? I'll not disappoint."

Her heart thumped in her chest.

Every nerve tingled.

"I fear you'll be overwhelmed," she whispered.

"I don't doubt it."

He kissed her with the firmness of a man in control, his mouth moving with such confidence in his ability to please it left her breathless.

Still, it left her wanting.

Wanting the vulnerable man, not the seducer.

Eliza dragged her mouth from his. "Roxburgh, I want *you* to kiss me, not some construct of a man who's rehearsed every movement. It's as if your soul is bound in shackles."

She feared she may have offended him, but Roxburgh laughed. "Are you certain you want the unbridled version? Untethered, I'll lack restraint."

"You don't think I can handle you?"

"I'm not sure you're ready."

Ready? She was a woman of five and twenty, not a missish debutante who blushed at the mere mention of kissing. She solved crimes for a living, lived in fear of her life. Perhaps he was the one not quite ready, not ready to kiss someone who cared.

"Why do you want to kiss me?" She was curious to know. "I want to kiss you because your lewd comments have woken a need inside me. I want to kiss you because you're an enigma I cannot solve. Because I'll most likely die in my fight with Jeremiah Black, and I'd like to know how it feels to kiss a man I desire."

His response sounded like a feral growl. "I've been waiting for you, waiting for as long as I can remember." He pulled her hard against him, capturing her in an open-mouthed kiss that tugged at the muscles deep in her core, turned her insides molten.

Yet beneath every erotic caress, beneath the yearning for carnal pleasure, she recognised a desire for intimacy. Roxburgh needed someone to care for him, someone to appreciate the man few people knew. He needed to taste genuine affection.

And so, as unskilled as she was in the art of seduction, she poured her heart and soul into the kiss. She embraced him with her lips, caressed him with her tongue, made love to his mouth, let him know it was him she craved.

Him.

Just him.

But she underestimated the power of lust, was unprepared for the urgent pleas of her body. Every intoxicating thing about him lured her from her planned path and sent her spiralling on a different course, to a place where gratification was the order of the day.

Indeed, the ache became unbearable. She ached to feel the heat of his body, to feel his hot hands on her bare skin. It was the impetus needed for her to break free from her own restraints.

She threw her arms around his neck and devoured his mouth like a wanton woman in need of tupping. Their tongues tangled in a hurried dance, her sex pulsing to the same erotic rhythm.

And yet, it wasn't enough.

Their breathless moans filled the night air.

And yet, she needed more.

She gathered her skirts and sat astride him, threaded her hands into his hair and tugged gently, fought to feed the hunger writhing within.

"Good God," he panted, breaking to catch his breath. "Love, you're beautiful when starving. You're yearning to feel full." He slipped his hands under her skirts and stroked her bare thighs. "I could ease your suffering."

Roxburgh could drug a woman with his kisses and sinful discourse. She'd never felt so desperate for a man's touch. Never wanted to crawl beneath his skin in a bid to cement their connection.

"Feel what you do to me, love." The devil gripped her hips, drew her back and forth over the hard length filling his breeches. "As a gentleman, I should be horse-whipped for my transgression. But I've never wanted a woman the way I want you."

The St George's bells suddenly clanged the first stroke of midnight.

The second strike awakened her addled brain.

The third pulled her to her senses.

Eliza scrambled off Roxburgh's lap. "I—I should leave." Her legs shook as she righted her skirts. "I—I never intended for things to go so far." How had a chaste kiss become a rampant frolicking in the hedge maze?

Why could she not resist him?

"Stay. Don't go." Roxburgh stood, brushing dirt from his coat, which she suspected was a ploy to address the bulge in his breeches. "Let's move to the rotunda and discuss the case."

She didn't trust herself in his presence, not when every nerve in her body thrummed with life. "Will you walk me to the door and summon a hackney?" Despite clinging to the last vestige of common sense, she'd not leave him alone in the darkness. "We'll resume our usual routine tomorrow. Don't expect more of the same. Tonight was an exception."

"Tonight was exceptional. Stay awhile."

"You know that's unwise." She swallowed past this confounding desire for him. "My mind is incapable of forming a rational thought, and so I shall bid you good night before we both do something we'll regret."

His lips formed a mischievous grin. "Running away won't help."

"Staying won't help. Now see me to a hackney."

"I'll summon my coachman, escort you safely home myself."

"Roxburgh! Just find me a hackney!" She'd likely enter his carriage a virgin and exit a woman with a wealth of experience.

He raised his hands in mock surrender. "As you wish, but leaving won't change anything. We'll both have a devil of a time sleeping tonight."

With her body strung as tight as a bow, sleep would definitely elude her. "Count sheep. I'm told it helps." She tugged his coat sleeve to ensure he followed her out of the maze.

"Are you sure I can't persuade you to stay?"

"Most sure." She was so keen to put some distance between them she didn't dare venture upstairs to pack her valise.

He didn't call for a hackney. He escorted her to the mews where Dobbs sat waiting atop his box, swamped in his greatcoat, reading beneath the light of the lamp.

"An educated coachman makes for a much better travelling companion," Roxburgh informed her. "I wasn't sure you'd have time to stay for the hour and told him to ready the coach come midnight."

Still wrestling with the urge to return to the garden, she quickly bid Roxburgh good night. "Down brandy if you struggle to sleep, though we'll need our wits tomorrow night if we're to protect Lillian."

He brought her hand to his lips. "Until tomorrow, Miss Dutton. Picture me when you've no option but to ease the ache."

One would think her heart would settle the moment the carriage clattered out of the mews and Roxburgh's handsome figure disappeared into the darkness. But the heady scent of his cologne filled the conveyance. It clung to her clothes, coated her skin, stirred her senses.

It would be easy to fall in love with a man who stoked her inner flame. A man as complex as he was captivating. A man she admired more with each passing day.

Perhaps Mr Daventry had another motive for giving her this case. Perhaps she had a secret mission to find the kind and compassionate man hiding behind the guise of a rogue.

One thing was certain. Roxburgh was misunderstood, and it would take the skills of an enquiry agent to unravel him.

CHAPTER 10

Dressed in evening attire, Adam stood in the hall of the Order's house in Howland Street, waiting to ferry Miss Dutton to Lord MacTavish's ball. Miss Trimble hovered beside him, sour-faced, and emanating an energy that could best be described as volatile.

One would need an axe to hack through the tension.

Miss Trimble grumbled again beneath her breath. The woman would be attractive if she wasn't such a grouch. She was but five years older than Miss Dutton, had a worldly air that made her the perfect person to play housemistress to female enquiry agents.

"Say what's on your mind, Miss Trimble." Adam had grown weary of her sighs and groans. "I'm old enough and wise enough to understand your gripe."

"Very well." Miss Trimble faced him, her cheeks red with indignation. "Miss Dutton has suffered enough and doesn't need you filling her head with nonsense. If there's a gentleman hiding beneath your rakish facade, you'll tell her you no longer require her to come to Hanover Square at midnight."

"But our meetings are relevant to the case." It wasn't a lie. They discussed many things during their late-night liaisons.

"Pish! It's a means for you to play your wicked games." Miss Trimble made no secret of her displeasure. "She was noticeably different when she returned home last night."

He was noticeably different since kissing her, too.

Never had a woman responded with such unadulterated passion.

He could still taste her on his lips.

He could still feel her essence filling his chest.

"We discussed personal tragedies as well as the case." That was a lie. She'd dragged him from the darkness but had revealed nothing new about the suspects. "Perhaps that accounts for the change you noticed."

Miss Trimble was about to whip him again when Miss Dutton appeared at the top of the stairs, dressed in vibrant blue satin. Her hair was styled in the latest fashion, accentuating her dainty jaw, drawing his eye to the delicate porcelain skin of her throat.

Her colleague Miss Wild stood behind, staring in awe.

He stared in awe. Every muscle in his body hardened. The crippling hunger surfaced, reminding him how desperately he wished to feed.

He closed his mouth as she descended, so as not to drool over the lush swell of her breasts rising up to greet him. Hell, he was in danger of losing his head tonight.

Adam bowed low. "You were right to refuse my offer. There isn't a modiste in London capable of creating such a breathtaking spectacle."

She wore exquisite sapphire and diamond earrings, and he was suddenly possessed with the need to shower her with lavish gifts, to afford her every luxury.

"Next to the sapphires, your eyes appear blue."

She offered him a bright smile, her gaze falling to his lips.

Damn. She may as well have told Miss Trimble he'd devoured her mouth last night.

"Miss Trimble has an assortment of costumes to assist with our disguises." She fingered the elegant earrings. "And these belong to Mrs Daventry, kindly loaned for this evening."

A lady with such beauty and grace shouldn't have to borrow jewellery. She deserved a chest full of treasures.

Miss Trimble's brows were knitted in frustration as she draped a midnight blue cloak around Miss Dutton's shoulders. "I shall wait up to ensure you arrive home safely."

The comment was aimed at Adam—the wolf out to ravish an unsuspecting virgin. Was it not a little late to worry about Miss Dutton's safety when she chased criminals for a living?

"There's no need, Miss Trimble. I shall see Miss Ware safe and settled in Hanover Square before returning home. I'm sure Lord Roxburgh will extend me the use of his carriage."

Adam inclined his head. "Certainly."

Miss Trimble glanced heavenward before mumbling for them to have a good evening, though hurled daggers of disdain the moment Adam met her gaze.

During the short carriage ride to Pall Mall, Miss Dutton spoke to Lillian about her script and the need to improvise, about exuding confidence. Adam spent the time watching every movement of her mouth, imagining when he might kiss her again, anticipating the moment she straddled him, took him deep into her welcoming body.

"If any of the suspects are here tonight, we should attempt to question them," Miss Dutton whispered, rejoining him after depositing her outdoor apparel in MacTavish's cloakroom. "Discreetly, of course."

"I imagine we may see Lord Wright and Daniel Fraser."

"Excellent."

Having purposely arrived late, they made their way into the lavish ballroom, pushing through those clambering to pay homage to the Duke of Dounreay. Few Scots wore traditional dress, but many wore a hint of plaid as a mark of respect. Adam noticed a waistcoat in the green Douglas tartan, a lady's gown trimmed with the red markings of another ancient clan.

Lillian gripped Miss Dutton's arm, muttering her fears.

"Stand straight," Miss Dutton instructed. "Paste the pretty smile that has all heads turning. Any sign of timidity will make it seem like you're guilty of committing a transgression."

Adam watched his sister transform before his eyes. She slipped into a costume he knew well—the vibrant garb of an arrogant aristocrat. Confidence was a skill easily mastered.

Miss Dutton's lips curled into a satisfied smile. Hell, she knocked him sideways, regardless of her expression. Yet this was her first grand ball, too. She wasn't the least bit intimidated, or if she was, she didn't show it. That's what made her remarkable.

Noticing MacTavish standing a head above most men, they skirted the dance floor to acknowledge their host.

MacTavish welcomed them, introduced his daughter Ailsa, then his wife, a comely middle-aged woman with hair as red as winter berries.

The lady gripped Miss Dutton's hands as if she were the honorary guest. "I cannae thank you enough, Miss Dutton." She made no mention of the offending article found in Ashbury's box. "We owe you a debt that cannae be repaid."

"Lord Roxburgh deserves some of the praise," came Miss Dutton's graceful reply. "Despite the difficulty of his situation, protecting your daughter was his only consideration."

Lady MacTavish expressed her gratitude. "Allow me to take Miss Ware under my wing tonight. She can accompany Ailsa. Upon my word, I have nae intention of letting my daughter out of my sight."

Though it would allow them to hunt for Daniel Fraser,

Adam felt a stirring of unease. He was about to decline the generous offer when Lillian spoke.

"I fear most people believe I behaved inappropriately," Lillian said with quiet confidence. "The mere association may tarnish your daughter's reputation, my lady. No one wants that."

"Nonsense. There's nae a person amongst our friends who would think such a thing." Lady MacTavish captured Lillian's chin briefly and whispered, "You've the makings of a Scot, Miss Ware. It takes a bold and brave lass to enter the fray with nought but a charming smile and a backbone of steel."

Lillian glanced at Miss Dutton. "The support of good friends is more valuable than an army of well-wishers."

Lady MacTavish grinned. "You'll spend an hour with me, Miss Ware, and I'll hear nae more on the matter." She called over her shoulder. "Dounreay, will you nae grant your hostess a boon?"

The tall gentleman with his back to them turned around. He was young, with thick brown hair and a physique that would put a Greek god to shame. Miss Dutton's sharp inhalation upon witnessing the man's good looks had jealousy writhing in Adam's veins.

When Lady MacTavish made the introductions, Adam realised the man he'd met on occasion had died prematurely, and this strapping fellow was his heir.

"You've nae put your name on any lady's dance card, Dounreay." Lady MacTavish surely knew the duke well enough to tease him.

The duke's assessing gaze swept over Lillian. "Perhaps Miss Ware would do me the honour of allowing me to lead her about the floor."

Lillian curtsied. "Your Grace, I would be happy to accept."

Lady MacTavish tapped Adam on the arm with her closed fan. "There you have it, Lord Roxburgh. We shall entertain

Miss Ware for the next hour or two. I assure you, she will come to nae harm."

Lillian insisted she would enjoy spending time with Ailsa MacTavish, and so Adam reluctantly conceded. With a sudden need to demonstrate his masculinity in Dounreay's presence, he drew Miss Dutton aside and asked if she'd care to dance.

"We should use the time to make some headway with the case. We should separate, each one of us find a suspect and probe him for information."

Adam cupped her elbow, yet felt a clawing need to touch her in a far more intimate place. "If you think I'm letting you wander about alone or question a suspected murderer in a dark alcove, you're sorely mistaken."

Miss Dutton lowered her voice. "After what happened between us last night, is it not wise to maintain some distance?"

Maintain distance? He'd hoped to get considerably closer. As for being wise, his obsession with Miss Dutton would see him stumbling about like a besotted fool.

"Are you not keen to explore our unique connection? Are you not curious to see if you can rouse the same enthusiasm you did last night?"

Her eyes widened. "I assure you, last night was a mistake."

So why did she seem fixated with his mouth?

"It didn't taste like a mistake. It tasted warm, seductive, a sensual delight on the tongue." With his thumb, he circled the soft skin at her elbow. "I've never tasted anything so satisfying."

Miss Dutton swallowed deeply. "And I wouldn't want to ruin the experience should the second time prove disappointing."

"Disappointing? Love, your passion knows no bounds."

"That's enough."

"That's not what you said last night."

She tugged her arm from his grasp. "One more word, and I'm leaving. Help me look for Mr Fraser, else in future, I shall avoid venturing to Hanover Square at midnight."

Adam clutched his chest. "You'd break an oath?"

"Where might I find Mr Fraser?" She was beautiful when annoyed. "At the gaming tables? Looking for excitement in the library? Where?"

Forced to surrender, he scanned the ballroom. "Mrs Stanley isn't his only source of amusement. Lady Winchester shares his interest in literature. That, and frolicking on the host's polished desk. I'm certain I saw her when we arrived."

"Then let's stroll around the perimeter, see if we can locate him. If not, we'll scour every dark corner of MacTavish's mansion house."

They spent ten minutes searching the ballroom, another ten minutes watching Lillian dance with the Duke of Dounreay. Her bright smile lit up the room, though Adam could no longer accurately gauge his sister's mood after discovering she admired Bloom.

"Lady Winchester is with her husband." Adam noted the couple's reflection in the mirrors lining one wall. "They're exchanging cross words. No doubt she caused the argument to give her an excuse to flounce away and find Fraser."

"Perhaps my father being penniless was a godsend," Miss Dutton mocked. "I don't belong in this world. It's nothing more than a sham."

Adam couldn't argue. "Wolves run in packs."

She looked at him. "You run with them, but that's not really who you are. I know something of the man hiding beneath, and you're not at all what you seem."

"Maybe I'm only myself with those I trust."

She touched him gently on the upper arm. "Then you should trust people more often." Something passed between them. Something far more potent than lust. "Come, let's hunt for Mr Fraser. Perhaps he's in the study waiting for Lady Winchester. I'd rather not find them in the act."

They ventured through the throng, noted the corridor was busy but recalled from their previous visit that the study was the first room on the right, and so meandered through the crowd.

"When I open the door ajar, slip inside." Adam stood with his back to the study, his hand wrapped around the handle. "I'll follow."

Unfazed, Miss Dutton nodded. She moved stealthily into the room while he quickly closed the door. He waited until the coast was clear again before following her inside.

Fraser *was* in the study, and the red-haired rogue had his wandering hands all over Miss Dutton.

"Get off me, you imbecile," she whispered through gritted teeth, evidently not wishing to make too much noise. "I'm not who you think I am."

Anger flared.

Adam moved swiftly, grabbing Fraser by the collar of his coat and practically dragging him off his feet. He threw the lout into the leather wing chair and pinned him by the throat.

"Touch her again, and I'll throttle the last breath from your lungs." He firmed his grip until the bastard gave a choking cough.

"I—I thought she was someone else," Fraser croaked, hitting Adam's hand with his fist. He coughed again when Adam released him. "It's dark in here, and my companion likes to tussle."

"Did you not hear her objection?"

"It's not uncommon for my friend to resist."

Miss Dutton brushed her skirts, then locked the study door. "Your friend can wait outside until we've finished our interrogation."

Fraser's eyes shifted nervously in their sockets. Clearly mistaking their intention, he gripped Adam's coat sleeve.

"Good God, Roxburgh. Don't hurt me. I swear, I'll not say a word about the incident with your sister."

Adam froze. Did Fraser think he had murdered Ashbury? And was he referring to Lillian finding the corpse in the maze or something else? "You speak of the incident where Ashbury ...."

"Threatened her and ripped her gown."

While hell's own fury turned his blood molten, Adam knew it was better to say very little and let this devil talk. "Go on."

"I would have come to you, but there seemed no point. The fellow was dead but an hour later." Fraser raised his shaking hands. "You have my word, Roxburgh. I'll not speak of it to a living soul."

"No, because I'll cut out your tongue and feed it to the dogs."

"Did you see anything else untoward that night?" Miss Dutton said, joining the interrogation.

Fraser stared blankly.

"Miss Dutton is an enquiry agent working to discover who killed Ashbury." Adam thought the truth was better than this fellow thinking she was his outspoken mistress. "You'll answer her questions, else our next call will be the Stanley household. I'd hate for Mr Stanley to discover he's a cuckold."

Miss Dutton firmed the threat. "Equally, I'm happy to wait for Lady Winchester and see what her husband has to say about your secret assignation. I can almost hear the discharging of pistols. Can almost smell the acrid scent of sulphur in the air."

Secret assignation?

Wait! Ashbury had attacked Lillian on the first-floor landing. If Fraser had witnessed the event, he'd been sneaking about upstairs.

"Where were you when you saw them?" Adam demanded to know. "If you lie, I'll have Miss Dutton fetch Lord

MacTavish, and you can explain it all to a horde of angry Scots."

Fraser gulped. "S-stretching my legs."

"You were upstairs in my house. Why?"

Fraser failed to answer.

Miss Dutton folded her arms across her impressive bosom. "If you cannot offer a plausible reason, we'll assume you were assisting Mr Ashbury."

Fraser squirmed in his seat.

The door handle rattled.

"Ah, perhaps we should invite Lady Winchester to join us?"

Fraser groaned. "I was merely looking around the house."

"For what?" Adam snapped.

"For no reason."

"Liar. Don't make me call you out."

The man whimpered but offered no explanation.

"Very well. Name your second."

"Wait! You'll call me out if I tell you why."

"I'll bloody well call you out if you don't."

Miss Dutton touched Adam's arm. "If he tells us everything he knows, might you show leniency?"

"Perhaps."

Fraser winced. "I was hoping to ... to steal something from your dressing room. It's that, or I shall lose my damn home."

Adam jerked his head. He'd have punched Fraser for his damnable cheek, but the last comment fed his growing curiosity.

"You're not short of funds. I've seen you gambling at the Sapphire. You'd find nothing of value in my chamber, nothing that would raise enough money to cover a substantial debt."

Fraser bowed his head.

Silence ensued, but then Miss Dutton said, "*Victor Ludorum*."

The devil jumped in shock.

"You wagered the deeds to your home." Her voice brimmed with pride for having pieced the clues together. "You were looking for something bearing Lord Roxburgh's crest."

It was a logical assumption.

Fear filled the man's eyes. "I had no choice. I entered naively, didn't understand the rules until it was too late. By then, I'd signed the damn contract."

Not wanting to appear ignorant, Adam offered a vague response. "Jeremiah Black never plays by the rules."

"And now I have no choice but to find a winning hand."

Adam was busy trying to make sense of the information, but Miss Dutton's mind proved superior to his own. "Something bearing the Duke of Dounreay's crest would win over Lord Roxburgh's heraldic shield," she stated.

Fraser nodded. "The King's crest trumps everything."

So this was a game of wits, a game where the best thief won the hand. Perhaps Fraser's secret liaisons were a means to rummage in drawers under the guise of conducting an illicit affair.

"Empty your pockets."

Fraser's eyes bulged in their sockets. Adam had to threaten him again before he reached into his coat, removed a gold seal ring and handed it over.

"I shall have to inform MacTavish."

"No! No! I'd no choice. I had to do something to beat my opponents."

"I want the names of these opponents. It's likely one of them killed Ashbury believing he already had the winning hand."

Fraser scratched his head and stared open-mouthed. "Ashbury was playing *Victor Ludorum?*"

Miss Dutton gave a curious hum. "You didn't know?"

"No. We're masked. We're not allowed to know their names in case we sabotage the game. Anyone who attempts to discover another's identity loses their place and their deed."

"Jeremiah Black ... is he ... is he the only one who knows?" Miss Dutton touched her hand to her throat. No doubt she'd just realised they had another pressing reason to call at the Sapphire.

"Yes."

"W-when is the game due to take place?" Her chin trembled as she spoke. "And how m-many players are there?"

"Next Saturday. There are four of us left now that Ashbury is dead."

One of them must have killed Ashbury.

One of them knew the identity of the other players.

Fraser must have arrived at the same conclusion because he suddenly whimpered. "I'll be next. The devil will find me and snap my neck in two. He could be here, lurking in the shadows, waiting to pounce."

"Guilty men often cast suspicion elsewhere," Miss Dutton said, having found her floundering courage. "You had a motive to kill Mr Ashbury. You were missing from the supper room at the time of the murder. You are the prime suspect."

Fraser shot out of the chair. "I'm innocent! Mrs Stanley can vouch for my whereabouts at the time in question. And I saw Ashbury arguing with your secretary moments before I entered the library. It's evident they knew one another."

Bloom knew Ashbury?

Adam considered the possibility they were acquainted. They were the same age. Ashbury was the grandson of a viscount, Bloom, the youngest son of a gentleman. Had Ashbury gone to Oxford or Cambridge? And why hadn't Bloom mentioned the connection?

"Do you take snuff, sir?"

"Occasionally," Fraser replied, again confused.

"Have you lost a silver box bearing your initials?"

"Not that I'm aware."

"You'll check when you return home and inform Lord Roxburgh should you find your snuffbox missing."

Fraser looked at the locked door. "Does that mean I can leave?"

"Yes, but might I suggest you remain indoors while the killer is at large? With luck, we hope to complete our investigation quickly but cannot guarantee your safety."

"I pray the killer is playing *Victor Ludorum*," Fraser said, crossing the room. "With one more down, it will better my odds."

"Unless the killer seeks to get rid of you," Adam countered.

Looking as if he might cast up his accounts, Fraser left in a hurry.

"Now we know more about the game, we must discover the identity of the other players," Miss Dutton said, glancing at the open door with some apprehension.

"It won't be easy." Not when logic warned against having any interaction with Jeremiah Black.

"No." Her sad sigh was like a blade to his heart.

Adam closed the gap between them and cupped her cheek. "I know you're scared, but you're not alone. Daventry won't let Black harm you, and I'll kill the cold-hearted beggar if need be."

Her strained smile conveyed her fears. "I doubt Mr Black would fight a duel, be it with swords or pistols."

"I'm a master of disguise, remember. I shall play a beast from the rookeries and slit the devil's throat in a dank alley."

"Where's the honour in that?"

Adam pressed a lingering kiss to her forehead. "Some things are more important than honour." Nothing was more important to him than her.

CHAPTER 11

They found Lord Wright alone on the terrace, taking long puffs on a cheroot. Between blowing smoke into the chilly night air, he grumbled to himself about the ballroom being full of Scots.

Eliza studied him while hidden behind the terrace doors.

Lord Wright was a man of middling years. The thick white streaks in his ebony hair made him appear menacing, not dashing. His hands were broad like his shoulders, his fingers as fat as the sausages from Smithfield Market. Were they nimble enough to clasp a man by the throat and snap his neck? That was the question.

The sudden touch of Roxburgh's hand on the small of her back drew her from her musings. Being unprepared, she couldn't stop the delightful shiver that ran down to her toes.

"Always so responsive," he whispered close to her ear.

"You caught me by surprise."

"As I did last night when my tongue slipped into your mouth, and you shivered in much the same way."

There was little point denying the truth. "Indeed. Did you find Lillian? I pray Lady MacTavish kept her promise."

"Lillian is dancing with Dounreay for a second time. A

third, and he'll have to make her an offer. Before that, she danced with the Earl of Lothlair. I'll not be surprised if she develops an affinity for the Highlands and begs I purchase a house north of the border."

Relief settled over Eliza, and she smiled. "Lady MacTavish is proving a useful ally."

"It was generous of you to suggest I played a part in returning the torn piece of her daughter's gown." His hand slipped a fraction lower.

The tightening in her core was impossible to ignore. "I knew you'd agree to put their minds at ease," she said, trying to concentrate on their present task. "You didn't need to voice your opinion."

"No, it was my soul silently communicating with yours."

"Or that you're predictable."

His light laugh breezed against her ear. "When we're at home in the maze, I shall do something unpredictable. But we need to question Lord Wright while he's alone on the terrace."

It would be impossible to sit in the garden with Roxburgh without remembering his hot mouth mating with hers, without wanting more of the same.

"Yes, though I doubt we'll get a sensible word from him." She referred to Lord Wright's dribbling mumbles. "I can't quite tell if he's daft or drunk."

She pushed open the terrace door, aware Roxburgh followed so closely behind she could practically feel the heat radiating from his body.

"Lord Wright?" Eliza turned her head swiftly when the lord blew smoke in her direction. She coughed. "We wish to talk to you about what you saw in Lord Roxburgh's garden last Saturday night."

Roxburgh closed the terrace doors and came to stand beside her. "Sir Oswald said you made a statement, said you witnessed the argument between my secretary and Ashbury."

Lord Wright dropped the remains of his cheroot on the stone floor and crushed it with the heel of his shiny black shoe.

"There's nothing more to say. I saw your man following Ashbury into the maze, heard them shouting. A little later, your sister came tearing out, raising a hue and cry."

Lord Wright spoke succinctly. He wasn't in his cups and so must surely be teetering on the brink of insanity. That, or he had something so pressing on his mind, he resorted to conversing with himself.

"Do you know why they were arguing?" she asked.

The lord cast her a disdainful glance, forcing Roxburgh to introduce her as Mr Daventry's enquiry agent. "You'll answer her questions. I throttled the last devil who refused to comply."

Lord Wright was not intimidated. He raised his meaty paws. "And these hands would crush your fingers long before you crushed my windpipe."

"Can they crush a man's neck?" Eliza dared to ask.

The lord's brow furrowed. "Ashbury cheated at cards and dice, but I didn't kill the scoundrel. I'd place my wager on Roxburgh's secretary. It sounded like he had every reason to curse Ashbury to the devil."

Mr Bloom didn't seem at all like a man who would lose his temper. Yet, one could not deny he looked strong enough to put up a good fight.

"You had a motive." Eliza pressed harder. Lord Wright might easily lose his temper, and angry men always complained about their problems. "You lost a substantial sum to a man you believe cheated. And you were drunk. Drunk men behave irrationally. Drunk men rarely remember their immoral antics."

Lord Wright gritted his teeth. "I wasn't drunk. That devil added something to my port during play, something to numb my senses, something to make me lose the last hand."

The more Eliza learnt about Mr Ashbury, the more she believed he was inherently evil. "If Mr Ashbury drugged you, how can you be sure it was Lord Roxburgh's secretary who entered the maze?"

Mr Bloom had no cuts or bruises to suggest he'd been involved in a scuffle. And with the limited light and him being somewhat woozy, the lord might be mistaken.

"Because I'd seen them exchanging cross words earlier, ten minutes after the clang of the supper gong. They were in the hall, near the study. The secretary seemed angry, while Ashbury was his darned arrogant self."

Eliza's heart sank.

That made two people who'd witnessed the argument. She doubted both men were lying. Lillian would have to be told, but not tonight.

"You're certain it was Bloom?" Roxburgh asked with an air of dejection. He would dread telling Lillian the truth, too.

"So certain, I would swear to it in court."

A brief silence ensued.

Two questions hung on the tip of her tongue. "Are you familiar with the Latin phrase *Victor Ludorum?*"

Lord Wright muttered the phrase numerous times. "Mildly familiar. It's a term bandied about at school during initiations."

Eliza studied him. "Do you ever gamble at The Black Sapphire?"

"Only a man with a death wish gambles at the Sapphire," he scoffed.

"So, you don't frequent Jeremiah Black's club?"

"No!"

Eliza's was the only chin trembling, and so she would have to take Lord Wright at his word. "If you think of anything else pertinent, you may visit the Order's office in Hart Street, Covent Garden."

"I told Sir Oswald all I know, and I'll say no more on the

matter." Indeed, Lord Wright said nothing more until they made to depart. "You didn't ask if I'd stolen back my vowel. One might assume you didn't ask because you know who robbed Ashbury."

Roxburgh stiffened. "Sir Oswald seemed convinced you had no part to play. Like you, I'm eager to learn what happened to our vowels." He bid the lord good evening, placed his hot hand at the small of her back, and guided her into the ballroom.

"We should find Lillian, thank MacTavish and return home." Roxburgh appeared agitated. "Two dances with Dounreay will quell the gossip. Three will spark a wildfire."

"I trust Lillian has learnt from her mistake and will avoid gaining the gossips' attention." She brought him to a halt and met his gaze. "But that's not why you're so tense."

He sighed. "Every lead points to Bloom being the prime suspect."

"Mr Fraser has a motive for murder, as does Lord Wright and, dare I say, Lord MacTavish. Let's not jump to conclusions before we've heard Mr Bloom's story."

"You're right." His brown eyes softened as his gaze slipped to her mouth. "You're always right."

"I was wrong about you. You're not the arrogant knave I expected."

"I'm still a man who gambles for the thrill."

She touched his upper arm. "And tonight, when we're alone in the rotunda, you may tell me why." Was it that his heart had died, and he hoped to jolt it back to life? Was it that he'd lost so much already, nothing else could compare?

His countenance brightened. "You mean to keep your promise?"

"We agreed. An hour every night so we might know each other better."

It had quickly become her favourite hour of the day. He was always refreshingly honest, always listened and showed an interest. Yes, she would miss their midnight meetings when this was all over. She would miss him—dreadfully so she feared.

"I'm recently of the opinion an hour is not enough," Roxburgh said in his usual languid drawl. "Where you're concerned, I'm a man who craves excess."

Despite being eager to respond, their flirtatious repartee would prove distracting, and so she scanned the ballroom, keen to leave and continue the discussion elsewhere.

"I see Lillian with Lady MacTavish." Eliza gestured to the group standing near the grand fireplace. A group that also included the Duke of Dounreay. "Let's steal her away before she takes to the floor again."

"Longing to have me all to yourself, Miss Dutton?"

"Longing to learn your secrets, my lord."

They spent twenty minutes conversing with Lady MacTavish. Roxburgh returned Lord MacTavish's seal ring, explained how they'd come by it and said he would name the culprit once they'd caught Mr Ashbury's killer.

"There were a few sly glances and muttered whispers," Lillian said as they settled into Roxburgh's carriage, "but two dances with the duke helped stem the gossip."

"Dounreay seemed quite taken with you." Eliza glanced at Roxburgh, who sat with his nose pressed to the carriage window, and she wondered why they were still stationary on Pall Mall.

"My affections are engaged elsewhere, though I shall always be grateful to the duke. I've invited Ailsa and Lady MacTavish to come to Hanover Square to take tea tomorrow."

"Wonderful." Eliza tried to concentrate on the conversation, but Roxburgh had caught Lord Wright's affliction and was muttering to himself. "Is something wrong, my lord?"

Without warning, he opened the carriage door and vaulted to the road. "Wait here. Remain with Lillian. If I fail to return in ten minutes, have Dobbs come and find me."

Panic seized Eliza by the throat. "Where are you going?"

"There's a man watching MacTavish's house. I saw him in Hanover Square this morning and mean to ask him a few questions." Roxburgh slammed the door, said something to his coachman and then marched across Pall Mall.

Eliza shuffled to the end of the seat and stared out of the window. Through the gloom, she could see the dim figure of a stocky man who walked away the moment Roxburgh crossed the road.

Roxburgh shouted to the fellow, and they both burst into a sprint.

Eliza rubbed mist from the window and craned her neck, only to see both men disappearing into the darkness.

"What's wrong, Eliza?" Lillian sounded equally panicked.

"Your brother noticed something suspicious." Every fibre of her being said she should follow and offer assistance, but she shouldn't leave Lillian alone. "I'm sure he'll return momentarily."

Minutes passed while she waited, near frantic with worry. Then the heavens opened, and rain hammered the window-pane, making it impossible to see beyond.

What if one of Jeremiah Black's men had taken to following her?

What if he hurt Roxburgh all because she owed Black a debt?

An image of the lord lying battered and bruised in the gutter forced its way into her mind. Her stomach twisted into knots, demanding she act.

"Lillian, do you promise to wait here if I leave the carriage?" She couldn't delay a moment longer. The need to see Roxburgh's confident smile, hear his teasing remarks left her restless with impatience.

"I shall come with you." Lillian had the makings of an

enquiry agent, for she gave no consideration to her reputation.

"And have the *ton* see you racing through the streets, soaked to the skin. You'll wait here." Eliza gripped the handle just as Lord Roxburgh yanked open the door. She might have fallen into his arms had he not offered a steadying hand.

Eliza scampered back onto the seat. He climbed inside, sat down and attempted to catch his breath. Water dripped from the lock of dark hair plastered to his brow. Water dripped from his nose and chin onto his sodden coat.

The carriage jerked forward, quickly gaining speed as they made the short journey to Hanover Square. Though damp, the feel of his arm pressing against hers settled her nerves.

"Did you question him?" Beneath the glow of the lamplight, Eliza studied Roxburgh's face and hands, looking for evidence of a violent struggle.

"The brute could only communicate with his fists."

"He hit you!"

"Of course not. I was champion pugilist at Cambridge three years in a row."

Eliza shook her head. "You might have told me that before you darted after a man twice your size."

"Why? Were you concerned for my welfare, Miss Dutton?"

"Extremely concerned."

"Rest assured. I am in perfect health." He gave her a teasing nudge, then spent the journey recounting his fight with the thug. "I should visit Jackson's and take up sparring again. The brute almost landed an uppercut to the jaw."

"Once we've solved the case, I doubt you'll have many opportunities to brawl in the street." No, he would return to his sophisticated life, perhaps take a new mistress, tour the best gaming hells in town.

The thought left her bereft.

UPON THEIR ARRIVAL in Hanover Square, Eliza accompanied Lillian upstairs while Roxburgh changed into dry clothes. After a lengthy conversation about Mr Bloom and the Duke of Dounreay, she removed her earrings and brushed out Lillian's hair, then hurried to the garden.

She found Roxburgh seated inside the rotunda.

Despite the rain, she took a moment to drink in the sight. He sat in the moonlight, wearing buckskins and a crisp white shirt gaping open to reveal smooth, golden skin.

Desire unfurled inside like a spring bud.

What was it about this man that held her spellbound?

"Be quick! You'll get wet." He laughed as he stood and beckoned her to hurry. Grabbing a blanket from the bench, he held it open, ready to wrap her in a comforting cocoon.

She laughed as she picked up her skirts and ran to the rotunda, blinking away raindrops. "I don't mind the rain. I find it refreshing. People are always so afraid of catching a chill."

Roxburgh draped the blanket around her shoulders, his fingers brushing the sensitive skin at her collarbone as he drew it across her body.

She held his gaze, the strange swirling in her stomach playing havoc with her insides. "Always the gentleman," she whispered.

"Presently, my thoughts are those of a rogue."

Lust took command of her tongue. "You wish to taste me, Lord Roxburgh?"

"More than you know."

Her breath caught in her throat. It wasn't what he said, but that he spoke with an intense longing she had no hope of satisfying. "For fear of breaking an oath and dashing away on the stroke of midnight, we should sit and talk first."

"First? Tonight might be an exception, too?"

"Kissing is quite addictive," she admitted.

He brushed the backs of his fingers across her damp cheek. "Kissing you is addictive. I've never much cared for it with anyone else."

Swept away by his comment, she came up on her toes and pressed her mouth to his. The slow melding was like the caressing of souls, so deeply moving, so different from their wild mating last night.

"Well," she said, being the first to pull away, "kissing you is a unique experience." The thought of kissing another man felt repugnant.

His smile brimmed with masculine pride. "Perhaps we should forget everything else and focus on our addiction."

"You know that's not possible." Her heavy sigh conveyed the depth of her disappointment. "Should I fail to solve this case, Mr Daventry will have me at the Servants' Registry, begging for a new position."

"And yet you're not here in a professional capacity tonight. You're here because you want me to reveal something I keep locked in a dark corner of my heart."

He made talking sound like a punishment. "I wish to help you."

"You already have, though I fear you've ruined me for other women. Nothing will ever compare to the time spent with you."

Good Lord! He knew how to make a woman want him. He knew how to make everything seem exciting and new. How to make her feel like a goddess, a princess amongst her peers when she was poor and plain and petrified.

"Are those the words you use to make women fall in love with you? You should know, my heart is imprisoned in a steel chest." Though she suspected he could pick the lock, slip inside like a thief in the night and catch a woman unawares.

"Lillian exaggerates when she's upset. Why would I intentionally hurt someone knowing I cannot commit?"

Eliza had come to learn something about him during their nightly conversations. He was not selfish, not a braggart, did not have inflated ideas of his own self-importance.

"That's why we are so suited." She'd always assumed they were nothing alike, complete opposites in every regard. "Neither of us wants anything more than a trusted friend and confidant. I'm certain we will grow tired of kissing, for it is merely a means to chase away the ghosts."

Yes, it all made sense now. When consumed with painful thoughts, a good dose of flirtation was the perfect medicine. Although, with her mind filled with fears of Jeremiah Black, she was in danger of downing a whole bottle.

"Let us sit," she said before he offered a different explanation. "You were going to tell me why you find gambling so thrilling."

"Speak words I have never uttered to a living soul?" he teased. "You must be mistaken."

"I think not." Eliza captured his hand and drew him to the stone bench. Casting the blanket aside, she sat demurely, waiting for him to begin.

Clearly feeling uncomfortable, Roxburgh rubbed the back of his neck. "You'll need to ask me a direct question because I am not sure where to begin."

"You don't have to tell me anything. We can discuss the case." She didn't want to force a confession. "But if you wish to open your heart, begin with the first thought that enters your mind."

Heaving a sigh, he dropped down next to her.

Silence ensued.

She chose to reveal a memory. "I remember the first time my father held a card party at the house. I crept out of my room and listened from the landing. Everything held my attention, the laughter, the cigar smoke, the sickly sweet scent of liquor." The house had felt warm and alive for the first time in years.

"Men have shot themselves after leaving such an event."

A small part of her feared her father had sought such an escape. "That night, when the house fell deathly quiet again, I heard my father weeping. He'd wagered and lost the pearl necklace my mother wore on her wedding day. It made no sense to me. It still makes no sense to me."

"Gambling is a way to fill the void."

"Is that why you gamble?"

"It's difficult to explain what motivates me to risk precious items." He paused. "It may sound confusing. I'm not certain I have fully rationalised the process myself."

"You're trying to find the logical in something illogical?"

He dragged his hand through his hair, and his shoulders slumped. "I am trying to find the answer to a question that has nothing to do with playing whist or piquet."

She reached for his hand, squeezed gently, appreciating the warmth. "I doubt I have the answer and will probably add to the confusion, but I would like to understand you, Adam."

Roxburgh inhaled sharply. "I find it impossible to refuse you, Eliza." He gripped her hand as if clutching a cliff edge. "The question is this. How can someone who professes to love you risk it all on an uncertainty?"

She straightened, unsure if she'd heard correctly. She had asked herself a similar question many times. How could a man gamble away his home knowing it would leave his daughter destitute?

"I suspect you will never know," she said quietly.

"Or put another way, how can someone risk losing everything they hold dear for the chance there's something more beyond the grave?"

Eliza had no notion how to answer.

"It must sound confusing when I'm the one who gambles, but I refer to ... to my mother taking her own life." He bowed his head, but she didn't need to look into his eyes to see his pain. It was there in every strained muscle, every ragged breath. "In her diary, she wrote of her need to see my brother, to assuage her guilt, to ensure he was not alone in the after-life. She gave up everything, wagered it all on an uncertainty. In short, she didn't love us enough to stay."

The sound of his anguish was like a blade to her heart.

In her mind's eye, she saw him running, dashing into the maze. It made more sense now. People lied. People proved false. And so he was better off relying on no one but himself. Better off alone.

That's why he hid behind a facade.

That's why he had no intention of marrying.

He saw his mother's death as a betrayal.

"And so, I gamble in the hope I might begin to under-stand her thought process, so I might feel her dilemma, so I might reach a point where I become numb to the risk." He snorted. "It's irrational and not at all the same as choosing to die, but perhaps I inherited that from my mother."

"It's not irrational," she said, her voice choked with emotion. "It's merely a way of coping with trauma. You want to understand, yet it all swirls around inside you, a maelstrom of confusion."

He sighed. "It feels rather like trying to trap a tempest in a bottle."

"You needed to confide in a friend. Instead, you built a maze."

"For me, the maze is a place of solace."

"Because it's where you hide from your feelings." She glanced up at the impressive domed structure. "What prompted you to build a rotunda? What significance does it hold?"

He fell silent.

"Adam?"

He reached out, drew her onto his lap, and cupped her

cheek. "It's where I sat at Glendale, where I vowed Lord Roxburgh would not be so weak as to cry over a woman. It's where I swore to lock my heart in a chest, never to see the light of day."

Eliza gripped his arm. "And yet here you sit, holding me close, telling me your darkest secrets. Trusting me."

"It seems I'm as weak as the next man when caught unawares." He curled his fingers around her nape, drawing her mouth closer to his. "You've bewitched me, Eliza Dutton, and I'm having a devil of a time trying to understand how."

"Why torture yourself?"

"Perhaps you know of a suitable distraction." Roxburgh stared at her mouth like he was famished. But when he looked up, when those dark, fathomless eyes met hers, her heart raced so fast she could barely breathe. "Might I kiss you again? It appears I have developed a new, rather compelling addiction."

Without hesitation, she closed her eyes and leant forward, anticipating the first heart-stopping touch. Yet Roxburgh was anything but predictable. She felt his lips against her temple, so soft and featherlike. She felt his breath breezing against her ear, his wicked mouth against her jaw, her neck.

"You have your own worries," he drawled, "yet are selfless in your desire to help me understand mine. For that, you deserve a reward."

The reward was not a kiss on the mouth.

It was a sensual adventure that began with gentle sucks of her earlobe, him whispering all the erotic ways he would touch her once he'd stripped her bare. The trail continued along the column of her throat, his hot kisses searing her skin.

"Roxburgh!" Her head fell back like a wanton.

"Love, I ache to be inside you. We'd be so good together." His words were as drugging as his kisses.

She ached for something more, too.

But then the sound of a discreet cough broke through the seductive haze. Roxburgh straightened and quickly set her from his lap.

"Perhaps the distraction serves us well," he said upon hearing the cough again. "I lose my mind when I'm with you."

"I'm just as reckless."

He laughed, then called out to the mystery cougher hiding behind the high hedgerow. "You may approach."

Greyson appeared, apologising profusely. "Forgive me, my lord. A boy arrived with a letter for Miss Lillian. I thought it pertinent to detain him should you wish to inspect the missive and the boy."

"A letter? At this late hour?" Roxburgh turned to her. "If it's from Dounreay, he's damn presumptuous."

"It could be from Mr Bloom."

"Bloom!" Roxburgh shot off the stone bench and hurried down the steps. He took the note from Greyson and examined the seal.

"Surely you won't open your sister's letter?"

"Of course not, but our work tonight is far from over."

"What do you intend to do?"

"Interrogate the boy and insist he lead us back to the sender. Let's pray it leads to my elusive secretary. After being in one fight tonight, I would rather not threaten Dounreay in a ballroom full of Scots."

CHAPTER 12

The desperate urge to break the seal and tear open the letter left Adam's fingers throbbing. While keen to know the name of the devil who dared send his sister a note at this disreputable hour, his main motive was getting rid of the impudent urchin sitting in his carriage.

"Was the gentleman's hair blonde or brown?" Miss Dutton stared at the boy, equally frustrated by his reluctance to provide answers. "Surely you can recall his likeness."

"There's some with blonde hair wot looks brown at night."

"Did he give his name? Was it Bloom?"

"I can't rightly remember."

She sighed. "Might another penny provide some clarity?"

"It might."

Adam reached into his pocket, removed a coin, and flicked it to the boy. "You'll give us a description else I shall put you out here." This was the closest he'd ever come to throttling someone half his age.

As instructed, they were approaching Newgate Street, the magnificent dome of St Paul's visible to the right. Eager to earn another penny, the lad had refused to name the coaching inn where he'd been hired to deliver the note. The nearest was the Bull and Mouth on St Martin's le Grand, but they couldn't afford to take any chances.

"He's got blonde hair, and he didn't bother givin' a name."

"But he's staying at the Bull and Mouth, you said?"

The lad lifted his weather-beaten hat and scratched his head. "It might be the Bull." Then he grinned. "But the cove, he gave me a crown for the hackney fare."

"I'll give you a sovereign for the room number." Adam removed the coin, held it between his thumb and forefinger, so it shone beneath the lamplight.

The lad grinned and stretched out his grubby hand. "Don't let it be said nabobs ain't generous."

"You'll get it once you've directed us to the right room."

The lad gave a cheeky wink, then thrust his head out of the open carriage window and informed Dobbs to drive to the Bull and Mouth.

They sat silently for a few minutes.

No doubt, the boy was busy imagining the host of mouth-watering meals he could purchase with a sovereign. Adam battled a hunger of a different kind. A need to feed his lust, to lay Eliza Dutton out like a banquet and feast like a king.

It didn't help that she was no longer possessed of the same inhibitions. Twice, she'd touched his thigh to steady herself when the carriage bounced through ruts in the road.

"You'll get your sovereign once you have shown me who sent the note," Adam informed the boy. While he suspected they were about to reunite with Bloom, he prayed Dounreay wasn't plotting an assignation.

"Wot if he ain't here?"

"Then I'll have to tear open the seal and hope he signed the note."

Doing so would place a strain on his relationship with Lillian. And after witnessing the hurtful comments written in his mother's diary, Adam had sworn he'd never read a person's private missive.

Dobbs drove through the arched entrance into the yard of the Bull and Mouth. With stabling for a few hundred horses, and an area large enough to accommodate thirty carriages and wagons, the inn was a noisy hive of activity, even at this late hour.

Dobbs parked close to the coffee room to allow two coaches laden with luggage to make swift departures.

The lad swung the carriage door open and leapt to the ground. He scoured the dimly lit yard, maybe looking for the mysterious sender or scouting for his next wealthy punter.

"You'll find the cove upstairs." The lad pointed to the upper gallery of rented rooms. "The green door above the coffee room." He offered his open hand as if it were a silver salver. "Pleasure doin' business, gov'nor."

Adam placed the sovereign in the boy's dirty palm, and the rascal scampered away into the dead of night.

He looked at Miss Dutton, wrapped warmly in Lillian's blue ermine-trimmed pelisse. It was the first time they'd been alone since Greyson's coughing fit in the garden. Yet the memory of his mouth on her soft skin was the most prominent thought in his mind.

"Should we dare to venture upstairs, Miss Dutton?"

With her brows knitted together, she looked up at the first-floor gallery. "It's unlike you to proceed with caution. Who else can it be but Mr Bloom?"

Compelled to touch her, he cupped her elbow. "Since we've admitted to being rather reckless in each other's company and because our interlude in the garden has left us both ravenous, I was referring to us being alone in a place with empty rooms for hire."

It took a moment for recognition to dawn.

"Oh!" She swallowed deeply. "I see."

"Forgive the scandalous allusion, but life is precarious.

When there is something I want this badly, to hell with manners."

She considered him for a moment. "A kiss has complicated matters, and I lack the experience necessary to please one so well-versed in the art of lovemaking."

"The ability to express oneself honestly is the only skill required." He liked that she was oblivious to her allure. He liked that she was unaware he was so hopelessly besotted.

Maybe his infatuation would wane.

Maybe anything more than a kiss would ruin a friendship.

"We're here in a professional capacity," she reminded him, then her gaze softened. "But you have a way of making me forget my troubles. I'm frightened, that is all."

"Frightened?"

"Frightened I shall grow used to your attentions."

Adam grinned. "You've nothing to fear. I'm yours whenever you want me."

"Always the libertine," she teased.

"I'm always myself when I'm with you." Yet he could lose himself in the depths of her grey eyes, in the warmth of her body, in the kindness of her heart.

"Let us deal with the matter at hand." She gestured to the coffee room, to the internal staircase leading to the upper floors. "Let's speak to Mr Bloom and discover why he ran despite having your protection."

"I imagine it's because two witnesses could attest to his argument with Ashbury. He knew it was only a matter of time before Sir Oswald returned to arrest him."

"I hope it's because he loves Lillian and wishes to protect her."

"Indeed." The cynic in him doubted Bloom had acted out of love. But he said nothing more as he escorted Miss Dutton upstairs to the green door on the first-floor landing.

He rapped twice, became instantly aware of a hushed

discussion in the room beyond. "If it is Bloom, he's not alone."

Anger flared. Indeed, he was prepared to rip his secretary's head from his shoulders, but the door creaked open and a young woman stared back. Dressed in a plain pink dress, her blonde hair fashioned in a chignon, she appeared pious and wholesome and was definitely not one of the doxies frequenting the coffee room downstairs.

Upon witnessing the woman's shocked expression, Miss Dutton cleared her throat. "Forgive the intrusion so late at night, but we come on behalf of a friend, a dear friend of Mr Bloom."

The woman glanced over her shoulder. "Henry. You should come to the door. We have visitors."

What sort of man permitted a woman to open the door in a rowdy coaching inn so late at night? Surprisingly, the fellow who appeared had a kind face, round cheeks, and a warm countenance.

"I'm Roxburgh," Adam said with some aplomb.

"Ah! We should have anticipated your arrival, my lord." The fellow winced at the sudden awkwardness. "Am I to understand you come in Miss Ware's stead?"

"Do you honestly think I'd let my sister venture to a coaching inn at this godforsaken hour? Do you think I'd let her wander the treacherous streets of London alone?"

The fellow frowned. "The note asks Miss Ware to meet us at ten o'clock in the morning on the steps of St Paul's. We assumed she'd bring her maid. It's Godfrey's wish to protect your sister's reputation. Hence why we're here."

"Perhaps *Godfrey* should have considered that before inviting my sister into the garden at a ball for a hundred guests."

Miss Dutton coughed discreetly. "Godfrey?"

"He's referring to Bloom," Adam replied, suddenly aware that he was guilty of dragging Miss Dutton out at a disreputable hour. That he'd been equally thoughtless when ravishing her in his damn garden.

"May we come inside?" Miss Dutton asked.

The couple stepped aside and welcomed them in.

Adam followed Miss Dutton into the room. It was clean, well furnished, with a small seating area adjacent to the hearth. The oak-framed bed looked comfortable. Although the noise from the yard would make it impossible to get a good night's sleep.

Miss Dutton introduced herself as an enquiry agent, though judging from the couple's indifferent expressions, Bloom had already informed them of the comings and goings in Hanover Square.

After giving their names as Mr and Mrs Ranson, Miss Dutton said, "You visit Mr Bloom at his house in Brewer Street. I interviewed Mrs Rampling next door, who described you both with startling accuracy."

Mrs Ranson nodded. "Godfrey is my brother." She gestured to her husband. "Henry was at Oxford with Godfrey. We met when he came to stay with us at our family home in Bourton-on-the-Water."

Henry Ranson moved to the seating area. "Shall we sit down?"

Adam drew Miss Dutton to the sofa and sat beside her. He wanted her close when this polite pair revealed why Bloom had taken to his heels and left Lillian distraught.

Mrs Ranson smiled at them from her fireside chair. "I should begin by saying that Godfrey holds a deep affection for Miss Ware. These last few months, they've become firm friends."

Miss Dutton gave a mocking snort. "So firm he left without telling her the real reason why. A friend does not disappear without first offering some reassurance all is well."

Just when Adam thought he couldn't be more infatuated

with Miss Dutton, she said or did something to deepen his ardour.

"No one could have predicted the sudden turn of events," Mrs Ranson explained, her expression growing solemn. "Only fate could have orchestrated such an outcome."

"It would help if you offered a more detailed explanation," Miss Dutton replied. "Perhaps Godfrey failed to understand the severity of the situation. In agreeing to meet an innocent woman in the garden where they were certain to be seen, he compromised her, leaving a permanent stain on her reputation."

Miss Dutton was a gentleman's daughter. The fact she was sitting with a rogue in a coaching inn in the early hours said how far she'd fallen. Indeed, the sudden need to play the gallant hero and rescue this damsel overrode all concerns about Bloom and Lillian.

Tears welled in Mrs Ranson's eyes. "You tell them, Henry. I'm not sure I can bear to repeat the devil's name."

Seated opposite his wife, Henry Ranson held her gaze for a moment before sitting forward. "The dead man, Ashbury. We were at Oxford together. His arrogance was often grating, but he invited himself to join our group, and four became five. Rather than visit his parents, he invited himself to our homes during the holidays and at Christmas, intruded at any given opportunity."

"We pitied him," Mrs Ranson offered. "Until he did something so unspeakable, my heart is full of hatred for the man."

Henry cleared his throat. "Godfrey was betrothed to Miss Clarke, a wealthy landowner's daughter from Chedworth. When Ashbury came—"

"He never mentioned the betrothal to Miss Ware," Miss Dutton interjected. "I assure you, he gave her no indication he'd been romantically attached before."

"We never speak of it." Mrs Ranson sniffed. She drew a lace handkerchief from her sleeve and dabbed her nose. "We never speak of it because Mr Ashbury eloped with Miss Clarke, eloped to Gretna Green."

"But Ashbury was unmarried, a bachelor." Adam knew he frequented brothels, bedded wealthy widows by the dozen. "He lived alone at the Albany."

Tears rolled down Mrs Ranson's cheeks, and she waved for her husband to continue.

"They didn't go to Scotland but to the Continent. We heard they were lovers but not married. Then all communication stopped. Godfrey wrote to Ashbury's parents, visited numerous times, but they insisted they knew nothing of Miss Clarke, insisted their son was on a grand tour with friends."

It wasn't difficult to piece together the rest of the story. "Bloom arrived in Hanover Square to see Lillian and happened upon Ashbury."

"He'd not seen Ashbury for four years. They argued. Godfrey followed him outside and near throttled him. But he swears he didn't kill him. He needed him alive so we might discover what happened to Miss Clarke."

Miss Dutton sighed. "He fled because he feared being arrested if Sir Oswald discovered their history. He had a motive for murder and was seen by witnesses."

Henry nodded. "Not just that. Ashbury gave him a clue to Miss Clarke's whereabouts." He paused. "Ashbury provoked Godfrey, said he'd sold Miss Clarke to a merchant in France. Godfrey left for Calais this morning in the hope of finding her and bringing her home."

"Calais? I see." Miss Dutton's hand slipped from her lap to where Adam's hand rested between them. Secretly, she gripped his fingers. Probably to ensure he kept his temper. But it was comforting, all the same.

"It's for the best, of course," Miss Dutton continued. "Strong-minded women can overcome obstacles. We shall break the news to Miss Ware when we give her the letter. She may have questions, and we ask that you wait on the steps of St Paul's should she wish to meet at the agreed time."

Adam couldn't find the words to support Miss Dutton's decision. While anger burned like hell's furnace in his chest, the devil taunted him for failing to protect Lillian. Good God! If a man couldn't trust his own secretary, who could he trust?

He glanced at Miss Dutton, noted her proud chin, the determined set of her jaw, and was suddenly thankful he had someone beside him offering assistance.

"Godfrey wants Miss Ware to know that she's too good for him. She deserves someone who isn't plagued by memories of the past."

Adam should curse Godfrey Bloom to the devil, but he'd be damning himself in the process. "Sometimes, the past is like an entity living inside us. It wakes us from slumber, intrudes at inopportune moments to make itself heard. I understand why Bloom was compelled to answer its call."

"Under the circumstances, my lord, that's rather magnanimous of you," Mrs Ranson said. "Although in an effort to correct one mistake, my brother has made another."

"Indeed." Adam hardened his tone. "Which is why he is never to darken my door again. If I see Bloom anywhere near my sister, his head will roll."

"Lord Roxburgh's primary concern is to protect Miss Ware's reputation," Miss Dutton said, reinforcing the point. "I would like to add that once you've spoken to her tomorrow, you do not play emissaries again."

The couple nodded.

Mrs Ranson offered yet another apology, rambled on about them all feeling somewhat responsible for the tragedy that had befallen Miss Clarke. That she was sorry her brother had abused his position in forming an attachment to Lillian.

Keen to leave—but not so keen to return home—Adam brought the meeting to a swift end. Anger prevented him from saying a word as he escorted Miss Dutton back to the coaching yard.

Miss Dutton brought him to a halt outside the entrance to the coffee room. "I think I'd rather face Mr Black than tell Lillian the truth about Mr Bloom. We should tell her together. It might help to soften the blow."

Adam clasped her upper arms with a tenderness that belied the fire boiling his blood. "While it's too much to ask of you, you'll know what to say to soothe her, know how to make everything right." He sighed, his breath turning misty in the cool night air. "For me, happy endings are a thing of myth. I lack the faith required to convince her all will be well."

Miss Dutton's eyes glistened with compassion. "Though I may spout wise words, I don't necessarily believe they're true. But Lillian is young, and she has you. I'm older and have no one. What else can I do but hope that tomorrow will be better?"

The sudden desire to make all her tomorrows magical was a novel sensation, a need he had never known.

"Like me, Lillian is resilient," she continued while he was still trying to come to terms with these odd bouts of sentiment. "I suspect her feelings for Mr Bloom amount to an infatuation. After seeing her with the Duke of Dounreay, I doubt she's in love with your secretary."

"How does one tell the difference?" He may be experienced in most things but was a relative virgin when it came to affairs of the heart.

Miss Dutton shrugged. "Infatuation is a feeling based on an illusion, a perfect image of one's ideal mate. Love, true love, is accepting of someone's faults and caring for them just the same."

"Interesting."

"And had Lillian been deeply in love with Mr Bloom, she would not have danced twice with the duke."

No. Adam couldn't bear the thought of dancing with any woman other than Miss Dutton. "You found Dounreay pleasing to the eye. No doubt most women think the same."

She narrowed her gaze, but her teasing smile vanished as she caught sight of something over his shoulder. Her eyes widened in horror, her face turning a deathly shade of pale.

"Good God. D-don't turn around." She gripped his arm while struggling to draw breath into her lungs. "Heaven help us. What the devil are we to do?"

"What is it?"

"Not what. Who? Jeremiah Black has just entered the yard." Her bottom lip quivered. "Roxburgh, he has us both in his sights and is heading this way."

CHAPTER 13

Like Satan, one look from Jeremiah Black could stop a woman's heart beating. One look from those soulless eyes could freeze a woman's blood. This was not a chance meeting. He had known to come to the Bull and Mouth, known he would find her there.

Eliza's stomach churned, twisting so violently she might cast her accounts over the yard. Yet her fears were not for herself. She had witnessed first-hand what Mr Black did to gentlemen who got in his way. And the sudden thought that something dreadful might happen to Roxburgh only intensified the urge to vomit.

"Stand straight," Roxburgh demanded, sounding much like she had when advising Lillian at Lord MacTavish's ball. "Paste the gorgeous smile that steals my breath. Don't let him know he intimidates you. Do you hear me, Eliza?"

"Y-yes," she breathed, though one glance at the gaming hell owner robbed her of rational thought. Jeremiah Black wore a red waistcoat and cravat. Was it to disguise the splatters of his victims' blood?

Roxburgh turned as if making to leave, but Mr Black was only a few feet away, close enough to fire a lead ball at a man's chest, close enough to slit a man's throat, close enough for either to prove fatal.

"Lord Roxburgh." Mr Black stopped dead in his tracks, his hulk of a henchman coming to stand beside him. "On a night such as this, you should be at home, enjoying the comforts of a warm bed."

"Surely you would prefer to be seated before a roaring fire," Roxburgh said, "counting coins after a profitable night at the tables."

"Business is business. I've come to collect on a debt. Heard the dodging scoundrel was returning to town on the late stage from Cardiff." His gaze moved to Eliza, and he doffed his hat, revealing the ebony widow's peak that made him appear so sinister. It didn't help that his pale skin had an almost silver sheen in the moonlight. "Miss Dutton, what a pleasant surprise. You never mentioned your acquaintance with Lord Roxburgh."

Suspecting this man knew everything about her, there was little point lying. "Lord Roxburgh is my client. He hired me to investigate the murder of a man in his garden."

"Investigate?" he said, feigning ignorance.

"I'm an enquiry agent, Mr Black, employed by Lucius Daventry. A woman has no choice but to seek a paid position when facing mounting debts."

"Perhaps you should consider taking a husband, Miss Dutton." While Mr Black's tone sounded mildly suggestive, his beady gaze was ghostly—so cold, so lifeless. "A lady should have someone capable taking care of her at night."

She might have said Lord Roxburgh was doing an excellent job caring for her needs, that it was inevitable they'd become lovers, but did not wish to put a noose around the lord's neck.

"Gentlemen do not marry forthright women, Mr Black." Deciding to use the opportunity to her advantage, despite every muscle in her body compelling her to run, she broached the subject she'd been dreading. "Indeed, I'm glad we happened upon you. Your name has been mentioned in relation to my current case. I hoped you might answer a few questions when you have time."

Jeremiah Black stared.

His menacing brows twitched, and still, he stared.

Stealing her courage, she added, "I can get a warrant from the Marlborough Street office, but as we're acquainted, I did not deem it necessary."

The air turned ominous, like the prelude to a storm.

Then Mr Black's rigid jaw softened. "You know where to find me, Miss Dutton. Come ask your questions. If it's about the Sapphire, most men in London have frequented the establishment at one time or other, including your cadaver Mr Ashbury."

Yes, but they did not all play *Victor Ludorum*, though she kept that information to herself for the time being. Nor did she question him about how he knew the name of the victim.

"It is just a formality, you understand." With every muscle in her body bunched tightly, she wasn't sure how long she could maintain her confident composure. "Would noon on Monday be convenient?"

"I shall make it so."

"How generous." She felt sick to her stomach for not voicing her true opinion. "Well, we have one more person of interest to question, and so shall bid you good night."

"Best be on your way. Coaching inns are dangerous places after dark."

The villain wished them luck in their endeavour. He fixed them with his hawk-like stare as they climbed into the carriage, looked almost ready to swoop when the vehicle turned in the yard before clattering out through the stone archway.

"Heavens! Could you not feel the tension mauling your flesh like a rabid dog?" Eliza could hardly catch her breath as fear burst through the barricade she'd built to keep it at bay. "He looked as if he might drive a blade through your heart and rip the organ right out."

"Meeting him was unfortunate," Roxburgh said calmly from the seat opposite, "but we'd planned to interview Black at some point soon. He saved us the trouble of begging for an audience."

"Yes, but I wish he'd not seen us sneaking out of the Bull and Mouth in the dead of night. He will assume we're conducting an illicit affair."

It must have looked like a lovers' tryst.

Roxburgh gave a devilish grin. "We are conducting an illicit affair. When our mouths meet, all thoughts turn immoral."

"You know full well I refer to a certain intimate act."

Roxburgh's smile died. "An act to be shared with your husband on your wedding night, not with a man you consider a libertine, and in a place frequented by cutthroats and thieves."

The odd comment obliterated all fears of Jeremiah Black, leaving nothing but confusion in its wake. An hour ago, he'd alluded to the possibility of them renting a room. Now, he'd practically told her to marry if she wished to experience anything more intimate than kissing.

"I thought we had agreed to speak honestly." Her brittle tone had him straightening in the seat. "Why fake piety? If you have grown bored with our association, simply say so."

"Bored?" He shook his head and gave an incredulous snort. "Bored! Miss Dutton, everything about you excites me. While a steep wager makes one's blood rush wildly, nothing beats the surge of anticipation when I think about making love to you."

The devil!

The man grew more confounding by the hour. "Then why say you don't want me?" He'd made it sound as if he had no intention of pursuing her. No woman, no matter how independent, wished to feel rejected.

Roxburgh laughed.

"You find me amusing?" she snapped.

"I find you delightful. I never said I don't want you—I want you so badly I cannot sleep at night—just that you should save yourself for someone better."

There was no one better. No one more intelligent. No one more honourable. No one she desired more.

She stared at him in the dark confines of the carriage. One did not need the skills of an enquiry agent to explain this sudden shift of opinion.

"Is it because my situation is similar to Lillian's? Because you're angry at Mr Bloom for taking advantage of his position and somehow think kissing me means you're no different?"

He lounged back in the seat. "It's because I like you far more than I should. Consider it a token of my esteem, not a sign of indifference."

"Can I not decide my own fate?" She was not a child in need of coddling. "I walk a different path to Lillian. I work to support myself and have no need of a husband. Should I choose to take a lover, the decision will be based on the depth of my affection, not the need for security, or to protect an already ruined reputation." Indeed, her affection for this man deepened by the hour.

He sat silently, his features partially hidden in the shadows.

"You don't need to protect me, Adam."

"Protecting you is my only consideration."

"What does the libertine want?"

"You know what he wants."

The air was thick with the need to act upon their desires. And yet both remained seated. Their shallow breathing cried of unsated lust, though neither spoke a word until the carriage slowed to a halt outside Roxburgh's house in Hanover Square.

Eliza sat there, wanting, waiting, the anticipation unbearable. "You might have told Dobbs to call at Howland Street first."

Roxburgh cleared his throat. "Being in a hurry to leave the Bull, it slipped my mind. But it's late, almost two in the morning. Perhaps you should sleep here tonight. Your room is as you left it, your hairbrush on the nightstand, your nightgown draped over the chair."

He had been in her room!

The sudden notion that he'd entered her private space, had touched her personal things, brought a rush of heat to her cheeks. "Miss Trimble knows I'm working late tonight. Dobbs can take a note to Howland Street, informing her of these new developments."

"We must speak to Lillian as soon as she wakes. It makes sense for you to remain here and catch what little sleep you can."

"Indeed." And yet she'd toss and turn until dawn, knowing he was sleeping in the room along the hall.

Roxburgh sat forward, his dark eyes searching her face, attempting to read her thoughts. It was a pointless exercise. Her mind was a maelstrom of mixed emotions: fear, lust, and something infinitely more terrifying.

She cared too much for this man, this libertine, this lost soul who had seduced his way into her heart. Consequently, she was in danger of losing more than her virginity.

Roxburgh alighted. He reached for her hand to assist her descent, the mere touch of his fingers making her skin tingle. He said nothing while escorting her from the safety of his carriage to a place where they might indulge in every wicked pleasure.

Carrying the candle lamp from the console table in the hall, Eliza entered Roxburgh's study. She wrote a quick note for Miss Trimble, blew gently on the ink, folded it in half and handed it to the man whose presence made her body ache.

Roxburgh snaked his arm around her waist, pulling her close. "Make no mistake, I am but a slave to your wants and desires, Eliza. You've been in command from the moment you entered my drawing room and agreed to take the case."

"Yet I am uncertain how to proceed." Not uncertain, afraid to risk her heart, to give herself completely.

He kissed her tenderly on the temple. "I shall give the note to Dobbs, then take a nightcap before venturing upstairs. You look tired. Get some sleep. We shall speak in the morning before Lillian rises."

He stepped away and left the room, robbing her of the heat of his body, of his soothing touch. Everything felt cold without him. Everything felt so bleak and desolate.

Loneliness enveloped her as she entered the bedchamber. There was no fire blazing in the hearth, no warm glow of a lit candle lamp—just the cold and the darkness and the ever-growing sense this was the closest she was likely to come to loving someone.

She undressed quickly, slipping into the nightgown she was certain Roxburgh had touched, but didn't climb into bed. Instead, she stood at the closed door, her palms splayed against the wood, listening.

Minutes passed before she heard Roxburgh trudge upstairs.

When he paused outside her door, she considered yanking it open and inviting him in, imagined what she might say to tempt him into accepting an immoral proposal.

Take me to bed, Roxburgh.

My virginity is an enticement to a man like Jeremiah Black.

Yet that was an excuse, not the real reason she would ask him to make love to her. The real reason would send him bolting for the hills. The real reason had her nerves skittering, too.

She didn't open the door.

Inexperience left her floundering.

A warm bed beckoned, but she hesitated. What did she have to fear? Roxburgh would not turn her away. Like always, he would know what to say to make everything right.

Tired of the constant chatter in her head, she reminded herself she was master of her own destiny. And so she brushed her hair once more, opened the bedchamber door quietly and tiptoed along the landing.

Pushing doubts aside, she slipped into his room and closed the door.

A fire burned in the grate, the flickering flames bathing the chamber in a seductive amber glow. Heat stroked her skin, calming her fears, settling her nerves, relaxing every tight muscle.

Roxburgh was not sleeping in the vast tester bed but standing at the window, staring wistfully at the garden he'd constructed because the lost boy had grown into a lost man who had never truly grieved.

He wore a burgundy silk robe tied loosely at the waist, stood swirling brandy in a goblet, but didn't bring the glass to his lips.

"Roxburgh," she said softly before stepping farther into the room, calling his name again when he didn't answer. "Roxburgh."

He cast her a sidelong glance, the sight of her pulling him out of the meditative trance. Inhaling deeply, he closed his eyes briefly as if battling a powerful emotion.

"Have I disturbed you?" It was a mistake to come, she realised.

His gaze met hers, then slipped slowly down the length of her body, leaving a blazing trail in its wake. He tossed back his brandy, swallowing the contents in one mouthful, hissing to cool the burn.

"I'm sorry. I shouldn't have come." She had been wrong to

believe he would welcome the intrusion. "I shall leave you in peace."

"No." He placed the glass on the nightstand. "Stay."

"You look like you would rather be alone."

He made no move to cross the room, did not beckon her forward. "Forgive me. I am merely fighting to keep the libertine on a leash." Those dark eyes caressed her in the muted light. "I've imagined you coming to me many times, so many it hardly feels real."

She wanted to run to him, to prove he wasn't dreaming. "I doubt you imagined me wearing a dowdy cotton nightgown. Perhaps that accounts for the confusion."

"You look remarkable to me," he said, facing her fully.

Her gaze fell to the opening of his robe, to where the firelight danced across his golden skin. He was surely naked beneath, and her heart quickened at the prospect of touching him.

"Compliments slip off your tongue like honey, Lord Roxburgh."

"If you knew me better, you'd know I rarely compliment anyone, Miss Dutton." He moved, his sleek steps bringing him a little closer. "Yet everything about you stirs these profound reactions in me."

One look at his bare feet and muscular calves said she was correct in her assumption. "That's why I've come. To know you better. To know you in every way a woman can know a man."

"In every way?" he teased. "Tonight, time is a constraint."

She couldn't help but smile. "Is there more than one way, then?"

"Indeed." He gave a graceful bow. "Permit me to be your tutor."

"That's why I'm here," she said, feeling so bold confidence oozed from her pores. "So you might ease this damnable craving. So I might give myself to a man I've come to admire and respect."

He clasped his chest, drawing her gaze back to every enticing inch of bare skin. "I'm thrilled to know I've risen in your estimation."

It was her turn to bridge the gap between them, and so she edged closer. "I admire your honesty most. Promise me something."

"Anything," he breathed.

"Don't make love to me like I'm a novice. Don't think of me as naive. Make me feel like this is a mutual meeting of bodies and minds."

"I suspect I shall be the one out of my depth." He seemed to drink in every inch of her, his face a perfect portrait of desire. "Come here. I want to show you how beautiful you look to me."

She moved, drawn by his magnetic presence. When she reached him, he wrapped his arm around her waist, held her so close her nipples hardened as they brushed against his silk robe.

"We'll take things slowly." He drew her to the full-length looking glass propped against the wall near the window. "Do you see why I like this nightgown?" Roxburgh stood behind her, staring at her reflection. "When the light catches it here, I can see the soft shape of your thighs." He touched her thighs through the fine material, caressing her in slow, teasing circles.

Eliza gasped. "Your hands are so hot."

"My blood burns to have you," he whispered against her neck, sliding his hands up over the flare of her hips. "I can see every delightful curve, see the tips of two pert nipples begging for the flick of my tongue."

Her breath caught in her throat as she anticipated his next move.

In the glass, she saw that her eyes were glazed, her lips

parted, saw his wicked grin as he pressed his cheek against hers and watched her reaction as he palmed her breasts.

"See how beautiful you are when I touch you." His thumbs grazed her nipples, sending hot pulses shooting to her belly. "See how you respond to me, how we respond to each other," he said when she couldn't help but moan with pleasure. "I'm so damn hard for you, Eliza, and we've barely begun."

"Whatever you do to me, I plan to reciprocate." Would his heart race, too? Would every nerve tingle? Would his body throb for her touch?

"Such a promise will bring our lovemaking to a sudden climax." Roxburgh pressed his mouth to the sensitive spot below her ear and sucked gently. "Let's see what I can do to prolong the experience. First, I need you out of this nightgown."

The comment hit her like cold water, dousing passion's flames. "But I shall be naked."

He laughed while nuzzling her neck. "Oddly, that's the plan. I want to see you when I touch you. I'll not miss a second."

The thought of baring every inch before the looking glass filled her with dread. "I can't look at myself."

"Close your eyes."

"Won't it be cold?"

"With your eyes closed? Not in the least." His hand slid down over the soft swell of her abdomen, down to stroke between her thighs. "I cannot do deliciously wicked things if you're shrouded in cotton. Trust me. I shall make you forget everything but the desire for pleasure."

"It's you I desire, not gratification." Yet as his fingers slipped back and forth over her sex, easing the ache became the primary goal.

"You'll have every inch of me, love, but it will be so much better this way."

She shrugged off her insecurities. "Do it then. Undress me."

Through the looking glass, he pinned her with his smouldering gaze while gathering the hem of her nightgown. She had dragged the garment over her head a hundred times or more, never had she shivered in delight, never had the anticipation almost killed her.

Roxburgh edged the material higher, studying her intently as he raised it past her hips, past her waist and breasts. "Love, you're perfect, perfect for me, perfect in every way." He removed her nightgown and threw it to the floor.

She closed her eyes and leant back against him.

He was the only man who would ever see her like this, the only man who would touch her as he did now, his hot hands stroking every inch of her sensitised flesh.

"I feel like a boy in a confectioner's shop," he whispered.

Suddenly, he was everywhere—caressing her left breast, nipping her neck, stroking her sex, drugging her with his kisses, hypnotising her with the sensual words he whispered against her flushed skin.

"If you knew how many times I've imagined touching you like this, where you're wet and aching and longing for me to make you come."

"Heavens! Don't stop," she cried between breathless pants as he pushed his fingers inside her. "Roxburgh!"

"Hush, love, you'll wake the household." His free hand left her breast, and he offered her his thumb. "Bite me if it becomes too much."

Those devilish digits worked some kind of magic. The thumb slipping into her mouth mimicked the fingers plunging into her core.

The force of her climax tore through her, forcing her to bite down on his thumb for fear the servants might hear her cries of pleasure.

She sagged against him, catching her breath.

"We must do that again soon," he growled, supporting her weight. "When you've grown accustomed to the feel of me, I shall take you like this."

"You've done that before?"

"Never."

Never? The word left her emboldened. "I'm sorry for biting you."

He pouted while revealing the evidence of her teeth marks. "There's a savage beneath that beautiful facade. I rather like her."

"Then let me play nursemaid. You might like her, too." She gripped his thumb, locked gazes with him as she sucked away his pain.

"If this is how you soothe wounds, Eliza, I may resort to self-flagellation. Indeed, you have permission to bite every inch of me."

"Do I have permission to undress you?" she said, wondering if the rest of him tasted so divine, so male. "It's my turn to watch you in the looking glass."

"Next time." He captured her hand and drew her away from the glass. "Come to bed. The need to be inside you will likely kill me if I'm forced to wait a moment longer."

He seemed so desperate for this union.

"Is it always like this?" Her heart raced. Her body begged to have him fill the emptiness. "Is it always so ... so wonderful?"

"Never. You make it special." He stood before her and untied his robe. "Everything about you is intoxicating."

She reached up and pushed the garment off his shoulders, set her hands to his hot skin and tried not to gasp at the sight of his jutting erection.

Nerves pushed to the fore, and he clearly sensed it.

"We'll fit perfectly," he hissed as she explored the corded muscles in his chest. "I knew it the moment I laid eyes on you." He wrapped his fingers around her wrist, guided her hand to his heart. "I felt it here. A place I thought would forever lay cold and dormant."

They stopped talking.

Roxburgh claimed her mouth in a scorching embrace, kissed her until she was drunk with desire. When she climbed into his bed, and he came down on top of her, when their bodies touched for the first time, the sheer joy of it choked her with emotion.

Like a skilled lothario, he massaged her sex until the bud throbbed, lavished her breasts until she was writhing beneath him, begging unashamedly for more.

"Don't stop, Adam. I need you."

"Where do you need me, love? Say the words."

"I—I need you inside me."

She would remember his expert touch in the morning. But the profoundly tender look in his eyes when he buried himself to the hilt for the first time—she would remember that until the end of her days.

Hypnotised by the sheer power of every taut muscle, she clung to him as he rocked in and out of her needy body, as his urgent thrusts took her closer to that heavenly edge.

She'd presumed the act would amount to a selfish grasp for pleasure, but every stroke conveyed the depth of his affection. Even when her climax tore through her again, and she had to bite his shoulder to muffle her moans, she felt ... she felt loved.

Roxburgh withdrew and groaned her name while spurting his seed onto her belly. He met her gaze, his slow, sinful smile warming her heart, sending heat lancing through her.

She wanted him. She wanted to enter the room in her dowdy nightgown and let him seduce her all over again.

After kissing her tenderly on the mouth, he collapsed onto his back. His breathless pants drew her gaze to his chest, to the light sheen coating his bronze skin, making it glisten in the firelight.

She was in love.

It was the only explanation for her growing attachment. He had withdrawn from her body, and still, she felt full with him, felt joined to him in inexplicable ways.

Lillian was right. Roxburgh had a gift for making women love him. The question was, would he do everything in his power to push her away? In a bid to protect his heart, would he quickly cast her aside?

Her pulse raced as she considered another possibility.

Might Roxburgh one day learn to love her, too?

CHAPTER 14

The summons to visit the Hart Street office came while Adam and Eliza were away from Hanover Square, ferrying Lillian to St Paul's so she might meet with the Ransons.

It had been an hour fraught with tension and tears. Eliza had shown the qualities that made her irresistible. Kindness. Compassion. Abiding loyalty. She'd stood on the cathedral's stone steps, holding Lillian close while the Ransons delivered the news of Bloom's sudden departure.

Truth be told, Adam was relieved. Perhaps Lillian might accept an offer from Dounreay and have a thrilling adventure in the wet wilds of Scotland. Perhaps she would be the only Ware to find true happiness, everlasting peace.

And yet happiness filled his chest this morning. Making love to Eliza had been everything he'd hoped it would be and more. The depth of her passion had made for a unique union —one that had touched him in impossible ways, confounding ways.

Indeed, he'd held her while she slept, battling the need to demonstrate the depth of his affection, plagued by a need to know she wanted him as desperately, too. Instead of satisfying his hunger, having her had only intensified his craving.

The question was, would she be willing to explore this maddening connection they shared? He couldn't see why not. At worst, it would be an exquisite affair, eventually cooling to an abiding friendship. At best, it would be something ... well, permanent.

Permanent.

Adam was mulling over what that meant when he realised his carriage had stopped outside the Order's premises in Hart Street.

"It must be distressing to see Lillian so upset," Eliza said, dragging him from his musings. "But she assured me before we left for Hart Street that she intends to take tea with Lady MacTavish today. The woman has a way of brightening a room and will cheer Lillian up no end."

Guilt surfaced. His sister's welfare was always at the forefront of his mind, but Eliza Dutton had taken up residence there, too. "While Lillian's happiness is an important consideration, you know what occupies my thoughts today."

Her cheeks turned a pretty pink, much like they had last night when he worshipped every inch of her magnificent body before the looking glass.

"You promised we wouldn't discuss what happened last night. You said we'd wait until our midnight meeting, that our focus must be on solving the case."

Yes, he had said that, merely to ease her obvious embarrassment this morning. "Come the first stroke of midnight, I want you in my arms. There'll be little time for conversation."

She pursed her lips, indecision furrowing her brow. "Perhaps we should refrain from making love again. It's rather like an obsession, an obsession that clouds one's judgement. I'm not sure I can sit in front of Mr Daventry and rouse a rational thought today. And I cannot afford to lose this position, Adam."

He would have told her she had nothing to fear. He would always make her welfare a priority. But she was already struggling with a range of emotions, and he didn't want to add to the confusion moments before their meeting with Lucius Daventry.

"Then, for both our sakes, let me help you solve this case. Our priority today will be planning how we mean to tackle the suspects. Perhaps Daventry, with his wealth of experience, can offer valuable insight."

As it turned out, it wasn't a private meeting with the master of the Order. Miss Wild sat in one of many seats surrounding the low table in the drawing room, her spectacles perched on the end of her nose. On the brocade sofa, Eli Hunter lounged beside a golden-haired woman who was surely his wife. And Evan Sloane, one of Daventry's gentleman agents, sat on a chair near the hearth.

"I'm so sorry we're late," Eliza said, sounding almost breathless with worry. She glanced at the items spread over the table: the snuffbox and miniature, to name but two. "We were dealing with a new development and didn't receive your note until half an hour ago."

All the gentlemen stood.

"We were just discussing the items found in Ashbury's box at the Albany," Daventry said, gesturing to the two chairs next to Evan Sloane. "But you should update us on these recent developments."

Eliza sat down, and the men followed suit. "We're certain Mr Bloom did not kill Mr Ashbury, though we're told he did assault the gentleman in Lord Roxburgh's garden."

She informed them of the late-night meeting with the Ransons. Revealed why Bloom had fled Hanover Square.

"Bloom needed Ashbury alive in order to find Miss Clarke," Adam added. "And I doubt he has the heart to murder a man."

Daventry agreed.

"While at the Bull and Mouth, we encountered Mr Black." Eliza's voice wobbled at the mention of the gaming hell owner. "I am to visit the Sapphire tomorrow at noon to discuss what he knows of Mr Ashbury."

"You're not to visit the club alone. Roxburgh will accompany you."

She shuffled uncomfortably in the chair. "I'm not sure that's wise. Mr Black's motive for me visiting fortnightly is unclear. Perhaps it would be better if Mr Sloane acted as chaperone."

Daventry frowned. "What you're really saying is that Black saw you with Roxburgh at the coaching inn and presumed you were there for other reasons."

Eliza cleared her throat. "Yes. I fear he believes I am romantically attached to Lord Roxburgh, which is a ridiculous notion, all things considered. I am merely his agent, nothing more."

Daventry was by no means a fool. Her protests only made her sound like a woman who'd come hard against a rogue's expert touch.

"A ridiculous notion considering you despise men who gamble," Daventry offered. "Although I have it on good authority, Roxburgh hasn't visited a gaming establishment this past month."

Eliza's gaze shot to Adam. "You haven't?"

"I haven't seen the need of late," Adam replied, knowing that would be the topic of tonight's conversation. How would he explain that his fascination with her was his current preoccupation? His permanent preoccupation?

"Then it's settled. You'll take Miss Wild and Roxburgh with you tomorrow." Daventry looked at the timid agent hiding behind her crooked spectacles. "If I'm to give you Lord Deville's case, Miss Wild, you must become accustomed to dealing with intimidating men."

Miss Wild nodded, though with obvious reluctance.

Eli Hunter coughed into his fist. "Black is ruthless and has committed many violent crimes. With all due respect, I'm not certain Lord Roxburgh is a suitable chaperone."

Adam relaxed back in the chair and pasted a confident grin. "If you want to strip off your coat, Hunter, perhaps a bare-knuckle boxing match might settle your fears."

Eliza scoffed. "I am assured of Lord Roxburgh's ability to defend his position. Last night, he fought with Mr Black's henchman and returned unscathed."

God's teeth!

Such was the admiration in her voice she may as well have said she'd given him the gift of her virginity. And it had been a gift. A gift that had warmed every cold corner of his heart.

"Hunter knows I have faith in your ability to assist Miss Dutton with this case," Daventry reassured. "Let us focus on analysing the evidence, not on proving one's sense of worth."

Hunter inclined his head by way of an apology.

As did Adam.

Daventry reached for his notebook and flicked to the relevant page. "Bower questioned Mrs Mitchell, the owner of the coaching inn where Lord MacTavish left money in a valise. It wasn't the first time Ashbury made such an arrangement."

Eliza seemed unsurprised. "Could she name his other victims? I get the sense there have been many." She went on to explain what they'd learnt from Fraser about the game called *Victor Ludorum*. "Mr Ashbury needed high-value items. Cufflinks bearing a duke's crest are considered a winning hand unless someone can steal from the King."

Daventry nodded. "As it happens, she remembered Mr Minchin, the fellow who wrote Ashbury the letter professing undying love."

"Minchin?" Adam muttered. "Why do I know that name?"

"He is secretary to Sir David Forsyth, Chief Baron of the Exchequer and a member of the Privy Council." Daventry gestured to his gentleman agent. "I had Sloane interview Minchin. He will tell you more."

Sloane faced them. His long hair made him look like a pirate, and his velvet voice was said to melt most women's hearts. "Ashbury targeted Minchin because he wanted him to steal private documents signed by the King. Minchin stole Sir David's snuffbox and told Ashbury it was the best he could do. Ashbury threatened to publish the letter in the scandal sheet which is currently making the rounds at every London soiree."

As Adam had yet to see a copy, he prayed Lillian's midnight escapade wasn't amongst the scandalous stories.

"Does Mr Minchin have an alibi for Saturday evening?" Eliza asked. "Based on the nature of his work and his liking for male companions, he had more to lose than anyone."

"Minchin accompanied Sir David to a private meeting with the Attorney General. We have no way of gaining confirmation. Besides, Minchin is five-foot-six and weighs nine stone. I doubt he had the courage or the strength to murder a man."

"Well, at least we know how Mr Ashbury came by the snuffbox. Did you have any luck tracing Mr and Mrs Harper?"

They had called at the Harpers twice this week to be told the couple were away from home. Come to think of it, Adam could not recall seeing them in the garden when he'd raced outside to inspect the body in the hedge maze.

It was Mrs Hunter, Eliza's colleague, who answered. "I spoke to Mrs Harper last night. They've been away at the coast for a few days. She bore witness to the argument between Mr Bloom and Mr Ashbury, and so, seeking a haven away from the din, they left Hanover Square and returned home."

Silence ensued.

Daventry rubbed his jaw while lost in thought. "You say

Miss Ware accessed the maze without leaving through the terrace doors."

Adam nodded. "Yes, she came through the servants' door at the far left of the garden. You can enter the maze there or continue along the path to reach the rest of the garden."

Daventry let out a sigh. "Someone could have followed Ashbury to Hanover Square and entered the house, seeking an opportunity to murder him. But why your house? Why that particular night?"

"Perhaps, like Mr Bloom, a guest recognised Mr Ashbury," Eliza said in her usual intelligent way. "There's no telling how many people he has blackmailed or ruined over the years."

God, Adam could listen to her talk all day.

Could listen to her pleasurable sighs all night long.

"P-perhaps someone playing *Victor Ludorum* discovered his identity and sought an opportunity to get rid of him," Miss Wild said, offering an alternative explanation.

"Or Bloom fled to France because he did kill his nemesis," Daventry suggested. "Nonetheless, the next logical step is to meet with Jeremiah Black and learn more about this high-risk game." Daventry moved to examine the evidence spread over the low table. "I shall take the miniature and the brooch to Lady Perthshore. She may help us in locating Ashbury's other victims."

The housekeeper arrived with tea, and they spent thirty minutes taking refreshment while discussing other potential lines of enquiry.

Adam found himself thinking about tonight. Not because he feared what Eliza might ask him. He had already shared his darkest secrets. But because, with her, he felt an inner peace he'd never known and was keen to explore the reason why.

"Once I've visited the Sapphire, I shall seek out Mrs Stanley." Eliza placed her teacup and saucer on the table. "She must have witnessed the argument, and it would be helpful to get her opinion."

There were so many avenues of interest, it might take a month to solve the case. Adam rather liked the idea of having Miss Dutton to himself at the stroke of every midnight hour.

Mine at midnight.

The problem was he wanted her every minute of every day.

Daventry suddenly pushed to his feet. "Report to the office on Tuesday, Miss Dutton, and we can discuss what you've learnt at the Sapphire."

Everyone made to stand, though Eliza gripped the arm of her chair as if her legs lacked the strength to support her weight. "W-what if Mr Black refuses to discuss the game?"

"You're an enquiry agent, Miss Dutton. You'll find a way to get the information you need, with Lord Roxburgh's help, of course. And Miss Wild is at your disposal."

Eliza swallowed deeply, every tense muscle a sign of the panic within. "You may be assured I shall use whatever means necessary."

"Excellent." Daventry clapped his hands together. "Sloane will ferry you and Miss Wild to Fitzroy Square. You'll stay there tonight. D'Angelo is to teach you both the art of self-defence."

Adam's heart sank as fast as a brick in a well.

The thought of sitting alone in the rotunda filled him with dread.

Eliza seemed equally stunned. "We're to stay with Mr and Mrs D'Angelo tonight, not in Howland Street?"

"Isn't that what I just said?" Daventry mocked. "Beatrice D'Angelo's father was murdered by a notorious moneylender. When she needed information, she arranged to meet the devil in Newgate. She can offer insight into how to deal with wicked men. It will serve you well for your meeting with Jeremiah Black tomorrow. Roxburgh will collect you from Fitzroy Square in time for your appointment at the Sapphire."

"But Miss Ware needs—"

"Her brother tonight," Daventry finished. He turned to Adam. "Roxburgh, I would like a moment of your time if you're happy to wait until we're alone."

How could Adam refuse?

There were two possible reasons why Daventry might make the request. He wished to discuss how to deal with Jeremiah Black or know intimate details of his relationship with Miss Dutton.

Before Adam could reassure Eliza that he would see her tomorrow, Daventry ushered everyone out of the room, bar him, and closed the door.

"Sit down, Roxburgh." Daventry gestured to the sofa, then moved to the drinks table and pulled the stopper from a crystal decanter. "Brandy?"

"Do I need one?"

Daventry laughed as he sloshed liquor into two glasses. "That depends. Do you have something to confess and need courage?"

"Perhaps you should simply make your point and save us both the unnecessary questions. If you mean to discuss Miss Dutton's progress, simply say so."

Daventry approached. "Miss Dutton's welfare is a topic for debate." He thrust a glass of brandy at Adam, then sipped his own before dropping into the chair opposite. "You have seduced my agent, and I want to know of your intentions towards her."

Adam coughed suddenly, though not from the burn. "Your deductive skills are rusty. I fear Miss Dutton has been secretly seducing me since the moment we met. She has a power unlike any woman of my acquaintance."

"You failed to answer the question. Avoidance is a skill wasted here. It is you who should speak plainly."

"Very well. I fail to see what business it is of yours." There, Adam could not be more direct. "Rest assured, I have nothing but the greatest respect and admiration for your agent."

Daventry narrowed his gaze. "Are you in love with her?"

Adam almost spluttered a quick denial at the absurd question. Though it was not absurd at all. He had been infatuated from the beginning. But love? Was he not immune to the emotion?

"You're struggling to answer the question," Daventry said. "Perception is something I've mastered, and you look at Miss Dutton as if she's a goddess amongst women. That tells me all I need to know."

"Then put your wisdom to good use and enlighten me."

"That would be too easy." Daventry tossed back his brandy. "A man must come to his own conclusions, recognise his own destiny. Who am I to convince you that you feel something lasting?"

Adam's mind was a whirl of confusion. How could a man tell the difference between infatuation and love when the woman he admired was faultless?

"Let us turn to the subject of Jeremiah Black." Daventry went on to curse the gaming hell owner to the devil, his anger a palpable thing practically bouncing off the walls. "I attempted to clear Miss Dutton's debt yesterday, but the bastard threw me out."

Yesterday? Jeremiah Black made no mention of it last night.

"We had a war of words. Threatened each other. He told me to keep to my own business, said that he sees Miss Dutton fortnightly merely because he has concerns for her welfare."

The thought of Eliza visiting Black these past months left Adam chilled to the bone. A man renowned for his evil deeds had not suddenly found an ounce of compassion?

"Like me, you doubt Black's integrity."

"Indeed. It's why I insisted she stay with D'Angelo. Until I know what Black wants with her, I have a duty to keep her safe. You're entrusted with her welfare when you visit the Sapphire tomorrow."

Adam would shoot Jeremiah Black if he so much as threatened to harm Eliza. "It's possible Jeremiah has a man following Miss Dutton. The thug I chased from Pall Mall was also lingering in Hanover Square."

In which case, it was wise to ensure she always had a chaperone. Adam was compelled to remain at her side, and yet Daventry had sought to keep them apart tonight.

"We must be on our guard without frightening her." Daventry considered Adam with his usual unnerving intensity. "We may have to take drastic measures to free her from his clutches."

"Drastic measures?" Adam swallowed his brandy. Daventry was no stranger to violence, and so Adam understood his meaning. "You believe we may have no choice but to murder the fiend?"

"Let's just say the case has become complicated. It's not simply a question of whether we want to find Ashbury's killer. Now, we have a duty to save Miss Dutton from a fate worse than death."

CHAPTER 15

Eliza had hardly slept a wink last night. She should have lain awake, eyes wide, tossing and turning, because she feared meeting Jeremiah Black. But the devil was far from her mind. Indeed, the handsome gentleman currently sitting opposite her in the carriage consumed every waking thought.

Her body was just as restless.

Roxburgh had handed her into his conveyance, his touch sending a charge of excitement straight to her heart. Never had the organ raced so fast it left her breathless. Now, whenever their eyes met amid the strained silence, she imagined his mouth on hers, imagined his body pressing her into the mattress, the feel of his hot skin, every smooth movement of his tongue.

Indeed, she was beginning to understand the nature of addiction.

Eliza cast her colleague a sidelong glance, wondering if Nora sensed the clawing tension in the air. "Are you well, Honora?"

"Quite well," Nora replied, but her pinched expression said she was scared to the marrow of her bones. She cleared her throat. "Lord Roxburgh, may I ask you something?"

Roxburgh glanced at Eliza before answering. "Certainly."

"What do you know of Lord Deville? If I'm to take his case, I should like to learn a little more about him."

"Deville?" Roxburgh began somewhat awkwardly. "Erm, Deville. I've not seen him since he left for the Continent four years ago. Being a second son, he worked as a diplomat for the government. His last position was in Naples."

Nora's countenance brightened. "A respectable man, then?"

Roxburgh's gaze shifted. "I heard he was injured in a duel. Heard he bears a scar, though I've not seen it myself. Deville never attends social functions, never visits his club."

"A scar!" Nora gulped.

"Quite a nasty one across his cheek."

"Good Lord." Nora pressed her hand to her chest. "If he's a second son, how did he come to inherit?"

Roxburgh practically winced before saying, "You should ask Lucius Daventry. I'm not sure he'd want your head filled with gossip when you need to think logically and remain impartial."

Just as desperate as Nora to know what sort of man her friend might be forced to endure, Eliza said, "Forewarned is forearmed. Is that not right, Honora? Surely it's better to be prepared."

Roxburgh's reluctance to speak waned. "They say he killed his brother and sister-in-law, pushed them both off a cliff in the dead of night, though Lady Deville's body was washed out to sea, never found. That's how he came to inherit."

Good heavens. Mr Daventry must believe Deville was innocent of the crime, else he would not consider sending one of his agents to Kent.

"When was this?" Nora croaked.

"A year ago."

A fraught silence descended.

Nora would refuse to take the case. Yet, once Mr

Daventry decided on a client, it was impossible to deny him. That's why Eliza had accepted Roxburgh's case, despite the thought filling her with dread. Now, she yearned for his company, longed for his touch.

Would a similar thing happen to Nora?

"Mr Daventry would never send an agent to work with a man he didn't trust," Eliza said, trying to calm her colleague before they ventured into Jeremiah Black's hellhole of a club. "He is an excellent judge of character and is rarely wrong. All will be well, Honora. I assure you."

If only Eliza could say the same about her dealings with Mr Black. As the carriage rolled to a stop on the corner of King Street, courage deserted her like a rat did a sinking ship.

"You will both follow my lead," she managed to say as they all alighted, though her knees trembled terribly. "My lord, it is better if you play the injured client. Show indifference to Mr Black's motives, and explain you simply seek the man who murdered Mr Ashbury."

Roxburgh tried to insist he take the lead, protect her where possible, but she couldn't let Mr Black think they were romantically involved.

"If you care anything for my welfare, you will do as I ask."

Heaving a weary sigh, he nodded. "I understand. I am to play the lord with the devil-may-care attitude."

"Precisely."

"Perhaps I might ask Mr Black a few questions," came the surprising comment from Nora. "As Mr Daventry kindly pointed out, I should strive to become accustomed to intimidating men."

"Yes, if you feel able. Follow my lead."

How Eliza found the strength to walk from the corner of King Street to the alley leading to the rear entrance of Mr Black's premises, she would never know.

She took her anxiety out on his paint-chipped door, pounding it hard, as she imagined doing to the devil's chest.

While they waited, Roxburgh placed his hand gently on her back, leant closer and whispered, "Soon, this meeting will be over, and we can focus on how we might occupy ourselves tonight."

He was so close she might have kissed him had they been alone. "You're supposed to say something to settle my heart, not make it gallop faster than a St Leger's winner."

The crunching of a rusty bolt against metal drew their attention to the door. A man as solid as a lump of granite yanked the door open and glared at them through stony grey eyes.

Eliza allowed herself to feel a moment's relief. "Good day, Samuel. We're here to see Mr Black and have an appointment." Samuel was the only one of Mr Black's men who possessed a personality.

"Afternoon, Miss Dutton. If you'd like to follow me."

They followed Samuel through a narrow corridor with damp walls and chipped floor tiles. Like the road to hell, it smelt of dirt and degradation, of sweat and shame and the sad fact no one escaped alive.

Eliza almost wished she could grab Lord Roxburgh, nuzzle his neck, inhale the irresistible scent of shaving soap and the clean smell of heaven.

"How is Reginald faring?" she said, for mindless conversation always settled her nerves.

Samuel tutted. "The devil escaped last night and climbed in through Granny Taylor's open window. She woke to find him sitting on the table, gobbling her provisions."

Eliza shouldn't laugh. "You'll need to keep him in a cage when you're at the Sapphire."

Roxburgh cleared his throat. "I assume Reginald is a pet."

"A monkey," Eliza took pleasure informing him, "given to Mr Black as payment for a debt. Samuel took him in lieu of wages."

"And the devil has cost me a tidy sum, I can tell you."

They reached the end of the corridor and the imposing black door of the office belonging to Satan's spawn.

Samuel knocked on the viewing window.

Someone inside raised the small blind and peered out into the corridor. A key turned in the lock, and the menacing beast who had accompanied Jeremiah Black to the Bull and Mouth, opened the door and beckoned them inside.

Eliza had revisited this room many times in her nightmares. It was dark and dank, as cold and as lifeless as its owner's soul. A person might think this was hell's antechamber. A place where the master of the underworld decided the fate of those with mounting debts.

Mr Black pushed out of the leather chair and stood behind his desk. It wasn't a polished mahogany piece bought at Bonhams, but a crude slab of wood, scratched and stained and sturdy enough to use as a chopping block.

"Always so prompt, Miss Dutton." Mr Black's depthless gaze fixed her to the spot. "And you've brought friends, I see."

Eliza had seen the light of life leave her father's eyes, had seen the doorway to the soul close. Though Mr Black still breathed, his stare was as vacant as a dead man's.

"You know Lord Roxburgh, of course." Eliza gestured to the handsome lord, praying he would behave as instructed. "And Miss Wild is my colleague at the enquiry agency."

"Another woman needing work?" Jeremiah Black gave a broad, humourless grin, drawing attention to his teeth and the sharp incisors capable of tearing through flesh. "And yet you look like you'd be scared of your own shadow, Miss Wild."

Nora raised her chin. "First impressions can be deceptive, Mr Black. As an agent, it serves me well. Most people doubt I'm capable of killing a man."

Mr Black's onyx eyes widened slightly. "Now, there's a wager that would prove most profitable." He studied her as if weighing up an opponent. "Were I a betting man, I might place my stake on poison."

"And you would find yourself lighter in the pocket, sir."

Impressed by Nora's sudden burst of confidence, Eliza attempted to take control of the meeting. "May we sit, Mr Black?"

"Call me Jeremiah." He gestured to the two wooden chairs, which had no doubt been the deathplace of many men. "Lord Roxburgh won't mind standing," he added, his tone condescending.

Eliza's heart missed a beat.

Should Roxburgh offer a scathing retort, Jeremiah Black would take it as a slap to the face with a gentleman's glove. The outcome would be considerably more violent than pistols at dawn.

"I'm accustomed to spending inordinate hours propped languidly against a ballroom wall," came Roxburgh's rakish drawl. "It's no hardship."

Excellent.

Jeremiah Black merely nodded. He sat before they did, lounged back in the chair like a man blessed with immortality.

"As I said last night," Eliza began, keeping the quiver from her voice, "we are investigating Mr Ashbury's murder and know he gambled here. Know he preferred games where the stakes were high."

Mr Black's expression remained indifferent. "Most men in London have frequented the Sapphire at some time or other. It's a gaming club, Miss Dutton. Am I expected to account for every man who finds himself dead because of a debt?"

Eliza paused. Did she play her ace card now or risk waiting for another opportunity? Wanting this matter over quickly, she decided to present the evidence.

Heedless, she reached into her reticule, not realising her

error until the henchman darted forward, grabbed hold of her wrist and towered over her with his hulking frame.

Roxburgh pushed away from the wall, ready to come to her aid. The movement was keenly observed by Mr Black, who assured them his man acted as a precaution.

"I wish to produce something we found in Mr Ashbury's apartment," she explained, tugging her arm free from the oaf's grasp. "I do not carry a weapon in my reticule if that is your concern." Eliza carefully drew out the card.

Mr Black waved for his thug to resume his post. He glanced at the card. "They can be found on every table in the club. And we have already established Ashbury gambled here." He tutted. "Really, Miss Dutton, you should take a husband and leave the enquiry business to Daventry's men."

Anger seethed inside her. "You speak prematurely, Jeremiah." She turned the card over in her hand. "On the reverse, it says *Victor Ludorum*. My father had a similar card. I'm assured it alludes to a private game where men wager the deeds of their properties in the hope they can produce a winning hand."

Mr Black stared.

"Strange how you had the deed to my home," she continued, the fire in her chest spurring her on, "and now you own the deed to Mr Ashbury's apartment at the Albany. We have the letter you sent to his parents, informing them of the situation."

A sly grin twisted Mr Black's mouth. "There's no crime in informing a man's parents that he'd wagered heavily and lost."

"How can Mr Ashbury have lost the game when it's not due to take place until Saturday?"

Jeremiah Black failed to hide his surprise but quickly disguised it by giving a contemptuous snort. "Ashbury cannot play because he's dead." He opened the desk drawer, pulled out a sheaf of paper, and handed it to her. "Ashbury signed a contract, a contract to protect the players. We can't have a man promising the world, then failing to attend."

"It's the first rule of business," Roxburgh offered.

"You see, Miss Dutton. Only a man understands what it is to live in a man's world. He knows of the struggles and strife."

Eliza ignored the futile attempts to humiliate her and concentrated on reading the contract the players were required to sign if they wished to play the game.

One article, written amid a host of legal waffling, forced her to catch her breath. "Those who cannot play forfeit their homes."

Memories of a muttered conversation entered her mind. Like Lord Wright, her father spoke to himself as he pottered about the house.

Yes, I shall hire a solicitor to rip apart the contract.

It can't be legally binding.

"My father signed one such contract."

Jeremiah Black shrugged. "Many men long to be crowned victor of the games. Somewhere there's a record. But I've been in business for twenty years, Miss Dutton. It might take some time to find the paperwork."

He did not need to rummage around in a dusty storeroom to confirm her suspicions. The glint in his eyes betrayed him. The arrogant tone of his voice screamed the truth.

"So any player who dies loses his deed?" Nora asked. "Regardless of how they met their end?"

"Gamblers are reckless by nature. I cannot risk my reputation on a man who might drown his sorrows in the bottle then stumble headfirst into the Thames."

"Surely you see the conflict of interest," Nora pressed. "You could have a man killed so you can take his property."

Even seasoned villains lost control of their emotions occasionally.

Mr Black thumped his fist hard on the desk and glared at Nora. "I shall ignore the insult on account of you being a woman of little experience. But don't dare accuse me of murdering a man."

Nora gulped.

Roxburgh stepped forward and placed a reassuring hand on Nora's shoulder. "Miss Wild is employed to ask logical questions, though she lacks the restraint an experienced agent might use when dealing with delicate matters."

Mr Black sat back. "Hence why she felt the sharp edge of my tongue and not that of a sabre."

Eliza attempted to steer the conversation back to the matter at hand without accusing Mr Black of a heinous crime.

"We're simply trying to ascertain if Mr Ashbury's murder had something to do with the game. We understand that the identity of the players remains a secret, that they're masked. Is it possible someone leaked information?"

Black's curious gaze slipped briefly to his henchman. "All players are told to meet at separate secret locations and are brought here wearing a hood. The only way anyone would know their identity is if one of my men turned traitor."

His lackey shifted his heavy frame uncomfortably. "No one would dare betray you, Mr Black."

Needing more information without angering the gaming hell owner, Eliza said, "Perhaps another player accidentally discovered Mr Ashbury was his opponent and killed him to better the odds. I trust the winner receives the other men's deeds."

"Yes, from those who sit down to play."

"How long does a game last?" Roxburgh said.

Eliza wondered why he'd asked. The risk of losing was significant indeed, an enticing prospect for a lord hiding from his grief.

"Players have two months to gather their hand." Black kept his gaze trained on her while answering Roxburgh. "Anticipating your next question, we play three games a year.

A man must feel it an honour to be asked to play in such a prestigious tournament."

Mr Black made it sound like a reputable game where the best players fought for the distinguished crown. In truth, he did not target society's elite but weak men consumed by their addictions.

"I think you can anticipate my next question," Eliza said, "but I shall ask it all the same. During other games, have men died by nefarious means before play commenced?"

Jeremiah firmed his jaw. "As I have already said, to play, a man must have a reckless streak."

His evasive response said other men had died, but it would be impossible to discover who. Though she knew of one other man who had lost his life while playing for victor.

"My father was shot while gathering his hand. He told me as he lay dying in my arms." It was a lie. He was dead when she found him. Still, her heart raced madly. In saying such things, she was courting trouble. But she might never get this opportunity again and the need for answers burned inside. "Therefore, another player must have known his identity."

Or you killed him, she wanted to say.

While his face remained a blank canvas, the brief flicker of excitement in his eyes reminded her of an ugly mural, a heinous painting depicting the story of his crimes.

"Your father was shot on numerous occasions before joining the game." Black pushed out of the chair. "Once by Mr Rainer because your father slandered his wife while sotted. Just a gentlemanly nick to the arm. A moneylender from Gower Street had his man shoot him for failing to pay a debt. Another timely scratch, for the man needed his money."

The pain of grief and disappointment brought bile bubbling to her throat. "He was a broken man and needed help, not an invitation to lose the only thing he owned."

Mr Black motioned for his henchman to open the door. "I

offered him a chance to make things right. He was riddled with debt. Several people might have delivered that fatal shot."

As much as she wanted to call him a liar, everything he'd said about her father was true. "And it all worked to your advantage. I suppose you've sold my family home and made a tidy profit."

"On the contrary, I hope to present it as a gift to my bride."

A cold silence chilled the room.

The hairs on Eliza's nape prickled to attention.

"Your bride? You're betrothed, Mr Black?" Why did she suspect he planned to marry her? That he would use whatever means necessary to achieve his goal?

"Indeed, though I have yet to present my bride with the contract." His voice rang with satisfaction, with a wicked sort of pleasure. He reached into his desk drawer. "I have a copy here if you'd like to see the document." He rounded the desk and presented her with a scroll.

With shaky fingers, she unrolled the parchment.

Her name was written clearly in elegant script next to Jeremiah Black's, a promise of marriage made by her father, who had scrawled his signature at the bottom. Failure to honour the contract resulted in a penalty—a fee amounting to thirty-thousand pounds.

Thirty-thousand pounds!

She could work a lifetime and still have no hope of paying.

"Good Lord!" Eliza clasped her hand over her mouth lest she wretch. No wonder Mr Black insisted she keep a fortnightly appointment. He must have been watching her for weeks. "As I had no knowledge of the contract, how can it be legally binding?"

She sensed Lord Roxburgh behind her. He inhaled sharply while reading over her shoulder. "Your father signed it in the presence of witnesses. Coleman is a justice of the peace, and

Hatchers is a respected firm that serve many aristocratic families wishing to secure the best settlements for their daughters."

"It cannot be legally binding because I have not given my consent, and I am past the age of majority."

Mr Black grinned. "Of course, you must agree. I had hoped to wait until you realised the enormity of your father's debt before presenting the options." He shot Lord Roxburgh a menacing glare. "Circumstances force me to act sooner than planned."

"You cannot make me pay my father's debt."

"No, but I can make you pay for breaking the contract."

"I shall settle the debt," Roxburgh suddenly blurted.

Mr Black narrowed his beady eyes. "It would mean paying the interest owed, including all—"

"No! The debt is mine." She would not give Jeremiah Black an excuse to kill Roxburgh. The devil would be at least thirty-thousand pounds richer, and Roxburgh would be dead. Lost to her forever.

The thought was like a knife to her breast.

"Lord Roxburgh is merely my client. No doubt he feels indebted to me for helping his sister, but he cannot afford to pay such an extortionate amount."

Roxburgh insisted he would do anything to release her from the contract, much to Mr Black's delight.

Wearing an evil grin, Jeremiah Black considered her while rubbing his jaw. Time ticked away, but then he said, "Perhaps Lord Roxburgh would like to make a wager. He can take Ashbury's place and play *Victor Ludorum*. Of course, he has less than a week to find a winning hand."

"What are the stakes?" Roxburgh said.

"Ignore him. Lord Roxburgh is not playing." Old feelings surfaced—the panic, the frustration, the never-ending sense of helplessness as she tried to persuade her father to stay at home.

"If you win, I shall free Miss Dutton from the contract," Jeremiah Black offered. "If you lose, you will leave London and remain at your country estate. You will agree never to meet with Miss Dutton again, the penalty for failing to comply being the utter ruination of your sister."

"No!" Eliza shot out of the chair. She clenched her fists at her sides for fear of pummelling the life out of the devil. "This has nothing to do with Lord Roxburgh."

"I accept the challenge," Roxburgh snapped. "I shall play *Victor Ludorum*, and you will crown me the damn champion."

Mr Black looked smug.

Eliza put her hand to her forehead, dazed and dizzy with shock. The men finalised the details. Then Roxburgh gripped her elbow firmly and escorted her out of Jeremiah Black's office while Miss Wild hurried ahead with Samuel.

Samuel showed them out into the alley. He shoved a small piece of paper into Eliza's hand and promptly slammed the door shut.

Eliza slipped it into her glove. A more pressing matter held her attention. "What the devil were you thinking?" she cried. "Are you so desperate for a thrill, you'd risk getting yourself killed?"

"Calm yourself, Eliza. We'll discuss this in the carriage." Roxburgh tried to guide her through the alley, but she tugged her arm free.

"Why agree to play? Does it have something to do with your mother's death?" She looked at Nora, silently pleading for help. "Tell him, Honora. Tell him Mr Black will bind his hands and feet and throw him in the Thames."

Nora pursed her lips. "I'm afraid it's too late. Mr Black will probably murder him if he fails to take Mr Ashbury's seat on Saturday. He will probably murder him because Mr Black has no intention of freeing you from the contract."

The contract!

What possessed her father to put his signature to such a

document? Losing her home was nothing compared to this wicked betrayal.

"Have faith, Eliza. This is one game I intend to win," Roxburgh countered, sounding more determined than ever.

"You lost at cards to Mr Ashbury. What makes you think you can win a game as complicated as this?"

"Daventry will ensure I have a winning hand." Roxburgh firmed his jaw. "Though I know of a much better way to free you from that rogue's clutches."

"A better way?" The cold realisation that he meant to wage war on Mr Black left her trembling to her toes. "What will you do?"

He looked her keenly in the eye, his expression darkening. "The only thing I can do under the circumstances. I plan to murder Jeremiah Black."

CHAPTER 16

"Murder Jeremiah Black?" Eliza whispered incredulously. She grabbed Adam's coat sleeve as if the sharp tug might make him see sense. "Have you lost your mind?"

Logic had abandoned him the moment Black produced the contract that may as well have been written in her father's blood. The moment he realised the devious blackguard wanted Eliza and was prepared to blackmail a justice of the peace to achieve his goal.

"We will discuss the matter once safely inside my carriage," he said, keen to have something solid between them and a henchman's pistol. He glanced back at the dank alley, relieved to find it empty.

"Listen to his lordship, Eliza." Miss Wild quickened her pace. "Hatred lives in Mr Black's heart. Once he's thought about his dilemma, I suspect he will kill us all."

Eliza said nothing more until they were inside Adam's carriage and had left King Street and The Black Sapphire behind.

"Why did you not heed my advice?" she blurted as if she'd been holding the question and her breath for far too long. "You were supposed to let him think we were colleagues, nothing more. A colleague does not offer to settle a debt amounting to thirty-thousand pounds. A colleague does not offer up his soul merely to free me from a fraudulent contract."

Adam glanced at Miss Wild to remind himself to hold his tongue, then thought to hell with it. "I offered to pay the debt because you're more than my colleague, more than my friend, more than my lover. I'd hang for murder before I'd let Black hurt you."

Eliza's pretty eyes widened in shock. She cast Miss Wild a sidelong glance, but the bespectacled agent had her gaze fixed on the window.

"I am not your lover." Eliza glared by way of a reprimand.

"Then I should see my physician. These hallucinations feel surprisingly real." He offered a teasing smile. "And I must have conversed with myself when journeying home from the Bull and Mouth. I swear you said you wanted me."

"Roxburgh," she warned.

He raised his hands, surrendering. "You're right. Miss Wild does not want to hear that we are so obsessed with one another we cannot keep our hands to ourselves. Indeed, I should be mindful of her delicate sensibilities."

Miss Wild was smiling when she met Adam's gaze. "I am not blind, my lord, nor have I lost the use of my other senses. I lived at the Pleasure Parlour for a month before Mr Daventry offered me a position. Consequently, I can perceive the thrum of desire in the air."

"The Pleasure Parlour?" Adam couldn't hide his surprise. He suspected Miss Wild was a woman of many secrets. And she must have hidden talents if Daventry believed she could deal with Deville. "Gentlemen pay an extortionate annual fee merely to gain entrance to the select club." He looked at Eliza. "Though I have never crossed the threshold."

"I was not one of Madam Matisse's ladybirds," Miss Wild

quickly confirmed, "but her maid for a time. The point I am trying to make is I am by no means a prude."

"Excellent. Then you won't mind me saying that my affection for Miss Dutton goes beyond the thrill one gets from a physical act between two people."

"Not in the least."

"Lord Roxburgh gets a thrill from teasing us." Eliza sounded far from amused. "He revels in our discomfort. Ignore him."

"On the contrary, we agreed to speak honestly. I don't care if the whole world knows how I feel about you."

She inhaled sharply, though her eyes softened to a dove grey. He took it as a sign of hope that she felt the connection keenly, too.

The carriage slowed outside the Order's house in Howland Street. He alighted and assisted both ladies to the pavement. The heavy ache in his chest pushed all other thoughts aside. He didn't want to leave Eliza, not while there were so many things left unsaid.

Bloody Daventry and his meddling.

"Roxburgh, wait for me in the carriage," Eliza said, barely looking at him. "I wish to have a word with Miss Trimble, then we must visit Mrs Stanley so she may corroborate Mr Fraser's account."

Relieved to know he was not spending the rest of the day alone, Adam returned to his conveyance and waited.

A few minutes passed before Eliza appeared.

She spoke to Dobbs, then climbed inside and closed the door. "I forgot to mention, Samuel slipped me a note when we left the Sapphire. Had I not been in a blind panic while fearing for your life, I might have recalled I had hidden it in my glove."

"Samuel? The man with the monkey?"

"Indeed." She clutched the leather strap as the carriage lurched forward and picked up speed. "He must have overheard our conversation because he scribbled five names on a piece of paper. Considering Mr Ashbury's and Mr Fraser's names are amongst them, it's fair to assume it's a list of those men playing *Victor Ludorum*."

Adam relaxed back against the squab. If he survived long enough to play the game, it would be helpful to know his opponents. Assuming Samuel hadn't been instructed to deliver a fraudulent note.

"Do you recognise any of the names?"

"Recognise them?" she began, struggling to contain her excitement. "Roxburgh, Mr Finch and Lord Wright are on the list."

"Finch? The odd fellow living at the Albany?"

"We have no way of knowing, but it cannot be a coincidence. That's why he was rummaging around in Mr Ashbury's apartment. I believe he knew his neighbour was playing."

Adam recalled how Finch had been desperate to tidy the apartment. Being overly helpful was a means of hiding his nefarious intentions.

"And what of the fifth name?" he asked.

"It looks like Weiland or Welland."

He thought for a moment. "It must be Justin Weiland, Sir Geoffrey Weiland's wastrel brother. I've seen him at the Sapphire. Perhaps we should find a way to question Samuel when he's away from the gaming hell."

Eliza nodded. "We shall mention it to Mr Daventry. He sent a note while we were out, asking us to call at Hart Street as a matter of urgency. We will have to visit Mrs Stanley later today." She lowered her gaze, a sheepish smile playing on her lips. "I hope you have no objection, but I asked Dobbs to take a detour."

"A detour? You have someone else you wish to question?" He suspected not. Based on the sudden flush staining her cheeks, she wished to discuss a personal matter.

"Yes, I would like to question you, Adam. Hence why

Dobbs will cross the river at Westminster and approach Covent Garden via the Waterloo Bridge. At this time of day, it should take an hour to reach our destination."

"Hmm." He would be alone with Miss Dutton in a carriage for an hour. While he longed for an amorous interlude, he guessed she wanted to discuss his need to join the game. "Did we not agree all questions of a personal nature should be addressed at our midnight meeting?"

She met his gaze, the sadness in her eyes dampening his ardour. "I doubt we will have another midnight meeting. Once Mr Daventry learns about the contract, he will insist I remain with Mr D'Angelo. I won't be free to join you in the rotunda again."

The information hit him like a tidal wave, robbing his lungs of air, knocking him back in the seat. He floundered, mentally thrashed about, knowing he would drown in this ocean of fear.

No more nightly meetings?

No more cherished moments?

No more kisses beneath the clang of the St George's bells?

Blindly, he grasped at an idea, hoping it might keep him afloat. "Once we've dealt with Jeremiah Black, you'll be free to continue our nightly meetings."

"I think that's unwise."

"Unwise?"

"Would you invest in a company that had no hope of success? No. You would not take the risk when failure was inevitable." Her gaze fell to her lap, to her clasped hands. "Neither of us want to feel the pain of loss. It is best to part ways now, save ourselves the heartache."

Dumbfounded, which was a rare occurrence for a man considered so articulate, Adam studied her. He drank in every inch of her divine form, silently pleaded with her to reconsider.

Then it occurred to him that he had a choice. Every loss

he'd ever experienced was due to circumstances beyond his control. But he could control this. When it came to Eliza Dutton, he would not lose her without a fight.

"Is that what you want, Eliza? To live a lonely existence because it's safer that way? Perhaps you've forgotten how it feels to confide in someone you trust. Perhaps you've forgotten how exquisite it is when my mouth settles over yours, when our bodies move in the same perfect rhythm, when I push deep into—"

"Of course I have not forgotten."

"I remember every detail, the soft touch of your skin, the sweet timbre of your voice, the teasing scent of your perfume. If I close my eyes, I'm there watching you in the looking glass, watching your lips parting on every little pant and sigh, your body shuddering against mine as you come against my hand."

She remained motionless, as if to move might stir her senses to life and remind her of every erotic sensation.

"Time makes lovers forget such things."

"Perhaps, but we share a deeper connection." So deep, his need for her went beyond the physical. The thought of not seeing her daily left him empty, bereft.

"What if it's just an infatuation?"

"It is not an infatuation."

These feelings were too intense. He was addicted to her smell, her laugh, the funny expression she made when annoyed with him. Her needs were more important to him than his own.

But did they have a future together?

Might she come to admire him in the same way, too?

He had no way of knowing. Life had been cruel to him thus far, but the thought of losing her was like a rude awakening.

"I'm in love with you," he said, despite feeling so exposed, so damn vulnerable, despite once swearing those words would never leave his lips. "And while I have no experience of the emotion, I am willing to risk further injury to my bruised heart in the hope you may come to feel the same."

Silence ensued.

Eliza stared at him as her shoulders relaxed, her gaze filled with tenderness and the same intense longing presently heating his blood. She didn't make a declaration, didn't spout flowery prose, a poem of undying love, didn't demand to know his intentions.

She spoke to him in a different way.

With deft fingers, she untied the ribbons on her bonnet. "I asked Dobbs to take the long route because I need to know why you have risked your life to help me." Carefully removing the bonnet, she placed it beside her on the seat. "Now the answer seems clear."

"I would die before I'd let Black force you into marriage."

"I truly believe you would," she said, puzzled, though set to work removing her kid gloves. "You do me a great honour. Regardless of what I said about you in the beginning, you're the most noble, most principled man I have ever met." She laughed as she began unbuttoning her pelisse. "Which is a contradiction in terms when one considers we're about to make love in a moving carriage."

Adam arched a brow. "We are?"

"Only if you want to, of course."

"If I want to?" Adam leant forward and tugged down both blinds. "Eli Hunter has a motto: acts, not words. Having pulled the blinds, you should be assured I am a willing participant."

"Remove your coat," she commanded, her voice husky. "I believe it's my turn to touch you, to watch you come apart."

Hell, the blood rushed to his cock at the thought of her pumping him hard. "I see the savage has returned," he teased, shrugging out of the garment. "What else is your pleasure, siren?"

She removed her pelisse and set it aside. "Unbutton your waistcoat and untuck your shirt. Show me that delectable ridge of muscle, that delicious trail of dark hair that tempts a lady to sin."

Needing to offer a reward for this spirited performance and say something erotic while slipping the buttons, he said, "When I next have you in bed, I shall suck that sweet little bud until you're bucking wildly."

"If you prove a disappointment today, Lord Roxburgh, I may have to decline." She drew her tongue across her bottom lip. "Show me. Show me, and I shall come and sit beside you."

"Minx." Adam dragged his shirt from his breeches, bunched the garment to his chest and ran his hand over his abdomen. "Happy?"

She hummed her approval. "Take yourself in hand."

Adam laughed. "Will you not do that for me, my love?"

"That's for me to decide. You're at my mercy now."

"So it would seem." He unbuttoned the waistband of his breeches, for it was easier to push them past his hips now than when she eventually straddled his lap, and he was desperate to plunge into her luscious body.

Eliza inhaled sharply when his cock sprang free. "Delightful."

"Delightful?" he mocked, stroking himself. "Love, it's thick and hard, a throbbing weapon longing for your touch."

She watched him, her arousal evident in her heated gaze, in the way she squirmed in the seat. Then the temptress touched her breast, and he almost came like a schoolboy spying on the maid.

"Having witnessed how events proceeded the last time we made love, I believe I need to take a different approach." Eliza gathered her skirts to her thighs, crossed the carriage and came to sit astride him. "I shall touch you once you've withdrawn, but I need to feel you moving inside me, Adam."

"Then you must have read my mind." After some

fumbling about beneath her skirts, Adam positioned himself at her entrance and pushed home.

The first thrust tore a moan from their lips. Hellfire. She was warm and wet and felt beyond divine. She hugged him so tightly, he prayed she would hold him like this forever, never let go.

Adam leant back against the squab, aware the rocking and rumbling of the carriage along the uneven road only enhanced their pleasure. He gripped Eliza's hips and showed her how to find a rhythm.

His minx was a fast learner.

She rode him hard while he pushed under her skirts and stimulated her sex. Soon they were lost amid a frantic frenzy of open-mouthed kisses, tangled tongues and breathless moans.

He fought his release, refused to come yet.

Her timely shudder saved him from losing control and flooding her with the depth of his affection. Her muffled cry of satisfaction was his undoing. He withdrew while she was still astride him, brought himself to completion, spilling over her petticoat like a young buck.

Eliza sagged against him, dazed from their lovemaking. She kissed his neck, hummed against his ear as she came down from the dizzying heights of her pleasure.

"I love you," she breathed sweetly.

Stunned, it took him a moment to respond.

"I love you," he replied, amazed that he had the propensity to feel so profoundly. Yet he was suddenly captured by a wave of intense emotions—a fear of losing her, a fierce need to protect her always, keep her safe, a surge of happiness so euphoric he could barely catch his breath.

And something infinitely more surprising.

For the first time in his miserable life, he felt content.

CHAPTER 17

No doubt Eliza looked like a woman who had recently climaxed in a moving carriage. Her lips surely appeared sore from the constant kissing. The stray tendrils of hair escaping her bonnet spoke of a wild and rampant coupling. Every movement teased her swollen sex and brought to mind the delicious memory of Roxburgh pushing deep into her body, filling her full.

And her heart—her heart sang so loudly everyone in London must have heard its joyous song.

Mr Daventry's inquisitive gaze swept over her face, then moved to Lord Roxburgh's creased coat as he welcomed them into the Hart Street study. The man was like a bloodhound and could sniff out sinners from five hundred yards.

"You seem flustered, Miss Dutton. A little breathless." The master directed her and Roxburgh to the two empty chairs opposite his imposing desk. "How did you fare at the Sapphire?"

Eliza touched her hand to her chest to calm her breathing. She didn't want to think about Jeremiah Black, only of Roxburgh's declaration and the prospect of them making love again on the journey home.

"I've agreed to take Ashbury's place and play victor of the games, assuming I survive until Saturday." Roxburgh spoke like death was nothing to fear, like it was a minor inconvenience. "I shall, of course, require help securing a winning hand."

Eliza swallowed a whimper. She couldn't lose Roxburgh, not now they had both declared their love. "The good news is I know why Mr Black insists I visit fortnightly. The bad news is my father signed a contract, a promise of marriage. Should I fail to uphold my end of the bargain, I must pay Mr Black thirty-thousand pounds compensation."

It was a ridiculous sum.

Mr Daventry didn't seem at all shocked. "The contract cannot be legally binding," he said, perching on the edge of his desk. "You're long past the age of majority, and you're not required to settle your father's debts. The contract is worthless. Nothing but a means of intimidation. A means to force your hand."

Roxburgh sighed. "Hatchers drew up the contract. Coleman bore witness. He's a justice of the peace who often presides at the Bailey."

"What the devil?" Mr Daventry straightened. "Then Black has something on Coleman and the solicitor at Hatchers. No doubt they expected him to force Miss Dutton to wed, then no one would be any the wiser."

"Or the contract is a forgery," Roxburgh said, his tone hopeful. "Black agreed to release Miss Dutton from the contract, but only if I win the game."

"Then you have every reason to suspect the worst. Black will kill you before he lets you walk out of the Sapphire." With some urgency, Mr Daventry snatched a piece of paper from the desk drawer. He dipped his pen in the inkwell and wrote a quick note. "Do I have your permission to move your sister to a place of safety? I shall have D'Angelo make the arrangements."

Roxburgh shot to his feet. "Good God! You think he'll hurt her?"

The horrifying vision of Jeremiah Black squeezing Lillian's delicate neck flashed before Eliza's eyes. "This is all my fault." Guilt surfaced. "I should have taken Mr Sloane to the Sapphire instead. Then we wouldn't be in this dreadful predicament."

"Black sees Roxburgh as a threat because you're in love with him," Mr Daventry said so matter-of-factly Eliza might have misheard. "Had Sloane gone to the Sapphire, we would still be wandering aimlessly in the dark." He glanced at Roxburgh. "Well? Can I move Miss Ware to a place of safety?"

Roxburgh sat down. "Do what you think is best."

"Permit me to visit Miss Ware in Hanover Square," Eliza interjected, "so I may explain what's happened. I don't want her to feel afraid."

"Very well." Mr Daventry sprinkled pounce over his note, folded it neatly, melted red wax and stamped it with his seal. "But you're not to go anywhere alone. Do you understand?"

"I understand."

He strode out into the hall and called, "Cole!"

Seconds later, Mr Cole appeared from the drawing room. He was an agent of the Order, his dark, brooding features the reason he had earned the moniker Raven.

"Send Bower to locate D'Angelo and bring him here." He thrust the letter into Mr Cole's hand. "Take this to Peel. Wait for a reply and offer your services should he wish to question Coleman."

The men continued to speak in hushed whispers.

Mr Cole left the house promptly.

Mr Daventry returned to the study and sat in the chair behind his desk. "I asked you here because a gentleman was found dead in St Martin's burial ground. When Sir Oswald searched the fellow's house in Drury Lane, he discovered a card for the Sapphire."

"With *Victor Ludorum* written on the reverse?" Eliza asked.

"Indeed. The victim is Mr Justin Weiland."

"Weiland?" Eliza gasped. She revealed the names written on Samuel's note and how they'd come by the information. "Samuel may have disclosed the players' names to someone else. I should visit him at his home in Holborn." She remembered Samuel saying he lived above Granny Taylor's wool shop in Fetter Lane. "See what he knows about the game and his employer's villainous deeds."

Mr Daventry shifted uneasily. "We must proceed with caution. But if Samuel did pass on the information, that person likely murdered Ashbury and Weiland."

"Then the murderer must be Lord Wright or Mr Fraser or perhaps even Mr Finch." Eliza wondered if they should warn the men to be on their guard, but how could they without informing the villain?

Mr Daventry pondered the information. "The three of us will visit Samuel tonight. I shall call for you in Hanover Square at eleven o'clock."

Eliza glanced at the mantel clock and noted she had eight hours until their rendezvous. "I must visit Mrs Stanley and take her statement. We cannot tiptoe around for fear of alerting her husband to her infidelity. And then I shall visit Hanover Square and assist Miss Ware."

"Agreed." Mr Daventry paused. "I have more news to impart." He reached into a drawer, pulled out the ruby brooch and the miniature of the young woman and placed them on the desk. "Lady Perthshore has never seen the brooch but recognised the woman in the miniature."

"She did?" Eliza mentally prepared herself to hear another sad story. If the woman was Mr Ashbury's lover, she had surely met a tragic end.

"Lady Perthshore believes it bears a distinct likeness to Lord Wright's illegitimate daughter Marianne." Mr Daventry looked at Roxburgh, his gaze turning pensive. The reason soon became apparent. "Marianne drowned. Her body was found in the river near Lord Wright's country estate in Thetford, Norfolk, almost two years ago."

Drowned!

While Eliza felt deeply for the poor woman, her heart ached for Roxburgh. The image of his mother's body was undoubtedly at the forefront of his mind. Indeed, his brow furrowed, and he breathed heavily.

Instinctively, Eliza reached for Roxburgh's hand and clasped it tightly, not really thinking about what Mr Daventry might say.

"Sir, while the love letters found in Mr Ashbury's apartment bore no name, they were written in February 1823. I recall the date clearly. Might they have been from Marianne?"

"Possibly. Marianne died in the April of that year."

Roxburgh cleared his throat. "Viscount Newton's seat is in Barnham. I think we can make the obvious assumption." He turned to Eliza. "Newton is Ashbury's grandfather. His estate is but a few miles south of Thetford."

Eliza built a brief story in her mind. Of Mr Ashbury visiting his grandfather upon his return from the Continent. Of Marianne, young and impressionable, swept away by the rogue's attentions and left broken-hearted.

"We must interview Lord Wright and confirm Lady Perthshore's story," Eliza said, though feared how Roxburgh would fare when forced to listen to the tragic tale. "There's every chance he murdered Mr Ashbury to avenge his daughter's death."

"At present, we must treat it as speculation." Mr Daventry returned the items to the drawer. "After gaining Mrs Stanley's statement, return to Hanover Square with Roxburgh. I shall meet you there. Questioning Samuel and ensuring Miss Ware's safety will be our primary goals this evening."

"Am I to sleep in Hanover Square or Howland Street tonight?" Eliza prayed it was the former. Time alone with Roxburgh was exactly what she needed, so she might persuade him not to play.

"Once we've questioned Samuel, you will remain with D'Angelo, Miss Dutton. Your safety is also a priority."

"And what about Adam?" she blurted without thought.

Before Mr Daventry could answer, Roxburgh gave her hand a reassuring squeeze and said, "I shall be perfectly safe in Hanover Square but will refrain from venturing about town alone."

Perfectly safe? Mr Black would walk into church when the pews were full and steal the gold candlesticks. He would enter the King's chamber and piddle in his pot. He had no conscience and would barge into a grand house in Mayfair as if it were an almshouse in St Giles.

Roxburgh was wrong.

He was anything but safe.

"DON'T WORRY ABOUT LILLIAN. Mr Sloane is an excellent agent. She will be perfectly safe with him and his wife in Little Chelsea." Eliza heard the clatter of horses' hooves outside and hurried to the drawing room window, wondering if it was Mr Daventry arriving in Hanover Square. "It's just a hackney cab."

Roxburgh tossed back what was left of his brandy and set the glass down on the silver tray. "Tonight, my sister showed a level of courage I didn't know she possessed."

"When I saw you talking to her in the garden, she seemed excited about leaving." Lillian had thrown herself into her brother's arms and hugged him with such affection it had brought tears to Eliza's eyes. "It certainly helped to lift your mood."

"Yes," he said, though did not explain what Lillian had said to improve his spirits. "I've never been more proud of her. I doubt I could love her more."

A lump formed in Eliza's throat as she studied him briefly.

How had she ever thought him arrogant and aloof? How had she not seen all his redeeming qualities? How much poorer she would have been for not knowing him. How her heart would have suffered such a great loss.

"I love you," she said, her voice breaking with emotion. "I know I said it earlier today while we were misbehaving in your carriage, but I want you to hear me say it when I'm not lusting after you." She paused. "My heart swells when I think of all the ways you're wonderful. I just want you to know how special you are, to Lillian, to me."

Roxburgh swallowed deeply. He tried to speak, but had to cough to clear his throat. "I love you." He crossed the room and cupped her cheek. "I love your strength and determination, your courage, love how kind and caring you are to Lillian, to me."

His mouth covered hers, and he kissed her deeply.

The clatter of carriage wheels outside forced them apart, though he kissed her desperately again on the mouth and forehead.

"I would have been moved beyond words had you said you liked me," Roxburgh whispered against her hair as they embraced. "The fact you feel something more is a dream beyond compare."

Every part of her wished to stay in the cosy drawing room, to settle on the sofa, relax into his arms and watch the flames dance in the hearth. But if she had any hope of saving his life, she had to discover which one of the players was a cold-blooded killer. Indeed, she suspected Jeremiah Black wouldn't sully his hands. Jeremiah Black would ensure the players knew Roxburgh was their competition, their enemy.

"Did you secure a statement from Mrs Stanley?" Mr Daventry asked once they were settled in his carriage. The master was dressed entirely in black and appeared much like a fallen angel.

"No." Mrs Stanley was as elusive as the Harpers. "Her butler informed us she was visiting her modiste. We returned later to be told she was dining with a friend. The butler refused to say where."

"Mrs Stanley won't admit to being in the library with Fraser," Roxburgh said. "We agreed that calling at the house was a mistake."

"Tomorrow, we will follow her and attempt to gain a statement."

"It's imperative you do." Mr Daventry relaxed back against the squab. "Tell me about your interactions with Samuel."

There wasn't much to tell. Samuel had the look of a man who'd fought his way out of the gutter. A person stumbling upon the beast in a dark alley might die of heart failure. Yet beneath his intimidating persona was a kind, caring man who did not belong at the Sapphire.

"Samuel once told me to leave London, to find the means to purchase a ticket to Boston before it was too late."

Mr Daventry thought for a moment. "If you want to leave England, I shall pay for your ticket and give you an allowance substantial enough to last a year. No one would think it cowardly to run from Jeremiah Black."

Beside her, Roxburgh stiffened.

Eliza had considered it many times, had enquired about the cost of the ticket, scoured advertisements hoping a lady of means might want a travelling companion.

"Everything that matters to me is here in London."

She looked at Roxburgh, knowing she couldn't bear to

leave him, though was unsure what the future had in store. He was a peer of the realm, and she solved crimes for a living. Ironically, she didn't have the heart to live as a man's mistress, and he had sworn never to marry.

"Miss Dutton has no need to worry." Roxburgh spoke casually, though went on to say something that stilled her heart. "I'll kill Jeremiah Black if need be."

A heavy silence descended.

"What men do for love," Mr Daventry mused.

"Indeed."

They spoke about the items Roxburgh would need to win *Victor Ludorum*, though he had to win more than one game. Mr Black had told Roxburgh he needed six high-value items, one for each round, plus one should there be a draw.

"You can have an item belonging to my father," Mr Daventry said. It didn't matter that he was the illegitimate son of a duke, just that a duke's personal possessions beat that of a marquess.

"I'll need something from the King if I'm to win."

Mr Daventry nodded. "I shall make the arrangements."

The carriage stopped on Fetter Lane, some distance from the busy White Horse tavern. Eliza cleaned the misted window with her glove and peered outside at a narrow four-storey building. The sign above the large bay window said it was Granny Taylor's shop.

They alighted.

Eliza studied the facade. "I know Samuel rents the attic room because he said Reginald likes to sit on the drainpipe. He has to keep the monkey on a tight leash when he's away from home."

Candlelight flickered in a first-floor window, though the rest of the building was shrouded in darkness.

"There's no means of entry other than through the front door." Mr Daventry thumped the sturdy wooden door. When he received no response, he hammered again. "Mrs Taylor?"

"Ain't you got your key?" came a croaky woman's voice. Granny Taylor had raised the first-floor sash and thrust her head out. "Is that you, Samuel?"

"Mrs Taylor?" Eliza craned her neck. "We must speak to you as a matter of urgency. Lord Roxburgh will compensate you if you come down and open the door."

"Lord Roxburgh, eh?" The old woman cackled. "Let's see the blunt."

Roxburgh delved into his pocket and removed a sovereign. "This is becoming somewhat of a habit," he muttered, referring to the cheeky scamp who'd also taken a gold coin from him this week.

"Wait there!" Granny Taylor shouted. "I'm bringing a swordstick, so don't try any funny business."

Mr Daventry snorted. "Perhaps she'd make a good agent."

They waited a few minutes for the woman to come to the door. The pointed tip of a blade appeared between the door and the jamb, followed by Granny Taylor's wrinkled face and floppy white mobcap.

"Give me the coin and state your business."

Roxburgh did as requested, then introduced them. "We're here to see Samuel. He's not expecting us, but if you explain who we are, I'm sure he will invite us inside."

"He ain't here." Granny Taylor tried to close the door, but Eliza rushed forward and thrust her booted foot in the gap. "Please, Mrs Taylor. He risked the wrath of his employer by doing a good deed. I'm concerned for his welfare. Do you know when he might be home?"

The woman hesitated, then sighed. "He came home an hour ago, but I heard him leave again. That damn monkey hasn't stopped making a racket ever since."

"You mean Reginald?" Eliza might persuade the woman to let her pacify the pet. "My mother had a monkey. I know how to handle them. The gentlemen may wait here while you show me upstairs." She hoped to gain Granny Taylor's trust and prayed she'd let them wait for Samuel's return.

Granny Taylor seemed keen to have someone silence the animal. "I can't afford to anger the other tenants, and he is clashing and clattering about up there." Through narrowed eyes, she assessed Eliza's clothing. "Come in then, but the men must wait outside."

Eliza waited for Granny Taylor to lock the front door and then followed her slow trudge upstairs. They stopped on the first-floor landing so the woman might catch her breath.

"Why don't I continue without you? I shall fetch you if there's a problem. I assure you, Samuel won't mind me handling his monkey."

How hard could it be? Reginald was probably hungry.

Granny Taylor gripped the bannister so firmly her gnarled knuckles turned white. "Go on ahead. These stairs will put me in my grave. Wait. I'll get the spare key."

A piercing screech echoed from upstairs, followed by a loud thud. The animal sounded distressed, not hungry.

The noises were enough to force Granny Taylor to hurry, and she returned to the landing moments later and thrust the iron key into Eliza's palm. "I'll follow. Best not leave you alone in Samuel's room. There's no telling what that beast will do."

She meant the monkey, not her tenant.

Eliza climbed up to the second floor and waited for the woman. Then took the narrow curved staircase to the attic. She moved to slip the key into the lock, but the door creaked open.

"Samuel?" Eliza called out, but received no reply. "Mrs Taylor, does Samuel usually leave his door unlocked?" Would he not be worried about Reginald escaping?

Eliza hesitated on the threshold before pushing the door slowly.

The hinges creaked again, or it might have been the

monkey whining. She peered inside the room, noted the stub of a candle burning in the pewter holder on the table. Why would Samuel leave it lit when Reginald roamed freely? Indeed, one glance at the empty iron cage said the beast was loose.

"Samuel?"

When Granny Taylor hauled herself up the last flight of stairs, Eliza stepped over the threshold. There were two tankards on the table, an overturned green bottle, dog-eared playing cards scattered over the surface.

"Does Samuel often have company?" Eliza feared pulling back the bed curtain lest she find the man sleeping with a lover.

"He drinks with a friend from the Sapphire most nights."

Then Eliza heard a groan, not from the animal that was yet to make an appearance, but a man's pained mumble. She hurried around the table to find Samuel lying sprawled on the floor, his face bruised, blood seeping from a deep wound to his head. His monkey sat quietly beside him. The animal took one look at her and screeched loudly, then leapt onto the table.

"Samuel!" Eliza dropped to her knees and checked the man's pulse. He was alive but badly injured. "Can you hear me? Who did this to you?" She looked at Granny Taylor, who was trying to calm the agitated pet. "Call my friends. We need help. Samuel needs a physician. Quickly."

Knowing it would take forever for the woman to reach the front door, Eliza dashed downstairs and alerted Roxburgh and Mr Daventry.

The master of the Order took control of the situation, sending his coachman to fetch a physician while he hurried upstairs to tend the wound and stem the bleeding.

Mr Daventry had Eliza boil water, had her take a needle and thread from the shop downstairs, had Roxburgh find strong liquor. He cleaned the wound and forced Samuel to sip Granny Taylor's gin.

"Can you recall what happened?" Mr Daventry said when Samuel's eyes flickered open. "Did one of Black's men do this? Was it because he discovered you revealed the names of the players?"

Samuel nodded weakly.

"Who did you tell?" Mr Daventry persisted, but Samuel seemed too frail to speak the man's name. "You must give us his name before more men die."

"Did you tell Lord Wright?" Eliza asked, hoping Samuel might nod in response.

But to their surprise, Samuel found his voice. He reached out, gripped Eliza's arm and whispered four faint words. "I t-told them all."

CHAPTER 18

Three days had passed since they had found Samuel beaten black and blue, and with a wound that might have killed him, had Lucius Daventry not cleaned and stitched it while awaiting the physician.

Three days had passed since Adam had spent more than a few minutes alone with Eliza. Fearing the worst, Daventry had insisted they both reside at Bronygarth, his secluded country home some miles north of London. Lillian had been brought to stay there, too.

Upon hearing of Justin Weiland's death, the men playing *Victor Ludorum* had gone into hiding. No one had seen Lord Wright, Fraser or Finch. And, according to her husband, Mrs Stanley had suddenly taken ill and was recuperating at her sister's home in Lincolnshire.

Adam stood on Bronygarth's terrace, watching Eliza and Lillian wander around the garden, arms linked, deep in conversation. They had become friends and confidantes, so much so he prayed his sister had not revealed his secret. When Adam asked Eliza to marry him, he wanted it to be a surprise.

First, he needed to rid the world of Jeremiah Black.

Indeed, he was considering how best to deal with the problem when Daventry's man appeared. "The master wishes to see you in the study, my lord." Jonah glanced at the ladies strolling around the lawn. "You're to come alone."

"Thank you, Jonah. I shall attend him shortly."

Adam caught Eliza's gaze as he made to leave, his need for her causing every muscle in his body to tense. God, he loved her. The sooner this matter was over with, and they could resume their midnight liaisons, the better.

Yet old feelings surfaced. Was he about to suffer another sudden shock and lose someone close to him? Would he have to live with the excruciating pain all over again?

The Wares were cursed, doomed to live a miserable existence. Adam's father had warned of their fate before dying, broken-hearted, mere months after losing his beloved wife. As a boy left to play lord and master and care for a six-year-old girl, Adam convinced himself it must be true. He'd had no reason to believe differently—until now.

After making his way through the house, Adam knocked on the study door, only to hear giggling from within. He waited. Moments later, Sybil Daventry exited, her red hair a little mussed, her cheeks flushed, her lips swollen.

"I beg your pardon, my lord. My husband is in a playful mood today. I'm sure that will change once you have ventured to the Wild Hare and questioned Lord Wright."

Adam was about to ask how the devil Daventry had found the runaway peer, but the gentleman called, "Roxburgh!"

Daventry was shrugging into his coat when Adam strode into the room. "Cole found Lord Wright at a coaching inn near Aylesbury," Daventry said. "The fool had his coachman deliver his correspondence there. Wright agreed to return to London on the condition I provide protection. Cole has him at the Wild Hare."

"If he's agreed to return, perhaps he's innocent of Ashbury's murder." Being the leading agent on the case, Eliza would need to question Lord Wright. The fact Adam had been told to come alone meant Daventry had another pressing matter on his mind. "But that's not the reason for your summons. You wish to discuss Jeremiah Black."

Daventry moved to close the door. "If we're to guarantee Miss Dutton's safety, we need to kill Jeremiah. While recuperating at Bower's residence, Samuel revealed two important pieces of information. First, Jeremiah ensures at least one player learns the identity of his opponents."

"Black uses the game as a front to steal deeds and build his empire. I'm surprised someone didn't murder him long ago." Black must have ruined many men during his twenty-year reign.

Daventry took a sheathed blade from his desk and slipped it into his boot. "Black has had men watching Miss Dutton since I employed her as an agent. He hoped she would find herself in trouble. That she would come to him for assistance, agree to accept his protection. The men watching her were to cause problems where possible."

"Black seems determined to marry her," Adam growled.

"If all else fails, he'll force her to wed."

Adam's blood boiled. The devil's own fury darkened his tone. "Then I shall speak to Samuel and discover Black's habits, kill him before we sit down to play for victor."

Daventry fell silent. "I despise injustice. I wish to save Miss Dutton from that fiend, but feel duty-bound to save your life, too. Be assured I will find a way out of this mess."

Ghostly whisperings of the past echoed in Adam's mind. People he loved always died tragically. Was his father right? Were they a family cursed to suffer one disaster after the next? Was Adam's happiness merely a brief respite before the axe fell again?

"Why not break into the Sapphire tonight and kill him?"

"According to Samuel, Black makes two of his henchmen sleep in his antechamber. We would have to kill them all. We might escape the noose for killing Black, but not for killing three men." Daventry paused, tension clawing at the silence. "If he kidnaps Miss Dutton, we have grounds to storm his premises."

Anger pushed to the surface. How could one corrupt man ruin so many lives and still go unpunished? They hanged children for stealing a hunk of bread.

A knock on the door brought Eliza, concern marring her brow. "Jonah said you're holding Lord Wright at the Wild Hare. That I'm to fetch a pelisse because we're to question him."

Daventry nodded. "Cole has him locked in a private dining room, so we should make haste. We'll wait for you in the carriage, Miss Dutton."

Suspicion marred her gaze as she studied Daventry, then Adam. No doubt she wished to know if there was news of Jeremiah Black. Still, she made no comment and only enquired as to who would lead the interview.

"It's your case, Miss Dutton. See what you can learn from Lord Wright. We will play a supportive role." Daventry reached into his coat and withdrew the miniature of Marianne. "Take this. It belongs with her family, not in a dusty drawer."

Eliza's fingers trembled slightly as she took the miniature. "I shall do my best to think logically, but my heart breaks for the man. I doubt I shall keep the tears at bay when speaking of his loss."

Love for her filled Adam's chest. Love for her flowed like blood in his veins. She was his life, his forever, and he would do anything to ease her suffering.

"I understand something of Lord Wright's plight," he said, closing the gap between them and capturing her hand. "I shall assist you should you find it difficult, reveal details of my own torment if necessary."

He never spoke about his mother's accident.

But he would if he thought it might help Eliza.

Heedless of Daventry's presence, Eliza held Adam's gaze. She looked deeply into his eyes as if memorising every golden fleck, as if to look away meant she might forget him. The strain of the last few days melted away as she pressed her body against his, came up on her toes and kissed him.

The taste of her made him lose his head, made him forget Daventry was standing there, and he was only briefly aware of the man's retreating footsteps.

Adam poured everything of himself into the kiss. He kissed her like it might be the last time he would know her taste, her touch. He kissed her so deeply the Lord would know the depth of his affection. Know it was time to release him from this damnable curse.

THE WILD HARE was located eight miles north of London on the Great North Road and had served weary travellers for almost three hundred years, or so Mr Daventry explained.

All romantic notions Eliza had about the quaint building left her the moment she entered the taproom. The pungent smell of fish assaulted her nostrils, quickly followed by a musty whiff of mildew.

Mr Daventry pointed to the flagons hanging from hooks in the beamed ceiling. "Whenever a duke drinks here, it's tradition to decorate the room with his empty flagon."

Roxburgh snorted. "Do they come with provenance? I might take one for the game tomorrow night."

Eliza didn't laugh. How could she when she feared losing the man she loved? When Jeremiah would murder Roxburgh before he would let him win?

If it wasn't for her conscience, she would beg him to run away with her. Tonight. Leave Mr Daventry to deal with the mess. They could take Lillian to Boston and begin a new life far away from the Sapphire and Satan's spawn.

"Rest assured, Roxburgh. I have six items that will guarantee success," Mr Daventry said, as if he spoke of nothing more taxing than a leisurely card game at Boodle's. "That's if we cannot find another means of doing away with Black and you're forced to play."

Eliza pursed her lips lest she convey her worst fears.

One could not kill the devil.

It was better to hide and hope he never found them.

A man approached. He was of average build but with a distended stomach and smelt of herrings and hard work. He leant closer and whispered something to Mr Daventry.

"Thank you, Stubbs. We won't require refreshment." Mr Daventry gestured for Eliza and Roxburgh to follow him, then slipped Stubbs a coin.

They stopped outside the door to a private room at the rear of the inn. Mr Daventry knocked three times, and the clip of booted footsteps brought a harried Mr Cole.

"I trust Wright has been no trouble and understands why you brought him here," Mr Daventry said to his agent.

"We had to stuff a kerchief in his mouth to stop him complaining." Mr Cole beckoned them into the room and quickly locked the door.

Eliza expected Mr Daventry to speak to the man tied to the chair, trying desperately to break free of his bonds, but he gestured for Eliza to step forward.

Nerves pushed to the fore, but she lifted her chin and rounded the large oak table. "My lord, you may remember me. We spoke at Lord MacTavish's ball, spoke about Mr Ashbury's murder. Please nod if you remember."

The lord's bloodshot eyes bulged in their sockets. The blue kerchief in his mouth muffled his angry mumbles.

"I wish to show you something I found in Mr Ashbury's apartment, but you must remain calm." She prayed it was

Marianne's likeness, a portrait given by an impressionable girl to the worst kind of wastrel, else they would have a devil of a time keeping Lord Wright quiet. "I shall remove the kerchief, then show you a miniature and explain why you're here."

Eliza nodded to Mr Bower to remove the gag.

Mr Daventry's man, who looked remarkably similar to his master and often acted as a decoy, untied the knot in the material and allowed Lord Wright to breathe freely again.

The lord gasped and coughed before throwing daggers of disdain in Mr Daventry's direction. "This amounts to assault and kidnapping," he hissed. "I'll have your damn head for this! I asked for your protection, not to be mauled by your hounds."

"We've been hired to solve a murder," Mr Daventry growled. "More men will probably die. Now listen to my agent, or Black's henchman might slit your throat in a graveyard."

"Untie Lord Wright's hands, Mr Bower," Eliza said before a fight erupted. "Please try to remain calm, my lord. I need you to study this likeness and tell me what you know of the young woman."

Eliza waited for Mr Bower to remove the restraints. She gave the lord a moment to rub his wrists before handing him the miniature found in Mr Ashbury's coal bucket.

Lord Wright snatched the portrait but started shaking the moment his gaze settled on the image. "Marianne. My darling Marianne." With trembling fingers, he touched the likeness of his daughter. Tears filled the lord's eyes, and he became lost in his memories.

Amid the bouts of silence and the lord's sobs, Eliza glanced over her shoulder to where Roxburgh stood, lost in his own morbid thoughts. She wanted to comfort him, run into his arms and remind him he was truly loved, but Lord Wright spoke.

"You found this in Ashbury's apartment?" Anger formed

the basis of the lord's tone, yet his eyes were still red and swollen from his tears.

"Yes. We also recovered love letters, though they bear no evidence of your daughter's name." Eliza kept her voice soft and low. "What you say here remains in the strictest confidence. I shall have the men leave if you'd prefer to speak privately." Then Roxburgh wouldn't be forced to reveal upsetting details about his own tragic past.

"I'll not discuss Marianne." Mentioning his daughter's name left him bemoaning her sad fate. He shook his head and mumbled incoherently.

Hating herself for having to remind him of his daughter's folly, she said, "We suspect Mr Ashbury wooed Marianne during his visits to his grandfather's estate in Barnham. We suspect he fooled her into trusting him, that he corrupted an innocent girl. We know she was found drowned in the river, but you suspect it wasn't an accident."

The man's face turned red with outrage. "Marianne drowned, and Ashbury as good as had his foot on her head. He killed her. He made false promises, and my poor Marianne believed his evil lies."

Eliza's throat constricted. She didn't know Marianne, but she knew how it was to feel foolish. She knew the desperation of wanting a man to change, the helplessness when realising goodness was beyond his capabilities.

"Do you believe Mr Ashbury killed her with his own two hands, or that his actions led—" She shouldn't say the words, but the truth was better out than left festering within. "Was her death a deliberate accident?"

Lord Wright shot to his feet, affronted. "Ashbury killed her regardless how she ended up in the river."

"My mother died in much the same way," Roxburgh said with an air of melancholy. "The coroner's report failed to reveal the depth of her suffering or her weak mental state at the time. It reads as if she stumbled too close to the water's edge. A silly mistake. A freak act of fate."

Lord Wright narrowed his gaze, clearly deciding if the revelation was a ploy to drag the truth from his pursed lips.

"I have a statue of Salus in my garden," Roxburgh said solemnly. "In Latin, Salus means safety, salvation. Daily, I touch the cold marble and recite a prayer, hoping she is safe and free of her pain."

Tears slipped down Eliza's cheeks, but they were not for Marianne. She had belittled Roxburgh, inferred the statue was the deity of gamblers. He might have shamed her and explained it was a means of communicating with his dead mother, but he had teased her rather than speak the truth.

She looked at him by way of a silent apology, vowed he would never have to suffer in silence again.

Lord Wright cleared his throat. "We do what's necessary to face the day," he said wistfully. "I suppose the purpose of all this is to prove I had a motive to kill Ashbury."

"You were on the terrace," Eliza said, focusing on the case and not her need to take Roxburgh to a private place and let him feel the depth of her love. "You lost your beloved daughter because of Mr Ashbury. He ridiculed you by drugging your port and taking your vowel."

"A vowel my sister stole because she wished to protect me," Roxburgh added. "A vowel I tossed into the fire because her reputation suffers for her foolish mistakes. I don't give a damn what people think about me, but I care what they think of my sister. I will do everything in my power to find Ashbury's killer, so I might bring her a modicum of peace."

Lord Wright thought for a moment. "Ashbury did not drug my port. Yes, he cheated at cards, but I lied about being incoherent."

"Because you killed Mr Ashbury?"

"No! Because I know who did."

The shocking statement robbed them all of a voice.

"You must understand, I was glad someone snuffed out that devil's light," the lord eventually said. "But if the murderer is arrested, I stand a chance of losing my London home."

Why would he lose his home if Mr Finch or Mr Fraser were arrested? Surely he could still play Jeremiah Black's wicked game.

"We know about the game at the Sapphire. We know the names of all those playing *Victor Ludorum*. Two are dead. Hence why you agreed to Mr Daventry's terms, providing he agreed to protect you. But why would you lose your home?"

The lord sighed. "My testimony would be used against me. I'm the only one with a strong motive for murder. The only one with a reason to cast the blame elsewhere. If I'm arrested, I cannot play Black's game and would lose my deed."

It seemed pointless asking the lord why he'd chosen to play. If Eliza had learnt anything since working this case, it was that people often behaved irrationally when battling their demons.

"Who killed Ashbury?" Mr Daventry demanded.

Lord Wright shuffled uncomfortably in the chair. "Ashbury was in his usual arrogant mood. He taunted me about winning my deed, knowing I couldn't wring his damn neck as I needed to play the game."

"Why did you not kill him the moment you learnt of Marianne's death?" Roxburgh asked.

"I had my suspicions about him, but no proof he was Marianne's lover until ten minutes ago."

"Who killed Ashbury?" Mr Daventry repeated.

"Ashbury provoked them. It was an accident."

"Them!" Eliza had heard correctly. Her mind scrambled to assemble the pieces of the puzzle, though it wasn't too difficult when one considered the remaining suspects. "You refer to Mrs Stanley and Mr Fraser."

To everyone's relief, Lord Wright nodded. "Ashbury saw

them entering the library. They must have followed him out to the maze, but they didn't pass through the terrace doors."

"They used the servants' entrance."

"I crept to the maze and heard them arguing. Ashbury threatened to inform Mr Stanley of their affair. He wanted Fraser to withdraw from the game. That was the price of his silence."

Mr Ashbury wanted better odds of winning.

His scheming had been the death of him.

"Fraser became frantic." Lord Wright blinked rapidly, as if suddenly witnessing the scene. "He said he would tell Roxburgh of the assault on Miss Ware. A fight ensued, though I cannot be sure if it was Mrs Stanley or Fraser who knocked Ashbury to the ground."

"But Ashbury died of a broken neck?"

Lord Wright shrugged. "Who can explain how a simple fall led to his death? But I swear that is how it happened."

A lengthy silence ensued.

No doubt Mr Daventry was at war with his conscience. No one deserved to die for killing a man as wicked as Mr Ashbury, but the veil of suspicion would forever fall on Roxburgh if they failed to pursue the couple.

Mr Daventry stepped forward. "We will, of course, have no option but to inform Sir Oswald. Perhaps your statement, and what we already know of Ashbury's misdeeds, might help them avoid the noose."

Lord Wright looked panicked. "I can't make a statement. Not until I've won the game and reclaimed my deed."

"If you play, you will lose." Roxburgh sounded much like the confident libertine. "I have been given Ashbury's seat and intend to win the game. Daventry has ensured I possess the King's own seal stamp."

Lord Wright blanched.

Being a man with a kind and generous heart, Roxburgh explained why he had no option but to play. "Jeremiah Black means to use the contract to force Miss Dutton into marriage. I have no option but to win the game and kill him if necessary."

During the lengthy pause, Eliza wondered when her father had realised he had no hope of winning. Or had he died without knowing she would be destitute? Had he been ignorant of Mr Black's intentions?

"I would have given my life to save Marianne." Lord Wright scrubbed his hand down his face and muttered something to himself. "But I cannot lose my deed. It seems there's only one option open to me, and helping another woman in need might ease my guilt."

"What exactly are you saying?" Roxburgh said.

"I'm saying we play the game and kill that rotten toad. I'm saying we both shoot the devil. It's the only way we can be assured of success. And it will be a damn sight more difficult to hang two peers for murder than one."

CHAPTER 19

Since leaving the Wild Hare yesterday, Eliza had seen little of Roxburgh. There had been much to do before the game, and so he had accompanied Mr Daventry and Lord Wright to London. They'd visited Samuel and learnt what they could about Jeremiah's habits and how he played *Victor Ludorum*.

Miss Wild and Mr Cole had gone to Lincolnshire, tasked with interviewing Mrs Stanley and bringing her back to London. Eliza wondered if the pairing served another purpose. A need for Honora to become accustomed to intimidating men.

Eliza remained at Bronygarth to assemble the items Roxburgh was to use in the game: a stamp bearing the King's seal, the Duke of Dounreay's cufflinks, the signet ring once belonging to the Duke of Melverley and inherited by Mr Daventry.

Amongst the other items collected, it was a winning hand.

Yet a sickening sense of trepidation warned that Jeremiah Black possessed the devil's own luck. Witnessing her father's road to ruin had stolen her faith, stolen her optimism. Bad things happened to good people, and she couldn't shake the terrifying thought that something terrible would happen to Roxburgh, too.

"It's cold tonight. You shouldn't be out here." Roxburgh's warm voice touched her like a comforting caress as he appeared behind her on the terrace. "I came to find you. I need to leave for London soon."

Nausea roiled in her stomach. She swung around to face him, knowing he would see tears in her eyes, praying it might persuade him to alter his plans.

"Please don't go to the Sapphire, Adam. Mr Daventry will find a way of dealing with Mr Black." She reached out and clutched his hand, a last plea to his sanity. He'd been back for a few hours and now had to leave her again. "Take Lillian. Go to Glendale, far away from London and this godforsaken mess."

"Far away from you? Never!" He captured her in a fierce embrace and kissed her madly. "Fate put us on this path, and we must follow it until the end."

"The end! The end will mean you gone, lost forever."

Roxburgh gripped her arms and forced her to look at him. "I shall return to you tonight. And when I do, we shall sit together on our favourite bench and make plans for the future."

"You speak of a future, yet your eyes tell a different story."

A story of a man who had found a reason to be happy, only to have it snatched from his grasp. If they were at Hanover Square, she would race into the garden, kneel at the statue and beg Salus to wrap her protective arms around him and keep him safe.

"I vow to do everything possible to rid you of Jeremiah Black." The sudden worry lines on his brow proved unnerving. "But should something unforeseen occur, I have given Daventry a sum of money and a valise full of valuables. I want you to take Lillian to Boston until Daventry writes to tell you it is safe to return."

"Boston?" Her stomach churned. She had felt helpless many times, but never as powerless as this. "What if I come with you to the Sapphire? We could lure Jeremiah into a trap, lure him into the alley and be done with him."

Roxburgh wiped away her tears. "I don't want you within a mile of that blackguard. You'll stay at Bronygarth with Lillian until Daventry returns. Promise me, Eliza. I cannot deal with Jeremiah Black while worrying about you." He kissed her tenderly on the mouth. "I need to know you're safe."

An internal war raged. She should abide by his wishes, but every part of her wanted to reach Jeremiah first and drive a blade into his wicked heart.

"Promise you'll wait here," he pressed. "As you're one of the few people I trust, you will give me your word." He waited. "Eliza!"

"You have my word. I shall wait here with Lillian." The last thing she wanted was to cause him further distress. "But why risk your life for me, Adam?"

He jerked his head as if it were a ridiculous question. "Because I have never felt a love like this, Eliza. Few people see beyond my facade like you can, few appreciate the complex man beneath. If it is my time to die, then I do so knowing the world is not ugly, but beautiful and magical, and I know that because of you."

Oh, her heart ached with love for this man.

Her heart ached at the cruelty of their situation.

She cupped his neck and kissed him, frantically so, thrusting her tongue against his, sampling the glorious depths of his mouth. She wanted to remember his taste, his warmth, the smoothness of his lips, the captivating scent of his skin.

"You're wrong," she panted, breaking contact. "There are not two men fighting for prominence. There's one man, one wonderful man who is simply the sum of his experiences. One man I love more than anything else in this world."

A discreet cough behind forced them apart.

"Forgive me," Daventry said, stepping out into the darkness. "You're due at the Sapphire in a little over an hour. We must make haste."

"Give me a moment." Roxburgh turned to her and kissed her once more—a goodbye kiss she feared would have to nourish her for a lifetime. "I love you," he said, too solemnly to bolster her confidence. "Never forget that."

And then he was gone.

"BLACK THINKS SAMUEL IS DEAD," Daventry said as his carriage rolled to a stop on the corner of King Street. "He has no reason to suspect you know anything about the game."

Adam sat forward, his stomach twisting into knots as he considered what was at stake. He reached into his top hat and pulled gently on the silk to reveal the false bottom added by Daventry's milliner.

"The pistol is loaded but not cocked." Daventry lowered the pocket pistol carefully into Adam's hat and pressed the silk-covered plate back in place. "Ironically, Black despises cheating. He will insist you store your playing pieces in your hat and keep them hidden from your opponents."

Adam's pulse pounded in his throat.

What if Black changed the rules?

What if Black took Adam's hat and left him unarmed?

That said, he still had a blade in his boot.

"Lord Wright has agreed to pull his weapon once the winner is declared. On condition he's guaranteed the return of his deed." Daventry gestured to Adam's polished Hessians. "You know how to slip the heel cover?"

"Yes." And he could open the folded blade with speed and

precision. "The blade will prove useful if Black throws me into his dank cellar and keeps me prisoner."

"There's nothing more I can do other than sit and wait and pray you're successful." Daventry sighed. "I have no wish to patronise you, Roxburgh, but you've surprised me with the strength of your conviction, the depth of your loyalty. You would make an excellent agent should you ever feel inclined to help those less fortunate."

Adam was touched by Daventry's faith in him. "I was under the impression eloquence was a weakness. But if I survive this, I shall ask Eliza to marry me. I can think no further ahead than that."

Daventry inclined his head, then pulled his watch and inspected the time. "It's almost midnight. Let us pray Fraser is still desperate to play for his deed. We may have this case concluded tonight."

Adam shuffled to the edge of the seat. A frisson of fear surfaced, not for himself. "Just promise me you will take care of Eliza and Lillian."

"You have my word."

Desperate to get this matter over with, he opened the door and vaulted to the pavement. "Save the brandy in your flask. If I make it out of the Sapphire alive, I'll need a stiff drink." Adam snorted, though there was nothing amusing about his predicament.

He reached for his hat and closed the door, entered the alley and hammered on hell's gate as hard as his heart hammered in his chest.

Being of average build, the brute who opened the door proved less intimidating than Black's other henchmen until one noticed he was missing an ear.

Adam introduced himself. "Mr Black is expecting me."

The fellow gave a toothless grin and beckoned Adam into the dimly lit corridor. "I'll need to frisk you for weapons, milord. Mr Black, he don't let no one enter the Blue Room without me roughing 'em up first."

Adam placed his hat and the velvet pouch of high-value items on the floor, then opened his arms wide. Black's lackey ran his grubby hands over Adam's body, patted and prodded, searched his coat pockets and slipped his calloused fingers inside the Hessians.

Satisfied Adam was not concealing a weapon, the lackey snatched the black top hat off the floor and peered inside.

Adam's heart almost stopped.

"You'll need to show me your playing pieces then put them inside your hat." The lackey thrust the hat at Adam. "If you ain't got good pieces, you ain't allowed to play."

Retrieving the velvet pouch, Adam showed Black's man all six items. "With luck, I'll have a good enough hand to win."

"Crikey! Is this the King's own seal?" The lackey examined the stamp before dropping it into the hat. "Happen you might prove lucky tonight, milord."

"That is the plan."

The lackey glanced nervously behind before leaning closer. "If you ever need to hire a man, milord, a man what's handy with his fists, you can find me at the Old Barn tavern near Seven Dials."

"I doubt Mr Black would approve of me stealing his staff."

"Things ain't good around here. I usually run errands, but some of the men left when they heard that Samuel—" The creak of a door had the lackey quickly straightening. "Best follow me, milord, before Mr Black has us both thrown in the Thames."

The Blue Room was located on the first floor of the Sapphire. Adam entered to find Lord Wright and Mr Fraser seated around a table covered in green baize. Both men looked shocked to see him, though Lord Wright's reaction was merely for effect. The men clutched their top hats possessively in their laps.

"Glad you could join us, Lord Roxburgh." Jeremiah slid out from the shadows like the devil's serpent. "I wasn't sure you would. You've been hiding these last few days."

"Not hiding," Adam snapped, hatred for this man knotting in his stomach. "Merely gathering my hand."

"You may take Mr Ashbury's seat." Black gestured to the space next to Lord Wright. "That's where Mr Dutton sat before he met such a tragic end. He was shot by a disgruntled player, I'm told."

No, Jeremiah had killed him because he had plans for Eliza.

Fraser's lip trembled. Fear had the fool shaking in his boots.

"Mr Dutton lost his deed," Adam challenged, dropping into the seat. "Why would a player have cause to shoot him?"

"Because Mr Dutton had lost every round, yet the hand he played in the last game denied a certain gentleman a draw."

There was no means of knowing if Jeremiah had killed Eliza's father unless one of his men confessed to murder. This was just a means to unnerve Adam before play commenced.

"It's of little consequence," Adam said, purposely blasé. "All that matters is I win the game, so I can marry Miss Dutton."

Jeremiah's nostrils flared, and he clenched his jaw. His anger was like a restless beast he had no choice but to contain. "What makes you sure you'll win? Your opponents have had two months to gather their stakes. You've had less than a week."

Adam leant on his aristocratic arrogance. "I have more to lose than anyone. That should tell you all you need to know."

Jeremiah's eyes darkened, but a sudden commotion on the landing stole his attention. He stomped across the room, yanked open the door, and glared. "What's the problem now, Evans?"

The lackey with the missing ear hauled Finch into the room. "He collapsed downstairs, Mr Black, crying like a babe. Finch wants to collect his deed and go home. Said if you'd just return it, he'd be on his way."

Finch looked as if he'd not slept since that day at the Albany. His hair was mussed but that was probably due to wearing a hood. His eyes were red and puffy. His creased clothes reeked of sweat and stale tobacco. The man was unsteady on his feet and appeared sotted.

Jeremiah grabbed Finch's cheeks and squeezed hard. "You signed a contract, Mr Finch. You're welcome to leave, of course, but that means I win your set at the Albany."

Finch whimpered and begged Black to reconsider, though one could not reason with a soulless man. "But I didn't know the rules when I signed. I had no means of gathering a good hand."

"Sit down, Mr Finch, before you lose something more valuable than your deed." Jeremiah practically dragged Finch to the table.

"Here's his hat, Mr Black." Evans came forward and placed the top hat on the table in front of Finch.

"You'll remain here, Evans. Woods will wait outside lest these gentlemen cause trouble." Jeremiah glanced at the mantel clock. "It's past midnight. Time to begin the game. Time to play for victor."

Strange it was midnight. The hour held a special place in Adam's heart. It signified honesty and true love. It marked the beginning of his life, not the end. Indeed, the thought of spending every midnight hour with Eliza gave him the courage to be bold.

Adam straightened. "Who is to start? I assume we take it in turns to stake a piece. The highest value piece wins the round."

A sly grin formed on Jeremiah's lips. "More or less, though

the house has the final say and can deem a piece worthless. It's in the contract."

Adam's blood ran cold. Thank the Lord he planned to murder the devil else he'd be done for. He thought to say he hadn't signed a contract, but Jeremiah might use it as an excuse to remove him from the game.

Jeremiah slammed dice on the baize. "The lowest roll starts play."

The men took it in turns to shake the dice. Fraser lost his temper when he rolled seven and was forced to reveal his piece first.

"Those dice are weighted." Fraser thumped the table with his clenched fist, but it became evident he was frightened, not angry. "I—I demand we roll again."

"Show your piece, Mr Fraser. Show it now, or Evans will throw you out."

Fraser grumbled as he examined the pieces hidden in his hat. He met Adam's gaze almost apologetically as he placed the silver letter opener onto the table. "It bears Lord MacTavish's coat of arms."

Adam grinned at the man's audacity.

Lord Wright played something belonging to his brother-in-law. "Viscount Grantham's snuffbox."

Fraser snatched the silver box and examined the heraldic markings.

Needing to beat a viscount and presuming Finch wouldn't trump him, Adam played the Duke of Melverley's signet ring.

Finch couldn't keep his trembling hand still long enough to reach into his hat. Jeremiah said he would pick for him and so Finch grabbed the first thing he could put his hand to.

"Viscount Newton's cigar case."

Newton? Ashbury's grandfather?

Finch must have stolen it from Ashbury's apartment.

Jeremiah Black scanned the items. "Lord Wright wins the hand. Newton's cigar case only bears his initials." Black smirked as he looked at Adam. "Melverley is dead. The rules state the owner must be living."

Adam gritted his teeth, though Fraser's panicked outburst said he also had pieces belonging to the deceased.

Jeremiah gestured for Lord Wright to show his next piece. And so it went on. Adam won the next two rounds, though he still had the King's seal stamp. Finch and Fraser could not contain their frustration, for it was impossible for them to win their deeds.

It was Finch's turn to start, and he grumbled and groaned while throwing a ruby stickpin down, claiming it belonged to Lord Mowbray, his neighbour from the Albany.

Fraser played a silver spoon bearing the Duke of Moreland's crest. Wright followed with a card case owned by Lord Montague, though insisted it had been loaned, not stolen. Adam offered Dounreay's cufflinks, knowing he had triumphed.

Indeed, Jeremiah begrudgingly said, "Roxburgh wins."

Fraser jumped to his feet. "I played the duke's spoon!"

"Moreland died without issue a year ago," Lord Wright informed them.

Fraser suddenly took leave of his senses. "I want my damn deed." He knocked over his hat, grabbed the letter opener, and launched himself at Jeremiah Black. "You evil bastard!"

But Jeremiah, having grown up in the rookeries, knocked Fraser to the floor with one swift punch. Woods, the beast who always accompanied Jeremiah, came charging into the room and dragged Fraser out.

Jeremiah cracked his knuckles and gave a mocking snort. "With Mr Fraser eliminated, Lord Wright may present his piece for the final round."

"It makes no difference," Adam said, slapping the King's seal on the table. "Lord Wright cannot beat me unless he has something belonging to the King."

Wright shook his head. "My best piece is the Earl of Loth-lair's fob, which I won last Saturday playing hazard."

Jeremiah pinned Adam to the chair with his beady gaze. "This is my club. I declare the winner. Maybe I'll say you cheated, Lord Roxburgh. What's to say your pieces are not forgeries?"

Adam's temper flared. "You'll keep your word and give me the damn contract. You will free Miss Dutton and concede defeat."

Jeremiah laughed. "You get to choose one man's deed, Roxburgh. That's the rules of the game. Take Finch's apartment at the Albany."

Evidently, there was only one way to free Eliza from this villain's clutches, and so Adam covertly reached into his hat, ready to pull the pocket pistol.

Finch shot out of the chair. "What if we all say you cheated, Mr Black? What if we spread the word in that scandal sheet making the rounds? People would soon stop visiting your club."

Black stared at Finch beneath hooded eyes. "You've no need for your deed anymore, Finch. Evans is going to escort you outside where Woods will have a little word in your ear."

No one could have predicted what happened next.

Finch pulled a pistol from his own pocket and aimed it at Jeremiah Black. "Give me my damn deed, or I shall shoot you dead."

Black glared at his man. "How the devil did he manage to conceal a weapon? You were supposed to search everyone."

Evans blinked rapidly. "Mr Finch near fainted. He was in such a state I brought him straight upstairs. He seemed harmless enough."

"My deed!" Finch pressed.

"Put the pistol down, you fool," Jeremiah Black cried before making two costly errors. He stepped forward, assuming Finch lacked the skill needed to hit a moving target.

He taunted the man, presuming Finch lacked the courage to fire.

"Do it, Mr Finch," Evans whispered. "Free us all from the beast's grasp. I'll swear you were defending yourself, and then you can get your deed back."

Finch fired.

Adam blinked against the sudden flash and loud crack.

Jeremiah Black did not cry out as the lead ball pierced his chest. His eyes widened, and his face turned ashen. He didn't fall to the floor gracefully, but with a heavy thud, like a carcass on a butcher's slab.

No one stepped forward.

No one attempted to save his life.

They all stood staring, waiting for the devil to die.

CHAPTER 20

Eliza stopped pacing before the hearth and checked the mantel clock for the third time in as many minutes. "We should have heard something by now. It's almost four in the morning."

"Lucius will send word as soon as he is able," Sybil Daventry said, her tone conveying utter faith in her husband. "I can only presume he's had to rouse Sir Oswald, maybe even Peel. Murder is a complicated business. His primary goal is to ensure good men don't hang."

Eliza tried to breathe, but her muscles were tense, her body braced to hear bad news. She glanced at Lillian sleeping peacefully on the sofa, so tired from crying she'd succumbed to the temptation to close her eyes.

"How do you live like this?" she asked Sybil.

"Like what?"

"In a constant state of agitation?"

Sybil thought for a moment. "I fell in love with Lucius Daventry. I find his conviction and his desire to save the innocent as attractive as his handsome countenance. I wouldn't want to change him. But it gets easier. And he promised me he would come home tonight, and I believe him."

"How I wish I had your faith."

Sybil smiled. "You're in the first bloom of love. You're allowed to feel afraid. When life has dealt you a rough hand, you're conditioned to fear the worst."

Eliza sighed. She had avoided Roxburgh for weeks before taking his case. Now she wished to spend the rest of her life in his arms. If only she had seen his redeeming qualities in the beginning, been more open to—

The sudden clip of footsteps in the hall captured her attention. A knock on the door brought Jonah, followed by Lucius Daventry and ... no one else.

Tears filled her eyes as a cavernous hole opened in her chest. She raced to Mr Daventry and gripped his arm. "Where's Roxburgh? Did he kill Mr Black? Did he survive? Tell me he's alive. Why has he not come home with you?"

Mr Daventry's gaze softened. He covered her hand with his own. "Roxburgh is alive and waiting for you in Hanover Square. Bower will take you and Miss Ware there now unless you would rather wait until the morning."

Alive! Oh, Merciful Mary!

Eliza exhaled the breath she had been holding for hours. "We wish to leave immediately. We wish to be reunited with him at once."

Mr Daventry glanced at his wife and smiled before turning his attention back to Eliza. "We had to involve Peel. The matter was too complicated to entrust to Sir Oswald. The man is incompetent."

Eliza's heart sank. "You're certain Roxburgh will not face charges for killing Mr Black?"

"Finch shot and killed Jeremiah Black. The stress of the last two months has left his nerves frayed. Though the witnesses claimed self-defence, he was taken to Bethlem Hospital as he's considered a danger to himself."

"Mr Finch!" She'd thought him a bumbling buffoon, not a man capable of murder. "Are you certain Mr Black is dead and is not like a cat with nine lives?"

"Quite certain," Mr Daventry said firmly. "Fraser is dead, too, killed accidentally during a scuffle with Black's henchman in the alley. He fell and cracked his head on the cobblestones. I did what I could, but it was impossible to save him."

Eliza could hardly absorb the information, but knew most of Jeremiah's men were vicious. "I'm sure Roxburgh will explain everything when we see him." After she'd spent a few hours locked in his warm embrace.

Indeed, she didn't dare ask Mr Daventry where she should sleep tonight and was soon relieved to be away from Bronygarth and huddled in a carriage with Lillian, charging back to London along the Great North Road.

They reached Hanover Square as the St George's bells chimed five.

Greyson could barely keep his eyes open when greeting them at the door. "His lordship is in the garden," he informed them while stifling a yawn.

Eliza gripped Lillian's hand, and they hurried outside to find Roxburgh standing in the moonlight, both hands pressed to the marble statue of Salus.

Sensing their approach, he turned around, and they ran into his arms. They stayed like that for a minute or more, the three of them muttering their relief, thankful their troubles were finally over.

It struck Eliza that this was the first of many dangerous cases, that she would likely feel terrified again. But for the moment, she was with Roxburgh, and her mind was at peace.

But Roxburgh was suddenly possessed by new worries. "Lillian, without a trial, there's no way to prove Fraser killed Ashbury," he said, releasing them from the comfort of his arms. "Peel believes Mrs Stanley will blame Fraser. And as

Lord Wright had a motive for murder, his testimony may be called into question."

Lillian understood what her brother was trying to say. "Adam, people will always presume you killed Mr Ashbury because we were found in the garden together. It's of no consequence as I have decided not to marry, at least not yet."

"Not even if Dounreay made you an offer?" Roxburgh teased.

Lillian smiled. "My heart is still bruised after Mr Bloom. And the duke has no plans to marry for the foreseeable future."

"Dounreay sent word he would call to collect his cufflinks tomorrow and enquired if you would be at home."

Lillian tried to appear indifferent, but Eliza suspected most women in London admired the Duke of Dounreay. "I'm sure he was merely being polite. Besides, I'm not at all interesting enough to hold the duke's attention. And when I do marry, I shall follow your example and marry for love."

Roxburgh's eyes widened in an almost silent chastisement.

Lillian appeared flustered and then quickly made an excuse about being tired. She bid them good night, and left them alone in the garden.

"I fear Lillian was a little embarrassed," Eliza said. "She wants you to be happy but fails to realise ours is a complicated relationship."

Roxburgh shrugged. "It's not complicated to me."

Ah, this was the moment she had been dreading. Now she would have to choose between a life of sin and losing him for good.

"Adam, love knows no bounds. Love does not discriminate. Love doesn't care that we walk different paths."

He frowned. "We walk the same path."

He would make it difficult, she knew.

"What I am trying to say is that I don't have the mental strength to be your mistress. Now I am no longer working on your case, I should not visit the house. It will only make matters worse for Lillian, and I do so want her to be happy."

Rather than rant about their need to be together, Roxburgh appeared confused. "Eliza, I would never disrespect you by asking you to be my mistress."

"Forgive me, but we have made love twice and are not married. I fail to see the difference."

He slipped his arm around her waist. "When I said I was proud of Lillian the other day, it had nothing to do with her going to stay with Sloane in Little Chelsea and everything to do with what I said to her about you."

"Why? What did you say?"

Roxburgh captured a loose tendril of her hair and let it slip slowly through his fingers. "I told her I'm in love with you and feel compelled to ask you to be my wife. I've never met anyone like you, Eliza, and refuse to spend another day without you by my side." He paused. "Marry me."

Eliza gripped his forearm to steady herself lest her knees buckled. "Marry you? But you're a peer of the realm, and I'm—"

"A gentleman's daughter. You're my match in every way. You're the only woman for me, and I intend to make you so happy, you won't regret your decision for a second."

Her thoughts became suddenly lost in a haze of excitement. "But you've sworn never to marry."

"And you've sworn never to live with a gambling man. It's time we broke our promises and made new ones. And you should know I will want children. I want them with you."

She felt so giddy with happiness she could hardly form a rational word. "What about my work for the Order?"

"Do you wish to continue solving crimes?"

Eliza thought for a moment. "I would prefer to become involved in Mr Daventry's charitable organisations." She admired his philosophy and wished to assist him in his cause. It's the least she could do under the circumstances.

"Does that mean you'll marry me? You'll be my wife?"

"Yes!" Tears filled her eyes. "I love you, Adam, and never want to be without you. I want to be your wife and bear your children."

"I promise we shall have a wonderful life together."

He sealed his vow with a kiss. A kiss that curled her toes and heated her blood. A kiss that banished all doubts and fears. A kiss that convinced her life with him would indeed be wonderful.

Ten days later
Hanover Square, London

"I ADMIT I'd made up my mind about him based on the scandalous gossip," Miss Trimble said before taking a small sip of her fruit punch. "I admit the gentleman has qualities that are not apparent to the untrained eye."

"So you approve of Lord Roxburgh?" Eliza teased.

She glanced across the drawing room at her husband, who was deep in conversation with his friend, the Marquess Devereaux. He looked magnificent in his black coat and pale gold waistcoat, though she could hardly wait to strip them off his muscular body and make love to him in the hedge maze. He didn't know it yet. It was her little surprise.

"Yes, I approve, Eliza. Everyone can see he's besotted with you. It's just that experience has taught me to distrust men."

Stunned that Miss Trimble had said a few words about her past, Eliza said, "I consider you a dear friend and am here if you wish to confide in someone."

Miss Trimble's smile faltered. She might have said more, might have told Eliza her real name, even though she had never admitted to using an alias, but Nora joined them, looking a little flustered.

Nora complimented Eliza's gown, spoke about the beautiful ceremony and how much she had enjoyed the wedding breakfast.

"Thank you, Nora." Eliza touched her friend affectionately on the arm. "Are you going to tell me what's troubling you, or would you rather discuss the flower arrangement?"

Nora shook her head. "Not on your wedding day."

"Now you've roused my curiosity, you must tell all."

Nora took it as a cue to open the flood gates. "I'm to meet Lord Deville on Friday to see if he will accept me as his agent." Her breathing quickened. "But I was in Monroe's bookshop on the Strand yesterday purchasing your wedding gift, and he happened in there."

"You spoke to him?"

"Of course not. Someone else did and mentioned him by name. And he had such a terrible scar on his cheek it had to be him. I hid behind the bookcase, watching, but he saw me."

Nora sounded more curious than afraid.

"Did he appear the most intimidating man you've ever met?"

"More than you can imagine. He fixed me with his penetrating stare, and my blood ran cold. The thought of working for him fills me with dread, but Mr Daventry seems to think it's an excellent pairing."

Eliza glanced at Julianna and Rachel, the other agents employed by Mr Daventry who had married their clients. She considered her own situation. The thought of working with Roxburgh had left her feeling much the same way. Fearful and secretly a little excited.

"People must stare at him all the time." Eliza decided not to suggest Nora might find herself attracted to Lord Deville. "That's why he glared at you. When he knows you're the one who is to help him, I'm sure he'll be charming."

They discussed why Lord Deville might want to hire an agent, but Eliza's attention kept drifting to her husband. Four times or more, their gazes locked, and they exchanged silent declarations of love.

Another two hours passed before the guests took their leave.

She stood with Roxburgh in the hall, bidding their friends farewell, though the feel of her husband's hand at the small of her back left her almost breathless with anticipation.

Lillian joined the Sloanes as they gave their felicitations and made to depart. "Mrs Sloane has invited me to stay in Little Chelsea tonight."

"Lillian, you don't need to leave." The last thing Eliza wanted was for Lillian to feel awkward. This was her home, too. "We will all dine together this evening."

"Would you mind if I went?" Lillian leant closer. "I'm to learn card games and taste rum and hear all about their wild adventure trying to locate lost treasure. If I'm ever to appeal to a man like Dounreay, I need to broaden my horizons."

Did Lillian not know how the duke looked at her?

Could she not feel the heat in his gaze?

"If I can offer you any advice, it's to be yourself," Roxburgh said. "Unless you're playing Sloane at cards. He's exceptionally good, so you may need to wear a mask of indifference else he will read your hand."

Mr Sloane teased Roxburgh about his losses at the tables.

Lillian hugged them both, then practically skipped out of the house. "Enjoy your evening!" she called before climbing into the Sloanes' plush carriage.

The second they were alone, Roxburgh pulled Eliza around to face him and claimed her mouth in a searing kiss.

"Let's go upstairs," he whispered against her cheek.

"Let's go to the garden."

"I think you mistake my meaning."

"I understand you perfectly well."

"Are you certain the garden is the right place?" His hot hands settled on her hips. "The need to be inside you is driving me insane."

Roxburgh could spark an inferno with his salacious discourse.

"I have a surprise for you. Something special arranged so you will always remember this day."

Roxburgh snorted. "You think I'd forget the day we married?"

"Of course not, but all will become clear." She stepped back and considered him thoughtfully. "You must wear a blindfold."

"A blindfold?" He seemed keen. "Here, use my cravat. I'll be removing it soon, anyway." He placed his sapphire stickpin on the console table, fixed her with his sinful smile as he untied the silk.

Eliza turned him around and attempted to bind his eyes. "Did Mr Daventry have any news to impart?" She tied the silk, but it kept slipping down.

"Only that the coroner examined Ashbury's body and found an old fracture to his neck. It accounts for why he died from a simple fall. Oh, and Coleman insists Jeremiah Black forged his signature."

Eliza attempted to tie the blindfold for a second time. "One way or another, Mr Daventry will discover the truth. Miss Trimble said he's hired Samuel to assist Mr Bower."

She had always felt that Samuel was a good man who'd simply made bad decisions. Unlike Mr Black's other henchman, who had been identified by a witness as being the man who killed Mr Weiland and dumped his body in the graveyard.

Though Eliza had no proof, she believed the same beast had shot and killed her father on Mr Black's orders. Still, she couldn't dwell on the past, not when she had such a glorious future.

"You'll have to hold the blindfold in place." She gripped Roxburgh's hand. "Come, I shall lead the way."

Taking unsure steps, Roxburgh followed her outside. They passed the statue of Salus, and Eliza uttered a silent prayer, wishing all their dearly departed were safe.

"You may remove the blindfold," she said, bringing him to a halt before the hedge maze. Lillian had agreed to help organise the surprise after their frank discussion about intimate liaisons. "On second thoughts, there's something I need to check first."

Eliza came up on her tiptoes and kissed Roxburgh on the mouth, slipping her tongue over his and stirring herself into a lustful frenzy.

"I recall what you said about being a man." She trailed her fingers down his chest and stroked the obvious bulge in his breeches. "Yes, I can confirm every inch of you is stiff and rigid."

Roxburgh hissed a breath and tore the blindfold from his eyes but blinked in shock when he noticed the maze.

"Welcome to my garden oasis," she purred, parting the silk curtains that acted as a doorway to the tunnels beyond.

Roxburgh looked at the assortment of curtains draped over the high topiary, creating a ceiling. "Are those the winter curtains?"

"Greyson arranged for me to use them today before they're aired and stored away until autumn." Eliza tried not to giggle as she parted the curtains and beckoned him inside. "Well, will you enter the siren's lair? Your wife wishes to show you what sensory delights may be found deep within the tunnel."

"And I intend to sample them at once." He followed her inside, where it was a little too dark, but she'd feared lighting the candle lamps while there was so much loose material. "Is that the chaise from the study?"

"Indeed. And the furs from your coach. It's our very own

bedouin tent. I have food and drink aplenty, enough to satisfy a weary traveller for hours. You may have whatever your heart desires, my lord."

Roxburgh moistened his lips. "I may ask for something scandalous. You do still owe me a boon."

"And I am more than happy to pay." She closed the gap between them, her eager hands impatient to have him out of his clothes.

Roxburgh captured her wrist. "Touch me at your peril."

"Why, what will you do to me?"

"Everything."

He kissed her passionately, kissed her until she was drunk with desire. They didn't feel the cold when they stripped out of their clothes and settled on the chaise. They'd been used to sitting outside during the midnight hour and the heat of his magnificent body soon warmed every extremity.

"You're mine, Eliza," he growled as he pushed deep into her body. "Mine at midnight and every hour after."

She clawed his back and called his name as he thrust to the hilt. "You're my love, my life. You're my everything."

She prayed that when he next came into the hedge maze, he wouldn't think about those dreadful two days spent all alone. She prayed he would remember that he was cherished beyond compare. That someone in the world truly loved him.

THANK YOU!

I hope you enjoyed reading *Mine at Midnight.*

Why does Lord Deville want to hire an agent?
How will Honora fare when faced with such an intimidating
gentleman?

Find out in ...

***Your Scarred Heart
Ladies of the Order - Book 4***

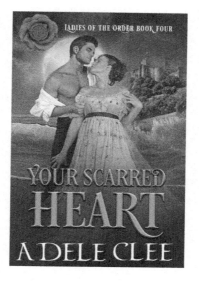

More titles by Adele Clee

Lost Ladies of London

The Mysterious Miss Flint

The Deceptive Lady Darby

The Scandalous Lady Sandford

The Daring Miss Darcy

Avenging Lords

At Last the Rogue Returns

A Wicked Wager

Valentine's Vow

A Gentleman's Curse

Scandalous Sons

And the Widow Wore Scarlet

The Mark of a Rogue

When Scandal Came to Town

The Mystery of Mr Daventry

Gentlemen of the Order

Dauntless

Raven

Valiant

Dark Angel

Ladies of the Order

The Devereaux Affair

More than a Masquerade

Mine at Midnight

Made in the USA
Monee, IL
24 January 2022